*continued . . .*

"A delightful yarn. Few amateur sleuths are as charming as this psychic mayor sleuth in a small coastal town where murder stalks the dunes and ghosts roam the Outer Banks. Kept me turning pages until it was done."
—Patricia Sprinkle, author of *Death of a Dunwoody Matron*

"This opening act of a new amateur sleuth is a wonderful mystery . . . The heroine is sassy and spunky . . . Joyce and Jim Lavene have . . . another hit series." —*Midwest Book Review*

"I could almost smell and feel the salty sea air of Duck as I was reading. The authors definitely did a bang-up job with the setting, and I look forward to more of Dae's adventures and the hint of romance with Kevin." —*A Cup of Tea and a Cozy for Me*

"This is a mystery with strong characters, a vivid sense of place and touches of humor and the paranormal. *A Timely Vision* is one of the best traditional mysteries I've read this year."
—*Lesa's Book Critiques*

## PRAISE FOR THE RENAISSANCE FAIRE MYSTERIES

# Treacherous Toys

"An engaging whodunit made fresh by changing the season . . . This exciting amateur sleuth is filled with quirky characters as team Lavene provides another engaging murder investigation."
—*Genre Go Round Reviews*

# Harrowing Hats

"The reader will have a grand time. This is an entertaining read with a well-crafted plot. Readers of the series will not be disappointed. New readers will want to glom the backlist so they don't miss a single minute." —*Fresh Fiction*

"The Renaissance Faire Mysteries are always an enjoyable read . . . Joyce and Jim Lavene provide a complex, exciting murder mystery that amateur-sleuth fans will appreciate."
—*Midwest Book Review*

# Deadly Daggers

"The Lavene duet can always be counted on for an enjoyable whodunit . . . Filled with twists and red herrings, *Deadly Daggers* is a delightful mystery."  —*Midwest Book Review*

"Will keep you entertained from the first duel, to the last surprise . . . If you like fun reads that will let you leave this world for a time, this series is for you."
—*The Romance Readers Connection*

"Never a dull moment! Filled with interesting characters, a fast-paced story, and plenty of humor, this series never lets its readers down."  —*Fresh Fiction*

# Ghastly Glass

"A unique look at a renaissance faire. This is a colorful, exciting amateur-sleuth mystery filled with quirky characters, who endear themselves to the reader as Joyce and Jim Lavene write a delightful whodunit."  —*Midwest Book Review*

# Wicked Weaves

"Offers a vibrant background for the mysterious goings-on and the colorful cast of characters."
—Kaye Morgan, author of *Celebrity Sudoku*

"This jolly series debut . . . serves up medieval murder and mayhem."  —*Publishers Weekly*

"A creative, fascinating whodunit, transporting readers to a world of make-believe that entertains and educates."  —*Fresh Fiction*

"[A] terrific mystery series . . . A feast for the reader . . . Character development in this new series is energetic and eloquent; Jessie is charming and intelligent, with . . . saucy strength."
—*MyShelf.com*

# A Finder's Fee

## Joyce and Jim Lavene

BERKLEY PRIME CRIME, NEW YORK

**THE BERKLEY PUBLISHING GROUP**
Published by the Penguin Group
Penguin Group (USA) LLC
375 Hudson Street, New York, New York 10014

USA • Canada • UK • Ireland • Australia • New Zealand • India • South Africa • China

penguin.com

A Penguin Random House Company

A FINDER'S FEE

A Berkley Prime Crime Book / published by arrangement with the authors

Berkley Prime Crime Books are published by The Berkley Publishing Group.
BERKLEY® PRIME CRIME and the PRIME CRIME logo are trademarks of
Penguin Group (USA) LLC.

For information, address: The Berkley Publishing Group,
a division of Penguin Group (USA) LLC,
375 Hudson Street, New York, New York 10014.

ISBN: 978-0-425-25231-4

PUBLISHING HISTORY
Berkley Prime Crime mass-market edition / October 2013

PRINTED IN THE UNITED STATES OF AMERICA

10  9  8  7  6  5  4  3  2  1

Cover art by Robert Crawford.
Cover design by Annette Fiore DeFex.

# Prologue

Dae O'Donnell, mayor of Duck, North Carolina, had been missing for three days. She'd closed her thrift store, Missing Pieces, and left a note for the UPS driver to drop packages at the Curves and Curls Beauty Spa next door on the boardwalk.

She left her grandfather a note to let him know she'd be gone for a few days.

And then she vanished.

"There's nothing I can do," Duck police chief Ronnie Michaels told Dae's worried friend, Trudy Devereaux. "She's an adult, and she has the right to get away for a while, if she chooses. She's probably off looking for that stuff she carries in her shop. I don't understand why everyone is so upset."

"Maybe because she left her cell phone and her bag at home," Trudy explained. "She didn't even take any clothes. It's just over a week until the election—*her* election. She should be out campaigning. Something's wrong, Chief. Can you look into it? Or—or do I need to do it?"

Only Trudy's fear for her friend could make her bold enough to talk to the chief this way.

Chief Michaels, a formidable ex-marine who still sported a graying flattop, got to his feet and gave the proprietor of Curves and Curls a scowl meant to dampen any enthusiasm for a nonsanctioned action. "If we receive more information that points to foul play, we'll investigate. And tell Brickman I mean it. None of you should take the law into your own hands. The matter is closed—at least for now."

Because his wife, Marjory, had just reminded him that morning that he should try to be more understanding and kind to people, the chief reached over and patted Trudy on the shoulder. He tried to arrange his face in what he hoped was a sympathetic smile. It was hard for him to tell. Then he sat down and went back to work.

Trudy had been startled when he'd reached for her. She'd tried not to flinch. But the truth was that he scared her. He always had.

It was Dae who was the brave one, the one who got them in and out of trouble. Who grinned cheekily at the chief like she dared him to do anything about their childish exploits. Maybe that was one reason she loved Dae so much. Dae was the person Trudy wished she could be.

Trudy huddled in her heavy coat as she left the police station and went out to her car. She'd received one important piece of information from Chief Michaels—she wasn't the only one worried about Dae.

She should have realized Kevin Brickman, Dae's beau, would be worried too. It had thrown her off when Horace O'Donnell, Dae's grandfather, didn't appear to be concerned at all. His words had almost perfectly echoed the chief's. But then, Dae's grandfather used to be the county sheriff. Obviously the two men thought alike.

Trudy drove to the Blue Whale Inn, which Kevin had been lovingly restoring since he'd moved to Duck. He'd been an FBI agent for twelve years or so. Surely he'd have some idea about what needed to be done—and there would be strength in numbers. She'd used up all of her individual strength confronting Chief Michaels.

One thing she knew—she'd been Dae's friend since kindergarten. Dae was as sturdy and dependable as any person she'd ever known (despite the cheekiness). That's one reason folks had voted for her to be the mayor.

She wouldn't leave this close to her own reelection unless something was wrong. And she certainly wouldn't go off without her cell phone or her toothbrush.

Trudy was surprised to see so many cars in the Blue Whale's driveway. It had been a cold October, which meant not many tourists were in town. Duck mostly closed down during this time of year, as did most of the Outer Banks. The hundred-mile-long strip of barrier islands was left to its inhabitants—in the case of Duck, not quite six hundred people.

Trudy parked her little car and didn't waste any time getting into the warmth of the inn. There was an ice fog that had chilled everything from the Atlantic Ocean to the Currituck Sound. Tiny frozen droplets hung from trees and houses. Only something as important as finding her friend would have brought her out on an awful day like this.

Duck police officer Tim Mabry was already sitting in the lobby of the old inn, his feet by the warm fire burning in the hearth. He was hunched over, staring into the flames.

*Of course!*

She should have thought about Tim. He'd want to help find Dae. He wasn't wearing his uniform either. That meant he wasn't *officially* working. She wouldn't want to get him into trouble.

Tim was a tall, thin man who'd once dated Dae when they were in high school. He'd dated Trudy too, truth be known, and almost every other girl at Duck High School. But for some reason he'd carried a torch for Dae out of school too.

Dae had never really cared for him in that way. If he'd asked her, Trudy would have told him he should move on.

He smiled and got to his feet when he saw her. Trudy was surprised when she noticed how blue his eyes were beneath the crisply cut blond hair. He had a nicer smile than she'd noticed in a while too. She'd seen him only a few days before but he *seemed* different.

She reminded herself why she'd come and quit smiling back at him. "Is Kevin here? I want to see him about Dae."

Tim sat back down when she was seated in a comfortable chair near his. "That's why I'm here. I have some vacation time coming. I want to use it to look for her. You know something's wrong for her to take off this way."

*"Exactly!"* Trudy warmed to her like-minded audience. "I went to Chief Michaels but he wouldn't listen. And I don't think her grandfather is even concerned."

"I know! I asked too." Tim admired Trudy's smooth silver blond hair and slender form. She'd always been a little too polished for him with her perfect clothes and makeup. Trudy was a beautiful woman, but out of his league—like a model or Miss America.

"So is Kevin worried too?" She slid a little closer to him under the guise of being nearer the fire.

"Oh yeah. He's been out looking for her the last few nights, since he couldn't reach her on the phone. He hasn't had any luck."

Trudy and Tim spent a few minutes looking awkwardly

at each other, trying to find something else to say about the problem. Both were relieved when voices from the entryway came toward the lobby.

"I'm telling you, Kevin, she's not herself. That's why she left this way." Ann Porter reluctantly carried a tray with sugar, cream and other coffee necessities on it. She was tall and gaunt with thin, straw-colored hair that hung down to her shoulders. "This is no time to be domestic. Dae needs help."

"What's *she* doing here?" Trudy whispered to Tim, moving a little closer again, noticing the scent of his aftershave. He was very muscular too, but not in an obvious fashion. It made her feel small and dainty to be near him.

Ann was Kevin's ex-fiancée and former FBI partner. They'd separated years ago when she'd had a breakdown and had to be hospitalized. She'd brought a hurricane of emotions with her when she'd finally tracked him down and found him living in Duck.

She'd moved to New York. Why was she back again?

Kevin Brickman put the coffee service down on a table and wheeled it close to the fire. "We need a strategy, Ann. We can't wander around the Outer Banks looking for her. I've been doing that. It's not working."

"Are there any cookies?" Seven-year-old Betsy Sparks joined them with a doll in one hand and a bottle of chocolate milk in the other. "When are we going to see Dae?"

Trudy glanced at Tim, who shrugged and shook his head. He had no idea why either of them was there. He knew Dae and Betsy had a special bond—Dae had saved her life. He also knew the girl was living in Richmond now.

Had she come to Duck with Ann?

Tim tried to reassure Trudy. "I'm not sure what's going on, but I know we're going to look for Dae. We're going to find her."

Neither of them was surprised when Shayla Lily stormed into the old inn, slamming the big front door behind her.

Shayla was also a good friend of Dae's. She hadn't known Dae as long as Trudy had, but they'd spent some time together. Shayla said she was a medium from New Orleans and had only lived in Duck a few years. Her shop, Mrs. Roberts, Spiritual Advisor, was on the other side of Dae's shop, Missing Pieces.

She was a little too big-city for Trudy's taste—smart-mouthed, always dressed in black. She'd never once asked for Trudy's help with her dark hair and cocoa-colored skin, but she always looked great. She was flamboyant rather than polished, and she always managed to make an entrance.

There was an older woman with her. She was plump and short. Her long black hair gleamed in the light. She was covered with gold and silver bangles that were interlaced with feathers.

Trudy had never seen her before but she thought there could be a family resemblance.

"Looks like we're all here for the same reason." Shayla glanced around the room then dramatically dropped her heavy coat on the circular bench near the doorway with a calculated shrug. "Good. Let's get started. I brought my Gram up from New Orleans to help find Dae."

Ann stared at Shayla, nearly her polar opposite. Her lips compressed into a thin, white line. "I don't think we need any mumbo jumbo to find Dae. Thanks anyway. She's lost in a powerful psychic hold that developed from a necklace she received. We have to find it and take it from her. Then we'll have to hope she's still normal. You never know what the aftermath of something like this will be."

"I don't know what you're talking about," Shayla said. "But you need to stay out of my way. We can handle this fine without the likes of you."

Ann put her hands into the pockets of her gray slacks as though to keep from hurting the other woman—which she was fully capable of doing. "Dae and I have a significant connection. I don't understand it but I know it's there. I know what happened to her, and I know how to find her."

Shayla's dark eyes flashed in Ann's direction. "*A significant connection?* You mean after you almost ripped her head off? I'm sure Dae will want *you* to find her."

"Ladies!" Kevin returned from the kitchen with a tray of chocolate chip cookies. He began pouring coffee into cups and passing them around. "I agree there's something odd going on, but fighting about who's going to do what won't help. We have to work together."

"You only need me and Gram," Shayla defiantly stated.

"Betsy and I can find her. I know you don't understand." Ann glared at Shayla. "But this is science. You know about science, right? They teach that here?"

"Please!" Trudy took Tim's hand in hers without realizing it (to his delight and consternation). "We need to work together, like Kevin said, so we can find her. We all care about her or we wouldn't be here."

No one disagreed with Trudy's outburst. They drank their coffee while exchanging angry scowls at each other anyway.

Trudy sat down, hoping everyone would think her flushed cheeks were from the fire and not her agitation. Tim squeezed her hand and smiled at her.

Kevin pulled out the old whiteboard he used in the kitchen so the staff would know what was on the menu while they were working. He was a tall man, over six feet, with broad shoulders and a disciplined physique he still maintained from his time in the military. He was hard in many ways from the life he'd led, and still prone to make snap judgments based on what his FBI training told him was right.

Being with Dae, and looking after his guests at the Blue Whale, had softened him during the time he'd spent in Duck. He didn't regret it. That other life was over. He didn't want to be that suspicious, paranoid person anymore.

"We know Dae left abruptly three days ago." He wrote the information on the board as he would have when he'd worked for the government—only this time he had to erase last night's main course and dessert first. "Ann and Betsy received a psychic flash at that time. They both saw her taking an amber necklace out of a wooden box. She was getting ready to put it on."

"The necklace is imbued with heavy psychic energy." Ann relaxed a little in the more familiar format Kevin had presented. She knew how to do this.

"Where did the necklace come from?" Shayla asked. "She didn't say anything to me about it."

"I think it had recently been delivered to her. Putting it on was probably a spur-of-the-moment decision," Kevin said. "I found the box in her shop. It was from Dae's father. Ann drew a picture of the antique necklace from what she saw in her vision and after she'd touched the box. However, she couldn't pick up anything regarding Dae's whereabouts."

"Let me see the box." Shayla took it from him. She closed her eyes and concentrated, but she was a medium, not a finder of lost things, like Dae and Ann. She was good at talking to spirits but not at communicating with inanimate objects. "I'm not getting anything."

"You had to sense the power in the necklace, like I did through *our* connection," Ann explained. "I tried to send her a mental message to leave it alone. But Dae, as you know, is easily blindsided by her curiosity."

"Like *you* know," Shayla sniped as she handed the box to her grandmother.

Flourine Lily shook all over as she handled the empty box, first with her fingers and then with her feathers and beads. "A *witch*. That's what we have here, *chère*. The necklace belonged to a powerful witch."

Everyone stopped and took that in. Trudy moved a little closer to Tim. He smiled reassuringly at her but had no clue what was going on.

"There are no witches around here, Gram," Shayla responded. "This isn't the bayou. And I'd know if there was a witch in the area."

"She lives not in our time, girl. The necklace and the power were brought forward from the past. It was preserved, waiting for the right person. Someone like Dae was the only way the witch could communicate."

"Dae isn't a medium." Shayla felt a little threatened that her friend might have taken on a new ability, one that might rival her own.

"She couldn't be," Flourine said. "This witch isn't a spirit you can talk to in your crystal ball. Her power is strong, but it all focuses in the necklace. She don't exist on any plane."

"Are we talking about possession?" Shayla's eyes narrowed. "Are you saying the witch from the past has possessed Dae?"

Flourine dropped the box to the floor. "It burns my hand to touch it." She looked at Ann. "You were right to be scared for her. She might be trapped in the past with the witch forever."

"There is definitely a time distortion surrounding the necklace." Ann wanted to get in the last word. "The entity— we wouldn't call her a witch anymore—was very strong. This was a psychic trap for the unwary. Dae certainly qualifies for that."

Kevin frowned at her. "Are you suggesting Dae has been

taken over by this witch since she put on her necklace? If so, we have to figure out what she wants. What's her endgame? What is she hoping to achieve?"

"There *was* a witch in Duck's past." Trudy shivered. "We all heard the story of Maggie Madison when we were growing up. She did some bad things to people and a storm washed her away. I think that was back in the 1600s."

Tim agreed. "She put a curse on someone's horses and made a cow go dry. I don't remember exactly."

"How do we track where she's taken Dae? How do we get rid of her?" Shayla asked.

"Normally, I'd say we'd use Dae's cell phone and credit card to track *her*," Kevin said. "But she didn't take them with her."

"Do you think Maggie Madison knew we wouldn't be able to find Dae if she made her leave those here?" Betsy was a little scared but holding up well because she didn't want to be sent to another room. She wanted to help her friend.

"It's possible," Ann said. "The entity has access to Dae's brain. She might be able to understand the ramifications of what that could mean for her, if not the technology itself."

"So what now?" Trudy asked. "Dae has to be somewhere. Everyone knows her. She can't hide out without someone spotting her. Maybe we should print up posters and have everyone search for her."

"The witch may be using her powers to disguise the poor girl." Flourine's eyes unfocused as she stared across the room. "I know a spell we could use for this."

"Not necessary." Ann got to her feet. "I can still feel Dae. She's not far away. I'm sure she's still here in Duck, doing the entity's dirty work."

Flourine had already dropped to the hardwood floor and was drawing a circle on it with chalk. Her eyes closed as she mumbled words no one could understand. She spit on her hand and rubbed it into the circle.

"Oh, for God's sake, Kevin," Ann whispered. "Seriously?"

Shayla got down beside her grandmother. She'd seen magic like this all of her life. If Gram said a witch was possessing Dae but she could find her, Shayla believed it, and she didn't care what anyone else thought.

The group was startled as the front door blew open, the ice fog creeping into the warmth of the inn. A hooded figure wearing dirty, torn clothing appeared in the opening. Trudy moved quickly to Tim's lap, a fact he didn't mind at all.

Kevin had started toward the open door when the figure threw back its hood.

"I hope those are chocolate chip cookies I smell baking," Dae said with a cheeky smile. "I'm starving."

# Chapter 1

I was back! It was warm and all my friends were gathered in one place. There had been times in the last few days that I'd been worried about how everything that had happened was going to work out.

The older woman on the floor let out a screech and got to her feet much faster than seemed possible. She ran forward, cannonballing right into me. I was knocked to the floor and trapped by her weight on my chest while my friends came to stare at me. I felt like a bug in a jar.

"Do you think it's really Dae?" Trudy had tears running down her face. "How will we know?"

"I'll know." Ann pushed forward through the others and pressed her hands on either side of my head. She pulled back after a moment of closing her eyes and frowning. "I can't tell for sure. The entity is powerful. It could be a trick."

"What could be a trick?" I found Kevin's familiar gray blue eyes in my line of sight and focused on him. "What's going on?"

"They think you're possessed." He said it as normally as if he'd said I had a cold. "That's as close an explanation as I can give you. How do you feel?"

"Hungry. Dirty. Tired. Will you get her off of me, please?"

I wasn't expecting this kind of reception. I'd only come by the Blue Whale to ask Kevin for his help. Everyone seemed to be upset that I was gone. It wasn't like I hadn't left a note.

"Not yet." Shayla's face replaced Kevin's. "How do we know you aren't the witch?"

"You mean Maggie Madison?" I laughed. "Those are old wives' tales about her. She wasn't a witch—just someone gifted like us. I was never her. She was never me either. I put on her necklace and I could see the world through her eyes. It was breathtaking—I can't even explain what it was like. But it was also very sad. I've been working to help her for the last few days."

"Working to help *her*? A dead witch?" Shayla sputtered. "That *has* to be Dae. I don't know anyone else who'd talk that way. Let her up, Gram."

I looked into the wrinkled, dark face close to mine and smiled. "I've heard so much about you. I'm Dae O'Donnell. Shayla talks about you all the time."

"Flourine Lily." She grinned from ear to ear. "I still smell that old witch on you, honey."

I was a little embarrassed. It never occurred to me that a crowd of people would be waiting for me. "I could use a shower. I've been digging over at the geothermal site for the new town hall. You won't believe what I found."

Kevin and Shayla helped Flourine to her feet. I wasn't sure she was very happy to see me there. She kept throwing feathers at me and mumbling words I couldn't understand.

I wanted to go right in and take a shower. No one else

liked that idea. They didn't think I should be alone. I thought longingly about the clean jeans and shirt I always kept there at the Inn. I finally decided that if they could stand it, so could I.

I'd never seen a group of people act so weird. When we all sat down at the big table in the bar area, everyone crowded in around me. Shayla and her grandmother were behind me, as though I might try to escape. What was wrong with them?

Kevin had leftovers from lunch that day, and warm cookies. I completely forgot about changing clothes and showering as I realized how hungry I was. I wasn't sure I'd eaten in the last few days. What had needed to be done had to be done quickly. I didn't mind. But suddenly, I was exhausted and near the end of my strength.

"Start at the beginning," Kevin said. "Tell us what happened."

"Well, you know about the amber necklace already." I spoke between mouthfuls of homemade bread and warm mulled wine. "My father sent it to me. It was the only real antique he'd managed to find in that whole mess he got himself into. He thought it was from the *Andalusia*."

*"The ghost ship?"* Trudy whispered.

"Yes. But when I held it, I realized it had never been on that ship. I made contact with Maggie. She was given the necklace as a gift from her lover before he left her."

"The *witch*?" Trudy could barely say the word. "Dae, you should've known better. You're the one always reminding everyone else about Duck history. Why would you do such a thing?"

"I tried to tell you to put it down," Ann said. "I guess you were too engrossed with the necklace by then to get my telepathic message."

"Maggie wasn't a witch." I could see the fear and suspicion

on their faces. "She had some special abilities. She could predict storms and heal people. Being different meant she was shunned by everyone else. She lived by herself until she met her sea captain, who left her the necklace then moved on. The witch rumors became worse after that."

"She had some powerful abilities." Ann interrupted again. "Betsy and I felt the connection between you all the way in Richmond and New York. Betsy's mother let me me bring her with me to help find you."

I smiled at Betsy. "I'm really sorry about that. I didn't know."

She came around and hugged me. "It's okay. I'm happy you're back."

She sat on my lap, leaning her head against my dirty shoulder. *Brave child.*

"After I put on the necklace, I realized what was wrong. I knew I had to move fast. It's taken almost a year to get everything in place for the geothermal system at the town hall site. They're ready to go on with the project now. Maggie's house is down there where they're going to drill the holes."

Everyone acted so strange that I didn't tell them that Maggie was killed there when a huge storm collapsed her house on top of her. No one ever bothered to see if she was trapped inside. They were just glad she was gone. "Maggie needs me to collect her bones and give them a decent burial."

Flourine spit on the floor. "Don't you believe them lies. That witch, she has something else in mind. Don't trust her."

Everyone started talking at once. I'd explained the situation as well as I could. I looked at Kevin. We had to get moving if we were going to get the bones. There was no more time. Tomorrow morning, the first hole would be sunk right where I needed to be.

I loved all of these people, my friends, but they were going to have to trust me. I hoped they'd help with the task.

"Look, no one took over anyone," I assured them. "Maggie wasn't a witch but she was gifted. In the fear and agony of her death, she managed to leave something of herself behind in the amber beads of the necklace. They survived and were passed from hand to hand until they reached me. I want to help her. I could use your help doing it."

"I'm sorry." Trudy shuddered. "It was really scary, you know? You said in the note you left for your grandfather you'd be gone, but you didn't take anything with you. Ann flew down here. We were all worried sick."

"I think we all get that part now." Ann was out of patience. "Where's the necklace, Dae? I'd like to see it for myself. I can't believe any object that old has so much power."

"I left it in my backpack by the door. I'll get it."

"No!" Shayla put her hand on my shoulder. "Let's not go through *that* again."

Shayla and Ann exchanged significant looks then tried to beat each other to the entryway. Too bad for both of them, Flourine was already there with her charms and feathers.

I'd heard some odd stories from Shayla, during the years she'd been in Duck, about her Gram. It was like meeting a legend— a *scary* legend.

Kevin came around the table and looked at Betsy. She'd fallen asleep against me. "She's exhausted. It's been a few long days for her. Maybe a nap will do her some good. I'll lay her down in her bed for a while so we can talk."

"You believe I'm me, don't you?" I asked him.

"I do." He smiled and touched my cheek before he took Betsy and left the room.

*Well, that was one for my side.*

Trudy and Tim were whispering to each other and looking like every word the other said was a matter of life and death.

"What do you need us to do, Dae?" Trudy finally looked up with a pretty blush on her cheeks. Her eyes were sparkling.

*Could it be?* After all this time, had Trudy and Tim found something together? Maybe I needed to disappear more often.

I started to explain my plan but was interrupted by Ann and Flourine fighting over the backpack.

"Let it go, Gram," Shayla advised. "It's okay."

"No! We need to put the witch down, *chère*. You know that. She can't be allowed to take hold of anyone else like she has your friend. Who knows what she really wants here?"

"Give me the backpack, old lady." Ann continued to struggle with her.

Seeing that my backpack was going to be shredded, I joined the fray. Reluctantly. Now that I wasn't so engrossed in finding Maggie's bones, and I'd eaten, I wanted to sleep for a few days.

I got up as the poor old backpack that had served me faithfully since college finally gave way. My collapsible shovel and lantern flew across the floor. The amber necklace spun up into the air. Like a charm, it came right into my hands.

Ann reached out and snatched it from me, putting it around her neck. Some of the gold filigree between the smooth amber beads caught in her pale hair. "It's beautiful. Look at the workmanship. It's like strands of sunlight."

"What do you feel? Can you see the witch?" Shayla studied her.

Ann closed her eyes and concentrated. "I can feel the power in it. It's like wearing a necklace made of electricity."

She abruptly opened her eyes. "But that's it. No witch's eyes. I guess she saved that for Dae."

"Let me try." Shayla reached for the beads.

"No!" Flourine cried out. Before anyone could realize her intent or stop her, she took out an old silver dagger and severed the necklace. Amber beads dropped on the wood floor around us.

I gathered them up as fast as I could and stuffed them into the pockets of my dirty jeans. I didn't know if it could be repaired, but I could feel that Maggie was still attached to the broken pieces.

The destruction of the beautiful old treasure brought tears to my eyes. I could still find the remains of the old house without it. I had a rough map I'd drawn to show me the way. I just hated to lose something so rare.

Flourine slid the old dagger into the side of her boot with a satisfied smile on her wrinkled face. "Won't do no more harm now. The witch can't speak."

Ann shrugged and went back in the bar to pour herself a tall glass of whiskey. Shayla smiled at me apologetically then coaxed her grandmother into joining her in the lobby by the fire.

Trudy and Tim, hand in hand, joined me by what was left of my backpack.

"Sorry, Dae," Tim said.

Trudy tried to be upbeat, like always. "Maybe it's for the best that you couldn't find the old bones. Who knows what might have happened? You should probably get cleaned up and sleep for a while. You'll feel better. Do you want me to take you home? I have my car here."

I picked up my lantern and shovel. "No. That's okay. I'll catch a ride home with Kevin. You're right. It'll be okay. I'll see the two of you later."

Tim finally stopped staring at Trudy long enough to say good-bye. It was funny how things happened. What didn't look like much yesterday could be worth everything tomorrow. That's what I had always loved about old things.

Kevin came downstairs. "Did I miss something? Where did everyone go?"

I explained briefly. "Let's go in the kitchen for a minute so I can look at these beads without someone trying to throw them away."

There were two assistant cooks working on lunch for a party that was booked for the ballroom. There was a wonderful aroma of onions and garlic simmering. After checking on how they were doing, Kevin joined me at the tiny table in the corner of the big, warm kitchen.

"Can you feel anything from the beads?" He watched as I set them on the table.

"Yes. It's not as strong, but it's still there." I told him about the map I'd created from what I'd seen in the past. "It was weird trying to figure it out. Once I put on the necklace, I was taken back to when Duck was an unnamed fishing village. Everything was in shades of gray. Some things were inverted or distorted. I don't think people could see me at all. It was like I was in Maggie's brain, seeing it all through her. I wish you could have seen it, Kevin. I think there were only about thirty people living here."

He took my hands. "I *did* see it, Dae. I dreamed about the whole thing. I couldn't do anything, but I felt what you felt. It sounds crazy, I know. Maybe working with you and Ann has rubbed off on me."

That was news. I knew he'd had dreams about things happening to me before. Could someone who didn't start out gifted end up that way?

"Are you sure all Maggie wants is someone to dig up her bones and bury them?" Kevin still held my hands as he stared into my eyes. "Shayla and Ann had quite a few other ideas about the necklace being a trap. All I knew was that you went off the grid. As soon as I woke up after that dream, I lost our connection."

"They're wrong. Maggie was gifted. We were in tune with each other. I could see what she saw, feel what she felt. It was breathtaking. And scary."

"I'm glad it was over before she was killed in the storm. Like always, Dae. You leap before you look."

"I guess it's part of who I am. Will you help me?"

"What do you need?"

That was one of the things I loved about Kevin. He was always there for me, no matter how crazy something was that I wanted to do.

"It's going to take a lot more than my collapsible shovel to get down low enough to reach her house. It's under about twenty feet of sand and mud. We have to get the bones out right away."

"And I have the small excavator to make the storm cellar bigger for storage." He nodded, understanding. "How are we going to dig over there, right off of Duck Road, with all the other activity going on? Surely the town manager, or someone who works for the contractor, will want to know what we're doing."

"That's why I've been digging at night. I've been sleeping in a tent next to the site during the day."

"With a camping shovel. It's going to be harder to disguise the excavator, even at night. We'll have to get some lighting too."

"I know. I have a plan for that." I smiled at him.

"It isn't one I want to hear, right? That's why you're recruiting me, right? You don't want anyone else to get into trouble."

Part of that was true. After all, Chris Slayton, the town

manager for Duck, would probably help me. He might lose his job if we were caught. What could they do to me and Kevin?

If I was caught digging up there, there might be some bad press for me. I was running for mayor against councilman Randal "Mad Dog" Wilson. But I figured people had already made up their minds about who they were going to vote for in just over a week.

Everyone loved Kevin and would do almost anything to keep the Blue Whale Inn open. I couldn't see a downside there.

He wasn't done with other ideas. "What about going to the historical society with this information? People have to stop work on construction projects all the time because of historic artifacts. This is about as historical as it gets."

"That would take too much time." I got to my feet, agitated by the idea. "We couldn't stop them from drilling fast enough. This is the only way."

Kevin stood up and put his arms around me. I was glad he cared enough to get so close despite the sand and who-knew-what-else I'd brought in with my clothes.

"Okay." His tone was gentle. "We'll do it your way. It's hours before dark. Take a shower. Change clothes. Get some sleep."

None of that was part of my plan. "I should be out there, protecting the site. What if someone disrupts my work?"

"The only way I'm going out there tonight is with Dae O'Donnell." He stared into my eyes. "If you can't slow down enough to get some rest, I might be forced to believe what Shayla and Ann said—that you're possessed by Maggie Madison. Let's not go there. Okay?"

# Chapter 2

I had no choice. I needed Kevin's little digging machine to reach what was left of Maggie's house before tomorrow morning. I didn't know how to run it. I couldn't stop the drilling process in time by myself. It had to be this way.

It had taken the best part of the last three days, since I'd put on the amber necklace, to figure out all the details. It had been hard overcoming what had seemed like a fantasy world. The area where I'd found myself was nothing like the place I lived. Nothing was where it belonged. I'd felt like Alice in Wonderland.

To begin with, it was all I could do not to be sick. I don't get motion sickness, but this was something entirely different. I wasn't aware of where I was for several hours. When I woke up from my first meeting with Maggie, I was shaking so hard I couldn't get up from the burgundy brocade sofa in Missing Pieces.

Gradually, I understood what had happened. When I put

the amber necklace on again, I was better prepared. But the process had taken too much time. When I realized what had to be done, I was already almost too late.

It looked like I was still going to have to wait to see this thing through. I tried not to worry. It was going to work out.

Kevin drove me home in his old red Ford pickup after our conversation. He had to be at the Blue Whale Inn for the party at lunchtime, so he'd convinced Ann to stay with me at my house. Obviously, he still wasn't quite sure about my story.

That stung a little.

Gramps was out with someone from the mainland in his fishing boat, the *Eleanore*. Talk about someone doing things that didn't make much sense. Fishing during an ice fog was dangerous and not worth whatever his charter had paid him.

Gramps and I were cut from the same Banker cloth, I guess. People who went back generations on the barrier islands did what they had to do to survive. He was proud and tough. I always hoped I was that way too.

He'd left some macaroni and cheese in the refrigerator along with a note telling me to call him before I went out again. I knew he worried about me, though he tried not to show it. We were the only two left in our family after my mother and grandmother had died. I tried hard not to make him have to wonder where I was, or if I was safe. Sometimes that wasn't easy.

The hot shower felt good as I washed three days' worth of dirt off of me. I put on a heavy sweater, jeans and thick socks when I was finished. It was barely two P.M. What was I supposed to do until it got dark?

Ann was sitting in my window seat, overlooking the Currituck Sound. I laughed as she fended off claws and teeth from Treasure, the black cat Betsy had given me last year. For some reason, he only seemed to like me, Gramps and Kevin. Most of the time, that was all that mattered.

"Will you put this thing in a cat carrier or something?" Ann yelped when Treasure bit her. "I'm not staying here and watching you sleep with it tearing me up. What's wrong with it anyway? Does it need catnip or something?"

I scooped up the cat I'd grown to love and sat down on the bed with him on my lap. "He doesn't like strangers."

"I can see that. What about the witch? Did he like *her*?"

Treasure hissed at her then settled down to purr on me. "I don't know what I can say to convince you. Maggie didn't take me over."

"So you have full recall of everything that happened to you, everything you did, in the last few days?"

I had flashes of total clarity, but I had to admit—to myself—that most of the last few days were a blur.

When Maggie and I had parted company earlier that day, I'd been at the town hall site, lying on the cold ground. I could see that I'd been digging—not very successfully— trying to reach what was left of Maggie's home. I suddenly remembered about Kevin having the excavating equipment and walked to the Blue Whale Inn.

I was sure I knew when I was looking through Maggie's eyes, and when I was on my own. As I'd told Kevin and the others, everything was gray and surreal when I was with Maggie in the past.

It was different when I walked to the Blue Whale. I knew I was in my own time and I knew what I was doing.

"So that's 'no' on that score." Ann sat down and looked out the window. "There's a good chance this entity was using you, Dae. I know your motives are good, but we don't know what her motives are. She may still be using you to get whatever she wants. Now you want Kevin to help you."

Her words brought a few doubts sailing along like clouds across the sea. The incidents of the past few days had been odd, even for me. It shouldn't have surprised me that Ann would point that out. I shored up my resolve and remembered that this quest meant a lot to Maggie. After hundreds of years, her spirit would be united with her lover's and a wrong would be put right for the people of Duck who'd hated her.

"Why are you being so stubborn about this?" Ann asked. "Is it personal, or just that Duck pride standing in the way of admitting you might be wrong?"

I lay back on the bed and forced myself to close my eyes. Everything inside of me was jumping around like I'd had too many energy drinks. I tried to relax. "I only have a few hours before we can work at the site. I should get some rest."

Her eyes narrowed as she stared at me. I didn't have to see her to feel her gaze. It was as sharp as a shard of glass trying to slice away my defenses. Ann was a powerful psychic. I wouldn't let her in.

"Yeah. You do that." She got up and opened the bedroom door. "And if there is someone else inside you, let me just say to her that you aren't alone anymore. Don't make us hurt you."

Ann left the room quickly after her ominous words. I waited with my eyes closed until I heard her talking on the phone downstairs.

I jumped out of bed and went into the bathroom, locking the door behind me.

"Are you all right?" I asked Maggie.

"I'm fine. You?" The words came from my mouth but the tone and dialect were different. Maggie had originally come from Surrey in England. That, and the old-fashioned English she used, made our voices very unique.

"I was worried. I didn't know if I'd lost you when the beads broke."

"Oh, my friend, there is so much more that binds us now than the beads. Is this your home?"

"Yes." I smiled. "The bathroom. Sort of a room for the bedpan."

She giggled. "What now? Do you hope to fool your friends?"

"That would be nice. I can better look for your lover's resting place without their aid." Her dialect was beginning to rub off on me. I had to watch it.

"Then I will do my best to stay hidden." She looked around the bathroom. "This is a place of wonder! And so many handsome men. Would that I could kiss them all."

Maggie wasn't a witch, but I'd learned she was a tavern wench who liked men a lot. Though she swore she'd given her heart to a sea captain named Thomas Graham, she liked to flirt. That had brought a whole other realm of trouble to her with the wives of Duck.

"Well, for now, let's keep it quiet. I don't want anyone else to guess what's happening."

"I can do that," she said. "It will be simple to sit back and look at your amazing life."

I went back to bed and must have fallen asleep right after because I was dreaming again of all the things I'd seen in the past with Maggie.

I hadn't expected their clothes to be so coarse and plain. Most of the dresses, trousers and shirts were shades of brown, barely held together with rough twine. The people were dirty and thin—some almost skeletal. It hurt to look at their frail, white-faced children.

Somehow I'd imagined my Duck Banker ancestors being a hale and hearty group, able to spit in the eye of hurricanes and keep on sailing.

Instead, they were a dour, unfriendly bunch—wary of strangers, fearful of anything or anyone who didn't look or sound as they did. Their dwellings were crude, barely able to withstand wind and rain.

How had anyone survived that time to get us to this one?

Then Ann was shaking me, telling me it was time to go. Kevin was already set up at the town hall site.

It was dark outside. Gramps was home. He wore his worried frown as I went downstairs in clean clothes and dry boots.

I still felt like a zombie, barely able to shake off the memories of my dreams. Maybe I looked like one too.

He hugged me tight for several long minutes while Ann tapped her foot impatiently near the door. "What's going on, Dae? Your note didn't say much and all of your friends were worried. Are you all right? Where have you been?"

There wasn't time to explain. Every moment of darkness we lost would make it that much harder to reach the remnants of the old house by morning. "I promise I'll explain when I come back. You have to trust me."

His broad face was an angry thundercloud. "I know we try not to step on each other's toes. We're both adults. But you're not going anywhere without me until I know what you've been doing. You look like death warmed over, as your grandmother used to say."

"Gramps—"

"I'm not kidding, honey." He put on his heavy jacket. "I'm going too."

Ann shrugged. "It doesn't matter. Let's go."

We took Gramps's golf cart down the silent streets of Duck toward the new town hall site.

Kevin had managed to find one of the big yellow tents that were being used by the contractor working on the geothermal site. He also had lights. The tent glowed like a beacon in the darkness. I hadn't counted on that problem.

I wasn't sure anymore that it was possible to do this and not get caught. I hoped I could keep everyone else out of trouble.

Even inside the tent, it was still cold. The ice fog hung on everything with its frozen breath. Shayla and her grandmother had come too, wanting to be there when we located Maggie's bones. Flourine had added even more beads and feathers. Shayla had opted for her usual classic black with no additions.

Everyone huddled in their heavy coats and jackets as Kevin started the small digging machine. Until that moment when I'd wanted everything to be quiet and secret, I hadn't realized how loud it was.

"This doesn't make any sense, Dae," Gramps said again—the second time since I'd basically explained what we were planning to do. "You can't be out here digging this close to Duck Road, in a restricted construction area, and not get caught. You could lose the election if you tell anyone what you're doing. You're playing with fire."

About that time, I wished I *were* playing with fire so I could get warm. "I'm sorry, Gramps. I have to do this. You don't have to stay."

He shook his head and muttered something about needing a permit but he didn't leave.

Kevin's excavator made my puny efforts at moving dirt and sand feel like wasted energy. That was the only real doubt I had about my relationship with Maggie Madison.

Why hadn't I thought about getting help? Why hadn't I thought about Kevin's excavator?

I'd labored out there—for however long it was—when I could've been done very quickly. I might even have had time to tell the historical society so they could help. The town would have been sympathetic, if approached through proper channels.

Was it because Maggie was thinking for me? Or had I still been mentally lost in the past where excavators and town regulations didn't exist?

It was as though when I woke up at the site I remembered there were better tools to work with. Maggie had lived hundreds of years in the past. She wouldn't have thought there was anything better than a shovel. Was that why I was out here digging with one?

I didn't say anything. I didn't dare let anyone know I had any doubts about what had happened. The group around me felt like tigers waiting to pounce on any weakness that might lead them to the *witch*.

I watched as Kevin plied the hard, sandy ground with the metal equipment. The pile of sand grew steadily around him. It wasn't long before he'd reached something.

"What's that?" Shayla squinted down into the dark hole.

"It doesn't sound like witch's bones to me." Gramps stood beside her.

Whatever it was had red paint on it. Bright red paint. I could only see about three feet of it, but nothing like it would have been here four hundred years ago.

"Let me take one more swipe at it," Kevin yelled over the noise of the machine.

I watched the bucket go down and come back with another load of dirty sand. The color was different this far down—more burnt orange than the pale sand on top. I knew that was because of sand washing away and the town replacing it every year. It usually wasn't even local sand. Archaeologists of the future were going to have a headache someday when they tried to figure that out.

As the bucket came up and moved away, something else

of what lay beneath us became visible. There was more bright red paint and the number twelve.

"It's the top of an old car." Ann sounded almost excited. "Are we going to have to go through a car to reach the witch's hovel? Did she mention a car was resting on her, Dae?"

Gramps peered hard into the hole. I held his arm as he almost got too close to the edge. "What is it?" I asked as he drew back.

"Kevin," he yelled. "Take one more swipe—to the left side a little. I think I know what this is."

"Sure, Horace. Stand back."

The excavator bucket went down again and came back. We all waited impatiently to see what more was revealed, standing as close as we could without falling in or getting hit.

There was a crashing sound—like shattering glass. The bucket seemed to be caught on something. Kevin couldn't get it to come back up. He had to play with it for a few minutes.

Finally, it broke free and came back to the surface. Attached to one of the tines on the excavator's bucket was a damaged car door that had been ripped from the vehicle. A partial, skeletal arm appeared to be waving at someone out the window.

"Old number twelve." Gramps chuckled when he saw the door. "That's Mad Dog's old race car. I wondered where that thing got to."

# Chapter 3

"A car?" Disbelief showed in Ann's flat face. "Why would a car be buried down there?"

"And what does this have to do with the witch?" Shayla demanded.

"Maybe that's one of her bones there." Flourine pointed to the car door and the arm bone.

Kevin shut down the digger and joined them. "I think this is probably someone else. It looks to me like someone was buried in the race car."

No sooner were the words out of his mouth than Duck police officer Scott Randall pushed aside the yellow tent flap. He stopped when he saw all of us there. "Mayor? Sheriff? Mr. Brickman?" He appeared a little bewildered. "What are you all doing out here this late? And what are you digging up?"

No one wanted to burden him with the tale of Maggie Madison. Gramps basically explained that we'd found the race car while looking for something else and stopped when we saw the door with the arm attached to it.

Scott was a very nice young man who was totally dedicated to Duck. He was also a little reserved and careful when it came to voicing opinions. He simply shrugged and said, "I'll call this in to the chief. He might want to talk with all of you."

Gramps put his arm around my shoulder. "I'm going to take Dae home, Scott. She hasn't been feeling well. The rest of you are welcome to come wait at the house until Ronnie gets there. I think we have some coffee, and I baked an apple pie yesterday."

Scott didn't question it. Gramps might not be the sheriff of Dare County anymore, but everyone still listened to what he had to say.

We slowly filed out of the tent. The cold air was like a blast of reality. I only thought it was freezing inside.

I was surprised when Shayla and her grandmother went along with the plan, but they respected Gramps's word too. Flourine rode to the house with us, sitting with me and Gramps in the front of the golf cart. It was a snug fit. I was pretty sure she was flirting with him too.

Shayla left her car at the Duck Shoppes parking lot, which was next door to the spot where the new town hall was being built, and rode with Kevin and Ann in his pickup.

I was confused and not sure what to do next. Obviously, finding a body in a car was going to put off trying to locate Maggie's bones.

It would also stop any further work being done at the town hall site, which was good. I didn't have to worry about anyone drilling a hole for the geothermal work through Maggie's house for now.

Finding the race car was completely unexpected. The

area would no doubt be a crime scene for a while until the police could figure out what had happened. I kept wondering what they would find. How could something that bizarre have been there? Who put it there and when?

I made coffee when we got back to the house. Ann called the local woman she'd left babysitting Betsy at the Blue Whale while she and Kevin went out.

It seemed Ann had changed a lot in the past year. I couldn't imagine her caring about a child's welfare when I'd first met her. I felt bad that she seemed to know so much about what was going on in my life while I knew nothing of hers.

As usual, everyone gathered around the big kitchen table. Its scratched and bumped surface had seen many late-night conversations between Gramps and other law enforcement officers down through the years. I used to sit and listen to them talk long after I should've been in bed.

I'd always looked up to Gramps and secretly wanted to be a police officer when I was a child. I'd never said anything about it, not sure if I would be allowed to join those exalted ranks.

Once I was old enough to consider it seriously, my mother had died and I'd dropped out of college. I began spending all my time collecting things that eventually went into Missing Pieces.

Now I knew joining the police wasn't for me. It took a certain mind-set that I'd noticed in Kevin, Gramps and even Tim, to a lesser degree. You had to have a suspicious nature and believe that the law was the best way to get things done.

I didn't always agree with that notion.

Shayla, Flourine and Ann were having a heated discussion about Maggie Madison and why we hadn't found her bones. Flourine was convinced that Maggie had manipulated the car to cover the spot where her bones were buried.

"That doesn't even make any sense," Ann argued from

her perspective as an ex–FBI psychic who'd once found missing children. "If you're saying the witch's bones have power and she'll rise again if we dig them up, why would she put anything in our way?"

Flourine, obviously a little angry too, shook her feathers and charms at her. "Don't act so high and mighty with me, miss. I can see right through you. You're like a ghost to me. I see all of you. And you are plain scared."

Ann rolled her eyes. "Even if I *was* scared—which I'm not—the race car takes out all of your theories about the whole event. You might as well go home and dig around in your root cellar for answers."

Flourine hissed at her much the same way Treasure had earlier. Shayla got between them, and the argument about Maggie's witchy powers went on among the three of them for a while.

Gramps was talking to Kevin in a corner of the living room. I noticed that Flourine insinuated herself between them, smiling up at Gramps, asking him what his favorite kind of pie was.

Kevin came into the kitchen to help me. "That's interesting." He nodded toward Gramps and Flourine then smiled.

"I know. Did you notice Trudy and Tim at the inn earlier? Romance must be in the air."

"You could've fooled me. Not much romantic about digging up a car out in the cold."

"I haven't thanked you yet for bringing the excavator out there even though I probably sounded like a crazy person and everyone thinks I'm possessed."

He kissed my forehead and put his arm around me. "I love you, Dae. There isn't much I *wouldn't* do for you."

My usually confident smile trembled a little as I said, "And you don't think I'm possessed, right? It would be okay to add that in."

"Something's up." He didn't quite let me off the hook. "I'm not sure what it is yet, but I'm willing to give you the benefit of the doubt. I wish you'd be honest with me."

That wasn't exactly the answer I was looking for. I wasn't ready to go into more of what had happened either. Before I could put my foot into it any more, there was a hard rap at the front door that drew everyone's attention.

I went to answer it, expecting to see Chief Michaels. He *was* on the front step, but he was also joined by another familiar face. Luke Helms had moved to Duck after retiring from his lucrative legal practice on the mainland. Last spring, when the district attorney for Dare County had given up his position due to illness, Luke had stepped in to take his place.

"Chief! We've been waiting for you. Luke, I haven't seen you in a while. I hope life as the DA is agreeing with you." I shook both their hands. I'd never felt less like the mayor of Duck than I did at that moment. There were too many doubts clouding my brain. I had to let my usual outgoing personality switch to autopilot and hope everything I said made sense.

Chief Michaels muttered something polite and immediately went to find Gramps.

Luke smiled and held my hand an extra moment when he stepped inside. He was a good choice for DA. He'd always been kind and helpful to everyone in Duck. I admired his expensive suits and confident handshakes.

"I haven't seen you for a while, Dae. How's the campaign going? You know you have my vote, right?"

"Thanks. I'm afraid I haven't put as much time and energy as I should have into the election. It always seems like something else comes up."

"Well, you must have good people working for you then. I've never seen so many signs in such a small place. Was that an airplane banner I caught the other day? I even noticed the Richmond paper had a story about you last week."

I was totally surprised by that. I knew Gramps and some of his friends from the pinochle group had put up a few posters they'd printed on our computer, and some high school students had held up signs during rush hour on Duck Road. That was as far as my campaign budget went. Who else would put money into my campaign?

I smiled and nodded then sidestepped the issue. "Why did Chief Michaels drag you out on this awful night?"

"I think we're about to hear the story." Luke nodded toward the chief, who was standing at the kitchen table. "I'll defer to him since he knows it better."

He was right. Gramps called us all into the kitchen, where he passed out slices of apple pie and mugs of hot coffee.

I wasn't hungry, but I felt the pressure of Shayla, Ann and Flourine watching me like it was some test of proving I wasn't possessed. I took a big mouthful of the spicy apples and crumb topping then swallowed. It almost choked me, but I washed it down quickly with coffee before I grinned at my audience.

"Now, I don't know what was going on out there tonight," Chief Michaels began in his usual semi-irritated voice. "I'm sure so many of Duck's illustrious citizens weren't out at this time of night simply vandalizing town property. So let me assume that our good mayor had a vision."

Of course, everyone was looking at me then. Not that it was a secret. I'd used my gift of finding things for the people of Duck since I was a child. I'd located hundreds of keys, wallets, earrings and watches. In more recent years, it was mostly missing cell phones.

Normally, thinking about what my mother had called my "service to the community" relaxed me. It made me feel that I'd done something useful with my life.

Not tonight.

Ann looked skeptical—she hadn't touched her pie, but no one was watching *her*. Shayla and Flourine still looked like they were ready to throw a net over me.

Gramps and Chief Michaels had their patient, long-suffering lawmen's looks on their faces. Gramps at least partially understood, because he'd lived with my grandmother, who was also a finder of lost things.

Chief Michaels put up with it, even acknowledging my help sometimes, but he would never understand. He usually tried to ignore the things I told him until he couldn't look the other way.

Kevin and Luke smiled at me encouragingly. Luke wasn't from Duck and had never had any traffic with the supernatural. I think he just liked me.

Kevin understood, maybe more than Gramps, after working with Ann for so many years. I knew he hadn't made up his mind about the possession problem yet. I could tell by the question in his eyes when we talked.

Ann stepped into the silence. "Dae hasn't been well. I'm sure one of us can explain."

"I appreciate that, Ms. Porter." Chief Michaels wasn't willing to share his show with her. "I'll get around to finding out why you're back in town later when I take your statement. Right now, I'd like to hear from the mayor."

I smiled at Ann, surprised that she'd tried to protect me. I might've once doubted why she'd done that, but I knew her better now. I'd been in her mind.

I never dreamed when we first met that she'd be sitting at my kitchen table, drinking coffee and trying to defend me. It would've made more sense for her to try to kill me, at least in her mind. She definitely didn't want to share Kevin.

I realized I'd made the chief wait long enough. He wanted to hear my story. I took another sip of coffee and leaned forward to tell it.

I was less than honest. The whole ordeal with my friends had made me a little sensitive on the subject of Maggie Madison.

Instead, I explained about the dream that had led me to look for a historic artifact crucial to Duck history. I couldn't lose with that argument. The chief knew I was crazy about finding things *and* Duck history.

I didn't go into a lot of detail. Chief Michaels was used to me trudging around the Outer Banks looking for items to put into Missing Pieces and the Duck Historical Museum. My story wouldn't surprise him.

"I didn't want them to drill through it." I tried to make it sound that what we were doing was the lesser of two evils. "Kevin—and everyone else—was helping me. We would've been in and out already, but we found the car."

Chief Michaels digested what I'd told him. "All right. I assumed this had something to do with your friends looking for you. You have to give some thought to letting people know what's going on. Tonight, for instance—"

"You know the proper channels would've been too slow to stop this." I felt some of my old fire. "Once it's lost, you can't get it back."

"There's still the issue of proper permits."

"That wouldn't have gone through until after tomorrow. Besides"—I smiled at him—"we found the car with a corpse in it. That must count for something."

He drew a deep breath and looked toward the heavens briefly. "It certainly does. That, and purchasing a permit for the work you've already done, plus paying a fine for digging on town property without permission, will keep you and your friends out of court."

"As to the matter of the car you found . . ." Luke wanted his say before the chief could pile any other accusations against me. "It seems this car has been at the center of an open murder investigation for a long time. Have you all ever heard of Lightning Joe Walsh?"

# Chapter 4

Everyone from Duck knew the legend of Lightning Joe Walsh. It came from back in the 1970s when local moonshine runners turned to racing. For a while, there was even a small racetrack in the Outer Banks. Nothing elaborate—just a dirt track and people sitting in lawn chairs watching and cheering local drivers.

The big local name at that time was Mad Dog Wilson. He drove his number twelve race car like a wild thing, uncaring if he rolled the car or skidded off the track to win the race. There was no real competition for him. He was the king.

Lightning Joe appeared out of the blue one day. No one knew who he was or where he came from. They said Mad Dog couldn't beat him because Joe was even crazier than him. What added insult to injury was that Joe didn't care about winning—at least not the applause, the trophy or the cash prize. He only seemed intent on being first, and making Mad Dog's life miserable.

Their final race seemed to bear out this conclusion. Mad Dog wrecked his car. It wasn't even as bad as other wrecks he'd had, but he was seriously injured. He gave up racing and had to walk with a cane after that. His badly broken leg had healed poorly. Mad Dog's number twelve car was hauled away by a wrecker and never seen again.

People thought for sure Lightning Joe would stop at the end of that race. His opponent was down and it would have been the sportsmanlike thing to do. He didn't stop—not for the thousand dollars in prize money or to see if Mad Dog was hurt. His car never returned to the racetrack either. No one ever saw hide nor hair of him again.

"Joe wanted to show up Mad Dog." Gramps finished his version of the tale for the people who weren't from Duck. "We always wondered what happened to him, the faceless driver who didn't care if he won or lost."

"How did you know his name if he never stopped?" Ann asked.

"It was written on the side of his black car with the number twenty-three," Gramps answered. "We never found out if he was local or not. He was gone with his car, and so was Mad Dog. Racing died out around here after that."

"Thank you, Mr. O'Donnell." Luke stopped the reminiscing. "We believe the skeleton you found in the number twelve car by the town hall may be that of Joe Walsh."

Gramps scratched his head. "That doesn't make any sense. Why would he be in Mad Dog's car instead of his own?"

"You remember the report that was filed when Mad Dog's car went missing?" Chief Michaels asked him. "Someone stole the car right off of the flatbed. People thought maybe fans did it, because Mad Dog swore he never saw it again. According to the mechanic who looked at it on the track, it was still running and could have been driven."

"That's right." Gramps snapped his fingers. "A lot of people thought Joe had taken it as a souvenir."

Luke pulled a thin file from his briefcase. "This report has been buried since that time. It's possible it wasn't ever received by the sheriff's department. We found it recently as the old records are being computerized."

I looked at the yellowed paper. Some of the typewritten words were a little smeared. But it was clearly a missing person's report filed for Joe Walsh of Manteo by his sister, Pam Walsh. *Six foot three, one hundred and sixty pounds. Black hair. Blue eyes. Anchor tattoo on his upper left arm.*

"You can see the report was filed the same night of the race Mr. O'Donnell was talking about, April 12, 1971," Luke pointed out. "In other words, Mad Dog's number twelve car and Joe Walsh went missing the same night."

"That's when you didn't have to wait forty-eight hours to report a missing person." Chief Michaels said it fondly, as though missing those days when he was a sheriff's deputy.

"I guess no one followed up on it," Gramps said. "We were overburdened in those days, since we were pretty much the only law enforcement on the island."

"There were ten subsequent reports filed by Pam Walsh." Luke pulled out more reports. "Miss Walsh tried to find her brother over the period of the next five years. We only found a few of those reports. No action was taken on any of them."

I felt bad for Gramps. He wasn't sheriff back then, but he was a deputy. I didn't know about the other reports, but the one Luke had given me was signed by Horace O'Donnell, Deputy.

The spotlight was on him now. As much as I hated everyone looking at me, I would've taken it back to give him some breathing room if I could.

No one said anything. It had all happened a long time ago—except that we found the number twelve car tonight.

"The medical examiner is doing tests on the remains as we speak." Luke put away his paperwork. "We hope to have a preliminary identification of the body very soon. As Chief Michaels mentioned, I'll need statements from each of you about what happened this evening. If the body in the car turns out to be Joe Walsh, you may each be part of a murder investigation."

"Has anyone spoken to Mad Dog?" Gramps asked.

"No," Luke answered. "And we'd appreciate it if none of you try to go around this process and contact him. My office, and Chief Michaels, will take care of that when the time is right."

Luke gave us each a sheet of paper and asked us to write our statements and sign them. I could only imagine what Flourine's statement would read—*Came here looking for a witch and found a dead man in a race car.* Would she go on to tell them about her own magical abilities?

I managed to put down what I'd told the chief in a neat paragraph, then signed and dated it. I knew what governmental bodies were looking for.

Everyone finally went home around midnight. I had a few stern looks from Shayla and Ann as well as a flutter of feathers from Flourine. Kevin hugged me before he left and said he'd call in the morning. Luke left with Chief Michaels.

Gramps collapsed into his recliner, exhausted. "That was quite a workout."

I sat on the sofa across from him. "Your name was on that report. I guess they won't hold it against you, huh?"

"Don't worry so much. Like I said, there was a lot going on back then. That's why most of the towns got their own police force. We didn't have the money or the manpower to keep up. We probably got hundreds of reports like that every week. It's a shame it had to be that way, but there wasn't much we could do about it."

"I'm guessing that was Luke's casual way of saying Mad Dog could be a suspect in Joe Walsh's death?"

"Sounds like it to me. I'm surprised Sheriff Riley wasn't out here with them. It was a case originally brought to the sheriff's department, which he could take to be in his jurisdiction, even though it happened before he was sheriff. Finding the car in Duck makes it Ronnie's case now."

"Do you think Mad Dog killed Joe Walsh? Could he have been that angry about him constantly winning?"

"I don't know, honey." He picked up the TV remote. He usually slept in the recliner with the TV on. "You should go up to bed and get some sleep. You've had a big day. Who knows what tomorrow will bring."

I told him good night and headed upstairs. Treasure was waiting for me on the bed. He yawned when he saw me and made room as I got changed. With his head settled against my shoulder, he started purring loudly.

Until Maggie decided to make her presence known.

"You meet as many young men as I did, but you don't have to serve them rum. Why don't you take advantage of it? Luke likes you. I could tell."

At that point, Treasure jumped and screeched before he ran downstairs.

"I don't want to take advantage of it. I love Kevin."

"I love Thomas too, but there's always time for a small dalliance, don't you think?" Maggie giggled.

"No. Not really. I need to go to sleep now. I'm exhausted."

She rubbed "our" hand across the sheets and my flannel pajamas. "These are so soft—like goose down. You are a fortunate woman, Dae O'Donnell, to be so wealthy."

"Thanks." I didn't go into the fact that I wasn't wealthy at all, except by her four-hundred-year-old standards. "Good night, Maggie. Mayhap we will have good fortune locating Thomas's grave soon."

Maggie subsided and I stared up at the ceiling. *Mayhap?* I had to do something about this blending between us or people wouldn't be able to understand me, although it did make it easier for me to understand Maggie.

Finding Thomas's grave might prove to be much harder than finding Maggie's resting spot, I realized. I had some idea where Maggie's bones were. But her ship captain, Thomas, could be buried anywhere along the hundred-mile span of the Outer Banks. I hoped I could keep my promise to reunite the lovers.

Of course now I couldn't go to sleep. I kept thinking about everything that had happened. Gramps just thought being caught digging without a permit would be a bad thing for the upcoming election. If Mad Dog was accused of murder, it would make him unable to continue. I would be the next mayor by default.

I didn't want to win that way, but I might not have any choice. Mad Dog and I had never been friends, but I hated to see him go down this way. If nothing else, it was a black spot on Duck's history. Despite the easy win, I hoped it wasn't true.

I woke early the next morning feeling like my old self. There were no unusual dreams, and I got dressed in warm clothes and went downstairs for breakfast. There was a brief moment when Maggie admired my blue sweater, but we quickly changed places. It was getting easier to go back and forth. I wasn't sure if that was good or bad.

Gramps was already gone. There was no sign that he'd eaten. The coffeepot was cold. It was unusual behavior for him. I tried not to worry about it though. He could've had an early charter.

"Looks like we're going out for breakfast." I grabbed Treasure and put him in the cloth carry-all I'd made. It was bright blue and had ducks all over it and a flap over the top, like a messenger bag, to keep him from jumping out. Not that he ever acted like he wanted to. He seemed to enjoy riding in it and liked being at Missing Pieces with me.

A pang of longing rose in me as I thought of how many days I had been away from the shop. I hardly ever went that long between visits, even if I wasn't working. I loved the shop and everything in it.

I walked quickly down the road to the Duck Shoppes on the Boardwalk. Cars honked at me and people waved. Most people here knew me. I waved back, happy to be going about my normal daily routine. The weather had turned warm again. The sun was shining down from a clear blue sky.

And a giant photo of me was smiling down from the side of the big, blue Duck water tower.

I stopped walking to stare up at it. I'd never seen anything else besides the town name on the tower. Sure, it was occasionally decorated for the jazz festival or Christmas.

But this was a political ad. I couldn't believe the town had okayed it.

How had it happened? I hadn't asked for it to be done, certainly hadn't paid for it. I felt sure the town hadn't meant it as an endorsement. I needed to ask a few discreet questions of the right people.

I stopped to pick up coffee and a cinnamon roll at the Coffee House and Bookstore in the parking lot of the Duck Shoppes. Jamie and Chris Slayton—they were married last spring—asked me about finding the race car. Duck had a fast-acting grapevine.

I couldn't tell them everything about finding the car or who the police thought might be in it, since Chief Michaels and Luke had asked us not to. They'd probably find out anyway, but it wouldn't be from me.

I sort of explained that I had been looking for something historical at the town hall site. I didn't go into detail. I didn't have to since people knew I was always looking around for something, usually inspired by my "gift."

Chris was our brilliant town manager. He wasn't happy about the news. "This will cost us another few months getting the town hall built. What artifact was so important, Mayor? I know you've been as excited as I have about finishing this project. We've had so many setbacks. Couldn't it have waited? I wish you'd come to me first."

"I didn't want you to be involved. I know you've tried to help me before and it didn't end well for you. I couldn't risk your job to find—the thing. It was better if it was all on me."

"I had to fine Kevin Brickman for operating that equipment on town property without a permit. There could even be legal ramifications. Councilman Wilson already contacted the town's lawyer to look into it. Kevin's my friend, Mayor. Or at least he *was* my friend."

I bit my lip, not happy about Kevin being fined. "If it had been the easy in-and-out project I'd imagined, none of this would've happened. But at least you weren't out there, Chris, and you didn't lose your job. We can't afford to lose you."

He continued scowling at me while Jamie held his hand. They were such a great couple.

"I guess you're right. I hated to send the fine out to Kevin. I know it's part of my job, but he's been so much help around town and he's a volunteer on almost every committee, not to mention working with the volunteer fire department."

"Don't worry. I'll reimburse him. He'll be fine."

"It's five thousand dollars. That's kind of hefty."

"Five thousand dollars?" I had no idea. I'd probably sat through that part of the lengthy ordinance creation—there were so many ordinances. I never expected to break any of them.

I'd thought it might be a few hundred and I could trade some labor at the Blue Whale for it. Five thousand was too much. I couldn't let that stand. There had to be a way to make some quick cash to repay him. I might have to sell something from Missing Pieces that I didn't want to get rid of.

"Maybe when the election is over, you could give him the money you've been spending on ads." Jamie smiled sweetly but her words were sharp. "That one on the water tower and the one that goes by on the charter boat twice a day must've been expensive."

"I don't know about the charter boat." Chris grinned. "But I charged your campaign agent enough to add some playground equipment to the park. Nothing personal, Mayor. You know you have my vote. I think an ad on the water tower should go for a premium price."

*What in the world was going on?* "That's okay. Who paid for the water tower ad?"

"Your campaign agent. I have his card back at town hall. I have an email from him with the ad specifications too. I can look that up and email you, if you like."

"That's okay." I didn't want to tell him that I didn't have a campaign agent. I wasn't sure who would have made that claim.

"Sure." Chris bent his head to kiss Jamie good-bye. "I think I can do lunch if you don't mind waiting until one or so."

"That's fine. Let me know later." She squeezed his hand.

I was so happy for them. Chris had been here for a few

years guiding Duck's growth and coming up with grants and ideas for wonderful projects like the new town hall and the expanded boardwalk.

Jamie had moved here to help her brother, Phil, save the coffee shop and had expanded the bookstore to include book clubs and other ingenious ideas. We would've lost our coffee shop and bookstore without her.

I walked with Chris up the stairs to the boardwalk that overlooked the Currituck Sound. A dozen businesses, including mine, Trudy's and Shayla's, were located here. Town hall was also in the small, cramped space.

That was one of the reasons everyone who worked at town hall was excited about the new building. We were all looking forward to larger spaces and a bigger meeting room for events. There would also be room for the Duck Police Department. That would get them out of the fire station farther down Duck Road.

I hated that I'd been instrumental in creating another setback to that progress. And now, besides finding a way to give Kevin five thousand dollars, I had something else to worry about.

I didn't know anyone who had the kind of money Chris was talking about to pay for election ads. I wasn't even sure it was legal to have someone else pay for them. That's why my advertising had consisted of computer-generated eight-by-ten-inch posters all over town.

I probably needed to go to the election board for answers, but it seemed kind of late. The damage had been done. I had no idea what people were going to think about seeing my campaign ad on the water tower. I was pretty sure it wouldn't be good.

Duck town clerk Nancy Boidyn was at her desk when Chris and I arrived at town hall. Nancy wasn't from Duck, but she was like Kevin—it was as though she'd always been there. She appreciated the summers, even though she hated storms. She was one of my favorite people.

"Dae! It's good to see you. What kind of trouble have you been into?"

Since I knew that she'd already heard, I didn't bother with much explanation. "You know me—always poking around where I shouldn't be."

Her eyes widened dramatically as she put her arm around my shoulders. I smiled at the pink bunny slippers she wore in the office and her slick, short new haircut that made her dark eyes seem so dramatic. Chris went back into his closet-sized office to look for the information.

"Sweetie, I'm so sorry about the fine. You know I didn't want to send it out, but I didn't have any choice. Councilman Wilson is breathing down my neck on this. Chris's too. He called a press conference for later today. I don't know who he thinks is interested enough to come. I don't think *Mayor looks for artifact without permit* is much of a news story."

"I expected as much. It doesn't matter. People who plan to vote for me know me. I don't think this will change their minds. It might throw a few undecided votes to Mad Dog, but that's all."

Chris came out of his office with a business card in hand. "This is the man who bought the advertising for the water tower. Whoever he is, he must have deep pockets. Maybe he can loan you the money for Kevin's fine."

I looked at the card with a growing sense of foreboding. I wished I were wearing gloves to touch it. Sometimes my gift of sight could be a hazard. "Thanks. I appreciate it."

I took the card from him. It was plain black letters on a white background. *Carlton Hughes*. Nothing fancy. Then the vision of its owner took over.

# Chapter 5

"Dae?" Nancy had a worried frown on her pretty face. "Are you okay?"

I always get a little shaky when I have a vision from something or someone I've touched. In this case, it was appropriate to be unnerved by what I saw.

The card belonged to a publicist from an advertising firm located in Elizabeth City on the North Carolina mainland. It was innocuous enough in and of itself. It was the money behind it that left me with a bad taste in my mouth. Dillon Guthrie had hired the firm for me.

Dillon was a big-time smuggler. His base of operations was national, but he had a soft spot in his heart for the Outer Banks. He and I had met last year over the sale of a rare antique pistol. He'd offered me money then for my campaign, but I'd turned him down. It was blood money, as far as I was concerned.

I'd had a few emails from him since then, but they were mostly questions about items he'd purchased and wanted my opinion on. He swore he respected my integrity and had begun treating me like his private antique broker. I hadn't actually done any deals with him, just given advice about antiquities.

Why had he decided to put money into my campaign, especially at this late date? It made me feel like he was a magician with something up his sleeve.

I thanked Chris and Nancy for their help, not sure if I'd already done so. I stuck the business card in my pocket and headed down to Missing Pieces.

The Currituck Sound was like a piece of blue glass, gulls dipping and wheeling over it. A few boats were out, their colorful sails trying to catch any early morning breeze. Two women were launching kayaks from the sand-bar near the boardwalk. Ducks paddled around in the cold water at the base of the piers that supported the structure.

All of the shops were open. There were even some early shoppers enjoying the day and, hopefully, looking for something from Missing Pieces they couldn't live without. I had a chance to make up for the time the shop had been closed.

August Grandin from the Duck General Store nodded curtly as he walked by me. He was never much of a talker. I waved to Trudy through the window of the Curves and Curls Beauty Spa as she worked on Annabelle Smith's hair. They both waved back to me.

Then I was home. *Home!*

It was always my first feeling when I opened the door to Missing Pieces and stepped inside. Maybe it was because I loved everything here. It would've all been at my house if it wasn't for Gramps suggesting I open a shop and sell some of it. I was very comfortable here. I might have lived here, if it were possible. The owner of the Duck Shoppes had a strict "no living on the premises" policy.

I opened the blind on the door and let Treasure roam through the shop. My burgundy brocade sofa beckoned, and I didn't even try to resist. I sat there in splendor and enjoyed my breakfast.

The sofa was a little old and a bit too big for the shop—Shayla frequently pointed this out to me. I didn't care. It was perfect. I worked around it as needed. It was pleasant having it there, sharing stories with friends and visitors when they came to visit. Sometimes I even spent the night on it. There wasn't a more comfortable sofa in the world.

That morning, even my sofa didn't bring me peace. I realized I was going to have to find five thousand dollars' worth of merchandise to sell and a ready buyer for it. Not allowing Kevin to pay for what he'd done for me seemed even more important than figuring out who my campaign benefactor was.

I knew there were several items worth that much. Some were worth much more. I took out a pair of silver bells that I had acquired and thought about them. The bells were made by monks in St. Augustine hundreds of years ago. There were actually three of them, but I hadn't been able to locate the third bell in the last year.

I knew I had a ready buyer who had the cash for one of the bells. Dillon had wanted to purchase the bell I'd found. I had refused to sell to him. Oddly enough, he already had the second bell and had given it to me—with the stipulation that I would let him buy the bells from me when I found the third one.

It wasn't a comfortable arrangement. I probably should have said no to it as I had his campaign contribution. I was weak and he knew how to trap me. I'd told myself that it didn't matter because I could find the other bell and that would be the end of our business relationship.

I knew my bell was worth a lot more than five thousand

dollars, especially since he had already had one. Maybe this had happened so I could free myself of him. He could buy my bell and take his own back. I'd be able to pay Kevin's fine and Dillon probably wouldn't be interested in me anymore.

I hated to give the bells up without finding the third. It wounded my collecting ego to let it go. But what was done, was done. Kevin had been fined because he'd been helping me. I had to get him out of the jam he was in.

I turned on my laptop and emailed Dillon to see if we could meet soon, before I changed my mind.

I sighed as the email left. Treasure jumped up on the counter and stared at me with a question in his beautiful green eyes.

"Yes, I'm a little sad about getting myself in this mess." My answer to the cat's unasked question seemed normal. It was as though I could tell what he was thinking. "Some times Kevin is right—I need to think a little more and act a little less."

He meowed and twitched his tail before he jumped down.

"It's not his fault. He wasn't being mean by saying it. He was trying to keep me, and possibly himself, out of trouble."

The shop door opened. It was Shayla and Flourine. Flourine was wearing a huge black hat that threatened to swamp her short body. I was fairly certain there was a large, *real*, raven on it. The bird looked as though it had been preserved through taxidermy.

"How are you doing today?" Shayla cast a knowing eye up and down my body. "Your chakras are better, though your aura is a little on the yellow side for you."

Flourine agreed. "Did you have some asparagus last night? That'll do it."

"No. No asparagus." I told them about the fine that was levied against Kevin. "I'm trying to come up with the money for him. It wasn't his fault."

"Fine?" Shayla held her head to one side. "Are you kidding me? After the two of you found that dead race car driver? Honey, they should be *paying* you for your services. Imagine the mess they would've had if they'd tried to do that geothermal thing *through* that car. It could've exploded. It would've been a disaster! No, ma'am. You need to take that to court. Sue the town."

I could always count on Shayla for the alternate opinion. "Not many mayors sue their own town."

"Then let Kevin do it. Don't sit around worrying about helping him. He can take care of himself. You need to get some rest so you can ditch the witch."

*Not this again.*

"Thanks for your advice, but I think I'll do things my way." I smiled at Flourine. "How long are you planning on staying here with Shayla?"

"I'm here until we run that witch out of town, missy. I don't cotton to witches taking over friends of the family." She leaned close to me and tapped my forehead with one of her charms. "You hear me in there? You're not fooling anyone."

"Really, there isn't a witch inside of me." I hoped I sounded calm and reasonable about it. I didn't want to make things worse. "Isn't there some test you could do to prove that it's just me?"

I thought it would be nice not to have them following me around and possibly telling voters that there was a witch inside me right before the election. I wasn't sure about Shayla, but I wouldn't have put it past Flourine.

Shayla conferred with her grandmother. "There are some tried and true ways to reveal a witch."

"That's right." Flourine was pleasant enough about it. "We could have her walk on burning tree sap. Or tie her to a tree out in the woods and see if birds peck out her eyes. They won't abide a witch, you know."

"Let me get back to you on that." Shayla smiled. "I'm sure there are less grisly ways of finding out the truth. But a word of warning, Maggie Madison. If we come for you, you're through on this or any other plane."

"That sounds fair." I swallowed hard. "Anything except birds or burning. Nothing painful. Or that could cause permanent damage. Let me know what you find out."

"Oh, we will." Flourine squinted at me. "Just you watch and see. That was a call for help if I ever heard one."

I was glad to see them go. I had wanted to meet Shayla's grandmother for years after listening to stories about her. Now I wished I hadn't been so eager.

Maggie traded places with me, obviously afraid of Shayla and Flourine's threats. "Would they really do those things? Even in my time, such things were not considered."

"You don't have to worry. They aren't going to do anything. I'll take care of it."

Once I was back where I should be, I worried about it. I didn't believe that Shayla and Flourine had any real magic. What if I was wrong?

I straightened up the shop and dusted everything. It didn't take long to get everything in order. I switched out some jewelry in the front case with new items from the storage room. I liked my customers to see fresh merchandise when they came in.

A man from Raleigh came in and bought a few Duck souvenirs. Another woman came in and asked for directions to the Hatteras lighthouse. Of course she was on the wrong end of the island for that. Instead, I told her how to go to the lighthouse in Corolla.

Stan, the UPS guy, brought a few packages in with his usual smile and joking manner. Treasure hissed at him, not liking his brown uniform. It was always the same with him and Stan. I had tried explaining that Stan was a nice person. Treasure didn't care.

The email from Dillon came in right before noon. I was about to close the shop and go to lunch. I checked for his answer one last time after a dozen other tries.

"Meet you tonight. Eight P.M. Missing Pieces. D."

So that was that.

I knew he'd be thrilled to have my silver bell for a mere five thousand dollars. He would've paid a lot more than that last year when he'd first offered for it. It was worth at least ten times that. The three bells together were estimated to be worth more than five million dollars.

I was responsible for Kevin's debt and I was going to pay it, I reminded myself. I put the bells away before I could change my mind. I put Treasure in my bag and locked the door to the shop behind me.

"Dae O'Donnell," a familiar voice hailed me as I stepped out on the boardwalk. "I was just heading in to see you."

It was Jake Burleson, a wild horse rescuer from Corolla. He'd rescued me from a bad situation and we'd spent some time together—only as friends. He popped in at the house from time to time to eat dinner with me and Gramps.

"Great. I'm going out for lunch. You can come too."

He smiled and put his cowboy hat back on his blond hair. He was tall and lean, muscular in that whipcord fashion that some men have. He lived his life off the grid—no phone or TV. He was a man from another time.

"I would never turn down that invitation." He held his arm out for me. I slipped my hand into it and we walked down the boardwalk together. "Where are you headed for lunch?"

"I was thinking about eating a sandwich out here and enjoying the weather before it turns again."

"Sounds good to me."

We ordered sandwiches and drinks at the little snack shop. They were low on everything since they'd be closing for the winter that week. Only the larger retail stores stayed open through the cold months. Most would open again in March or April.

Jake and I sat at a wood table and chairs, weathered by air and sea to a soft, gray patina, overlooking the water. A breeze had begun ruffling the sound, and the number of sailboats had increased. The smell of the water mingled with the odor of cooking onions from Wild Stallions Grill at the other end of the boardwalk.

We talked about a new wild horse he'd adopted. This one was lame and probably would've been shunned by the herd. The wild horse conservation group kept an eye on those types of situations. People like Jake took those horses and tried to nurse them back to health.

"I have a favor I'd like to ask of you, Dae." He finished his sandwich. "I found something remarkable at an old homestead that's on my property. Could you come out and take a look at it?"

"Sure. I'd be glad to."

"I can come and get you one evening and make *you* supper for a change. I'm not a gourmet cook like your boyfriend, Kevin, but I make a mean plate of beans you won't forget anytime soon. Bring Horace, if you like."

I laughed at his description. There was no comparison between him and Kevin in any department. Jake was like a crazy wild breeze coming in from the Atlantic. He smiled a lot and was a little on the edge of the rest of the world.

Kevin was stable, dependable. He was world-weary because he'd seen so much during his time with the FBI.

He'd created a new life for himself here, but the memories of that past life were always in his eyes.

"That sounds good—except for you picking me up. I'm not a horse person. Last time I rode back from Corolla with you, I could barely walk the next day."

"Well, you're in luck." He grinned lazily at me. "I finally got my old pickup running again. That should make the trip easier. She's not stylish but she goes where I need her to."

I agreed to take a look tomorrow night at what he'd found at the old homestead. I still had some cleaning up to do after being gone for three days, and I had to meet Dillon tonight.

"All right then. I'll pick you up about seven, if that's okay?"

"That sounds fine. I can't wait to see what you found."

He got up from the table. "Maybe I can persuade you to take a short ride on one of the horses. No wild galloping like last time."

"I don't know. No promises."

"You don't have to worry. I have the answer for sore muscles. You have someone slather on some liniment, massage it in real good and then take a long, hot bath. It does wonders." He winked at me. "I'll see you tomorrow."

"We eagerly await your coming, good sir!" Maggie suddenly blurted out.

It had been all I could do to keep her from interrupting the whole time Jake had been there. She couldn't let him leave without saying something that was going to embarrass me.

Jake laughed and kept walking. I muttered under my breath about my constant companion who was making my life difficult. I was going to be glad once we found her bones and reburied them.

I sat at the table a few minutes more after he was gone.

I could see Missing Pieces, so I knew there were no customers waiting to get in. As I was about to get up, Nancy joined me, putting a smokeless cigarette in her mouth. She'd recently given up the real thing.

"Hey there, sweetie. Was that the same cowboy who rescued you last year?" She grinned. "Sorry. I couldn't help but peek out at him. He's something special."

"Yes. Jake Burleson. We've kept in touch."

"I'd like to keep in touch with him, if you know what I mean. What a hunk! You're still with Kevin, right?"

"Of course. Jake and I are just friends."

Nancy patted a strand of her bright red hair that had been blown out of place by the breeze, even though it was barely an inch long. She was such a nice person, wonderfully organized, but she had no luck with men. She'd been divorced for a long time. She was always dating someone, but nothing lasting ever came of it.

"How about next time he comes to be friendly, you introduce us," she suggested. "I like those quiet cowboy types."

"Sure. I'd be glad to. Maybe he could convince you to ride horses with him."

"Anytime. I don't know a thing about horses, but I could learn."

"It's rough riding one, I can tell you that. Jake says the cure is liniment, massage and a hot bath. I don't know if I'm willing to try again."

Nancy's expressive eyebrows rose. "He offered to do that for *you*?" She puffed her fake cigarette a little faster. "Sounds like he might be thinking of you as a *little* more than a friend, Dae. Better keep your boots on."

We both laughed about that. Nancy went back inside, saying that her hands were freezing.

I thought about what she'd said about Jake. I doubted

that he had any romantic feelings for me. He knew I was dating Kevin, and he'd never stepped out of bounds in that direction. Sometimes people saw more than what was there.

Treasure and I went back to Missing Pieces. I gave him a tuna treat and he ran around the shop with it for a while. I watched him for a few minutes, enjoying his pleasure. Then I finished straightening up.

There were no more customers, and I knew I had to go home and face the real mess I'd left behind. There was a ton of laundry that needed to be washed and cat litter to change. I'd done the fun stuff, the work at Missing Pieces, first. Now it was time to go home and do the things I didn't want to do.

I packed up Treasure again and we headed down the boardwalk to the parking lot. A large crowd was standing around outside the coffee shop and bookstore. A few of them applauded as Councilman Randal "Mad Dog" Wilson drove up in his custom-made golf cart.

He waved and approached the crowd. I knew when he got up on the porch above the people that he was about to make the speech Nancy had told me about. I still didn't see any media there, but that had never stopped him. No doubt he planned to denounce me and urge people to vote for him.

Some of the people on the blacktop applauded again. Most seemed to be standing around waiting to see what was happening. Mad Dog held his hands out for quiet. I waited to see what he planned to say.

Out of the corner of my eye, I saw a Duck police car pull into the parking lot on one side of the group. I couldn't imagine that Chief Michaels planned to give Mad Dog a hard time about holding a gathering there. Duck wasn't that kind of place.

Instead, as Mad Dog began speaking about bad leadership, Officers Tim Mabry and Scott Randall approached him from either side.

"I'm sorry, folks," Chief Michaels said from the porch. "I'm afraid Mr. Wilson is going to have to come with us."

"What? This is outrageous," Mad Dog loudly complained. "What about freedom of speech?"

Chief Michaels put his hand on his shoulder. Mad Dog, at six foot four and almost three hundred pounds, dwarfed him. "I'm sorry, Randal. You're under arrest for the murder of Lightning Joe Walsh."

# Chapter 6

"That's ridiculous! I didn't kill anyone. You have no right," Mad Dog yelled as he struggled with the officers. People in the crowd started pointing and trying to figure out what was going on. More people came out of the coffee shop to see what all the commotion was about.

It wasn't a pretty picture. There was no way Tim and Scott could hold him, not with any kind of respect. Mad Dog was strong and bullheaded, according to Gramps. Once he got an idea about something, or someone, he didn't let go.

Tim and Scott kept looking at the chief, obviously wondering what he wanted them to do. Mad Dog seemed intent on kicking them down the stairs, but he was a town council member. The two young officers were a little bewildered by their duties at this point.

Chief Michaels finally bent close to his old friend. He whispered something and put his hand on Mad Dog's shoulder, as if trying to calm him.

I had no idea what he'd said to him, but immediately, Mad Dog released Scott from the half nelson he'd had him in. He removed his foot from Tim's chest.

Mad Dog stumbled to his feet and held his hands in front of him like a tame albeit dazed gorilla. The chief put on the handcuffs then walked beside him down the stairs and to the car.

It was a sad day for Duck residents to see one of their own, a man people looked up to for many years, led away with his head down and wrists cuffed. Some people in the crowd booed and protested their candidate being taken away.

I wished there had been another way to do this. I knew the chief was only doing what he had to, but maybe he should have waited until he had Mad Dog by himself. It wasn't like the councilman was a flight risk.

He'd be taken to Manteo, to the county jail, no doubt. I was sure he'd be bailed out right away. His family owned property and was well off. Besides, what bail bondsman wouldn't take the word of a town council member?

Mad Dog had been committed to the good of our town for as long as I could remember. Our ideas on how that good should be done clashed sometimes, but it was impossible to imagine he'd killed a man and buried him in his car. Even though I'd seen the skeleton and the car, it was very hard to take in.

Randal "Mad Dog" Wilson was a lot older than me, so I didn't really feel like I knew him personally like Gramps and Chief Michaels did. I wanted to believe the best of him even though the evidence must have been substantial for the chief to take such strong action.

I avoided the coffee shop as I skirted around the crowd. I knew everyone would have questions. I didn't want to be the one they asked. It was too obviously in my favor for my opponent to go to jail.

Instead I continued home with Treasure to do my laundry and consider how trying to find a dead witch had led me to a dead race car driver.

"Pardon me," Maggie interrupted. "I was never a witch. I thought you understood that."

"Sorry. It was because everyone keeps calling you that. I'll try not to let it happen again."

She exclaimed over the curtains in my bedroom and how they would make a lovely summer gown. I asked her to step back again and let me get finished cleaning up.

Gramps finally got home at about six thirty. I'd spent the rest of the day dusting, mopping and scrubbing. Everything smelled clean and fresh. My laundry was washed, dried and folded in the same day for once. I'd even changed the sheets on our beds and washed them too.

Gramps sniffed appreciatively as he came in the back door in his stocking feet. That meant he'd left his smelly fishing boots on the porch. "Smells like supper. Is that my granddaughter's famous corn fritters and beans?"

"It is." I heaped the fritters on a plate. "And there's apple cobbler for dessert."

"I should go away early without breakfast more often." He looked up at the light over the kitchen table. "And no cobwebs. You've been busy."

"Yep." I put out the casserole dish of beans and waited for him to wash his hands at the sink. "They arrested Mad Dog at the coffee shop today. It was terrible."

"I know." He took a seat at the table. "I met with Ronnie, Tuck Riley and Luke Helms early this morning. I knew it was coming. They were only waiting for the judge to sign the papers."

"So Sheriff Riley got in on it too. He wasn't at the coffee shop today."

"Ronnie insisted it was a town arrest, but Tuck said it

was a county cold case. They're like a couple of sharks going after a piece of raw meat sometimes." He chuckled. "I'm glad I'm not part of that anymore."

"I guess the evidence was overwhelming, huh?" I passed the beans after Gramps had taken his fill of corn fritters.

"I don't know about it being overwhelming, Dae. But those were Joe Walsh's remains in Mad Dog's old car. The medical examiner hasn't said what cause of death is yet, but Mad Dog is the logical suspect. I would've done the same thing."

"It's hard to believe someone you've known all of your life could do something like that. You know, we always tend to think the bad stuff comes in with the people from outside Duck. Was Mad Dog that different back then? I know he's belligerent sometimes, but killing someone is different than being cranky."

"Ronnie and Tuck will look into it." Gramps believed every word he said. "They'll figure out what happened. That's their job. Not ours."

"I know." Gramps was a stickler for letting people do their jobs, especially when it came to law enforcement. Apparently, he felt like too many people had put in their two cents' worth while he was sheriff. He wasn't stepping on anyone else's toes.

Changing the subject, he said, "How was your time at the shop today? Sell anything?"

I told him about my customers but not about planning to meet Dillon this evening. It would've been too much explaining that would have left us at odds over repaying Kevin for the fine. Gramps certainly wouldn't want me to talk to Dillon, much less sell anything to him.

Gramps would've said Kevin knew what he was doing when he agreed to help me. He'd pay the fine, like a man, and go about his business.

At least that's what he'd tell me.

Of course I knew this wasn't a two-way street. If Kevin had done something similar for Gramps, Gramps would be trying to figure out some way to pay him back. He might not turn to someone like Dillon for help—especially since he knew Dillon was a criminal. Gramps took a dim view of me spending time with anyone outside the law.

After we'd finished eating and done the dishes, I put on my jacket and started toward the door. "I'm going to finish something at Missing Pieces. Don't wait up."

He put down the dish towel and said, "You don't have to lie to me, Dae."

For a brief moment, I wondered what I'd said that had given me away. Did I look guilty? Was it his famous radar that always knew when I was in trouble as a kid?

"It's all right for you to meet Kevin. You don't have to sneak out or lie about it. You're an adult now. Although I do wish he'd come around and pick you up to take you out. There are still some rules about a man courting a woman. I would never have guessed Kevin Brickman was that kind of man."

I was so relieved that I hugged him. "Thanks. I guess I don't think about it that way. You're so old-fashioned!"

He sat down in his recliner. "I saw Jake Burleson this morning. I think he might want to give Kevin some competition. Did he drop by to see you at the shop?"

I explained about Jake taking me to Corolla tomorrow night. "He wants me to look at something. You too, if you want to come."

"I don't want to get between a man and a woman he might be interested in. Besides, I've got a Lions Club meeting."

"Believe me, you won't be interrupting anything. I'm dating Kevin. Nancy said the same thing about Jake today. I haven't gotten that feeling from him at all."

"Well, we'll see. At least he's picking you up at your

home, like a man should." He switched on one of the old shows he liked to watch. "Don't stay out too late."

I assured him that I wouldn't and slipped out the door.

I thought about Jake on my way down to Missing Pieces. I hoped I hadn't given him the wrong impression. Kevin and I weren't engaged or anything, but there was an implied exclusivity to our relationship.

I wondered if there was something I could say to Jake that would make him understand, in case there was a problem. I didn't want to awkwardly ask him if he was interested in me as more than a friend.

It was a strange, slightly exhilarating experience to deal with. I had never had the opportunity to wonder if a second man was interested in me. In school, I was always the weird one whose grandfather was the sheriff. Tim had been the only boy who ever asked me out.

It wasn't fair to lead Jake on though. I liked him and enjoyed his company, but not in that way.

There was a big chicken and dumplings dinner at one of the local churches near the house. It seemed to be a popular event. Traffic was heavy on Duck Road. I had to walk around some of the cars that were parked too far in the road. There were no sidewalks.

It was going to be awesome when all of the boardwalk was complete so everyone could get around town without walking along the narrow, sometimes crowded road.

There were a few cars at the Duck Shoppes. Trudy's Beauty Spa was closed and dark. I couldn't tell if anyone was in Shayla's shop—there were always dark curtains on the windows. A small group of people were outside at Wild Stallions, talking and nursing their drinks as they looked at the lights across the sound.

I opened the door to Missing Pieces, but before I could go inside, someone tapped me on the shoulder. I looked back and found a person-sized mirror right up in my face. I took a step back, almost tripping over the threshold into the shop. The mirror followed me like it was possessed.

"Jump out now while you can, witch," Flourine yelled with a vigorous shaking of her beads and charms.

"You're kidding, right?" I looked around the edge of the mirror at Shayla. "I can't believe you think something like that would work even if there were a witch inside of me."

Flourine frowned. "It always works. You can see the witch inside when you look in the mirror. Everybody knows that."

"I guess you forgot to tell the witch inside of me." I grinned at Shayla but was secretly terrified. Would that really work? "What next? Rubber chickens? A green umbrella?"

"I never heard of those," Flourine confessed. "How do they work?"

Shayla put down the mirror. "Come on, Gram. She's just making fun of us."

"No. Really." I laughed to disguise how close they were to the truth, but my heart was pounding. What would happen if they found out about Maggie?

"Okay. Laugh now. We'll see who laughs last." Shayla's usually melodic voice was harsh. "Oh, and by the way, watch out for Ann. Her idea was electrocuting you to reveal the witch. Maybe she's got the right idea. At least you wouldn't be *laughing* right now."

*That was scary.* "Maybe you should give it up before someone gets hurt."

"Somebody like that *witch*." Flourine huffed.

"Let's remember that even if there is a witch in me, I'd still be here. Hurting me would be bad."

Flourine squinted into my face. "You threatening me, witch?"

70

I glanced at Shayla. "Seriously? I think this has gone far enough, don't you?"

I didn't wait for an answer, just turned and continued into Missing Pieces, closing the door behind me. I felt a little sick. Maggie might not be a witch, but I didn't know what Shayla and her grandmother would have done if they'd seen Maggie in the mirror.

I needed to get back to the construction site and find those bones before one of Shayla's stunts hurt either Maggie or me. I wasn't sure about Flourine's magic, but usually Shayla's was more hoodoo than voodoo. I didn't want to find out that I was wrong.

I hoped Dillon wasn't outside waiting for me and witnessed the whole thing. It had been dark on the boardwalk. I might have missed him. That would be embarrassing.

I took out the silver bells—as soon as I felt sure Shayla and Flourine were gone. I looked at them one last time before I packed them up. I'd been so sure all three bells would find their way to me. I'd boasted of it confidently, especially after Dillon had given me the one he'd located. I would really have liked to see them all together, even if I didn't get to keep them.

"Your friends are very stubborn." Maggie appeared as I looked into the old mirror on the wall.

"They are. We'll get a lead on Thomas's grave soon. So much has happened, it's been hard to find time. I'm sorry."

She laughed, tossing "our" head back in a way I would never have done. "Don't worry about me. I'm having a wonderful time. Perhaps I'll stay awhile longer."

I started to argue with her (a complicated procedure), then I heard the door to the shop open and close. I straightened my shoulders and went into the main area. I plastered a big smile on my face, sure this was the best thing to do.

# Chapter 7

"Hello, Dae."

Dillon Guthrie was no doubt a bad man, but he looked more like a comic book superhero with his thick dark hair and square jaw. His icy blue eyes swept over the shop. Maybe he was making sure we were alone.

"Mr. Guthrie. Thanks for coming." I admitted to being a little scared of him. He'd never done anything to me personally, but I had it on good faith that he was a killer, smuggler and thief.

"Why so formal?" He removed his gray wool coat and tossed it to the nervous-looking young man who closed the shop door then ran to catch the coat. "I thought we were through the courtship phase. You know me. I know you. Call me Dillon."

I thought of him that way, when he wasn't around. Face-to-face was a different story.

He sat on one of the wood chairs near the burgundy

sofa. His suit and shoes might have been worth more than everything in the shop—except the bells.

"I got your email. What can I do for you?"

"I wanted to discuss some business with you. And there's the little thing about my giant face on the water tower."

He smiled at me like a shark might smile at its prey before swallowing it. "What's the problem? You don't like the artwork? I think they did a good job capturing your likeness. Think it's too small?"

"You've been financing my mayoral campaign ads, haven't you? I need you to stop. I don't think it's legal."

"Legal?" He laughed. "Of course it's legal. I'm your Super PAC. Anybody can pay for someone else's campaign now. You have nothing to worry about. Not that you didn't take care of it yourself. Getting your opponent framed for murder was brilliant."

"I didn't know the race car was down there. I was looking for something else."

"Well, it was fortuitous then, wasn't it? Looking for treasure? Did you find something? Is that part of the business aspect of this conversation?"

"In a manner of speaking." I didn't plan to let the conversation get away from my problem with him. "I appreciate that you were trying to help me with the election, but I can't accept it."

"Okay. I get your point. When I offered you cash for what you needed last year, you turned me down. I'm your friend. I didn't want to see you lose."

"I can take care of it myself, thanks." I watched as he signaled the thin young man, who brought him a bottle of water.

"What else can I do for you?" He took a swallow of water and smiled at me. "Have you found the third bell?"

This was the part I hated most. "I need to raise some capital. It's a lot for me—not something I can take out of the cash register."

I told him about Kevin being fined and that I wanted to return the money to him. "What I'm proposing is selling you my bell from the St. Augustine monks. Of course, you can take yours with you too."

He whistled. "For five thousand dollars? You and I both know that's a steal. You must really love Brickman. What is it about him? Maybe the law enforcement connection—like your grandfather?"

That brought my chin up. I needed his help financially. I didn't need him to tell me who I should and shouldn't see. "That doesn't matter. My personal life is personal. Will you help me or not?"

"I would rather spray-paint the *Mona Lisa* than take those bells away from you. You convinced me that the third one is coming your way. I'm not buying your bell, or taking mine. What I can do is loan you five thousand on account. You can pay me back when you're ready or when we get the third bell."

I thought about his proposal. I probably shouldn't have, but I shouldn't have been there trying to sell the bell to him in the first place. I was holding his property. It was worth a lot more than five thousand dollars. Maybe it would be okay this once to take advantage of his generosity.

Gramps or Kevin could never know this had happened. They would never understand. But my heart was lighter as I shook Dillon's hand on the deal.

"Thanks. I really didn't want to give up the bells."

"Yeah. I figured as much. You're transparent, Dae. Or it's just that we think so much alike. Except for the streak of righteousness you have running through you. It's probably just the way you were raised."

The thin young man quickly got Dillon's coat for him then held the door. "I'll have the money to you right away. Cash, I think, if you're comfortable with that. Checks leave such messy trails. See you later."

I watched them leave and sank down on the sofa. With that problem solved, my next question was how to give Kevin five thousand dollars without him asking where it came from.

I knew Kevin had his eye on an antique desk for his office, but it was too pricey for him to fit it into his budget. Five thousand dollars. I spoke with the man from Charleston who was selling it, and he offered me a great deal.

Because I could pay cash, it was delivered late the next morning. I followed the truck to the Blue Whale in the golf cart, filled with a combination of excitement and dread. I wasn't sure how Kevin would take this gift. He wouldn't want it if he knew where the money had come from. I'd be stuck with an expensive desk I couldn't use and an angry boyfriend.

Kevin came to the loading door at the back of the inn. He'd just finished unloading some supplies for the week. He was understandably surprised to see me there with the man from Charleston and the big desk.

"Is that what I think it is?" He grinned. "I don't think it's my birthday yet."

"Lucky you, it doesn't have to be." I gave him a quick kiss and kept my tone light.

As the man was unstrapping the desk, Kevin walked me away from the dock. "This is kind of pricey, isn't it?"

"I got a really good deal on it." It wasn't the truth—the seller wouldn't take a penny less than the asking price of five thousand. But I hoped my little white lie would make

Kevin feel better. "I knew you wanted it, so I jumped on it. I guess it's your birthday, Fourth of July and Christmas present wrapped into one."

"This is nothing to do with the fine from town, right? The desk was listed at five thousand dollars—exactly the price of the fine. No coincidence there?"

"Maybe a little one." I hugged him. "I wanted to say thank you for everything. I hope you like it."

He searched my eyes for several long seconds as though he might be able to fathom whether I was telling the truth. Finally he laughed. "I don't know what I'm worried about. I know you don't have that kind of money. You must've done some extensive bartering. Thank you, Dae. I appreciate it."

It wasn't exactly the same as giving him the five thousand dollars to pay the fine. On the other hand, it was a nice trade, since he'd admired the old desk for months. And it was the only way I could think of to do any sort of reparation for what had happened. My trader instincts told me our score was settled. That would have to be good enough.

After the desk was unloaded, I thanked the man from Charleston for bringing it so quickly. Before we came here, we'd already settled the money with the envelope full of cash that Dillon had dropped off at the shop for me. I had left nothing to chance.

Kevin and I walked inside to see where the best place would be for the desk. Ann and Betsy were on their way downstairs with luggage in hand.

"Let me help with that." Kevin grabbed the suitcases and took them outside to his pickup.

"You're leaving?" I tried not to sound as relieved as I felt. Shayla and her grandmother were bad enough trying to discover the witch. I didn't need Ann trying to figure things out as well.

"Betsy's mother wants her back today," Ann said. "Since

nothing seems to be going on besides a routine forty-year-old murder, I thought I might as well go home too."

"How's your psychic detective agency working out?"

"First of all, I'm not a detective. I'm a consultant. We make way more money. And it's going well. The FBI has thrown a few cases my way. That, and some back pay they owed me, has set me up. You should come see me. You'd like New York."

"I'll put that on my list of things to do before I die."

She smiled a little in her sardonic way. "Yeah. That's what I thought. Stay out of trouble, if you can. Don't lead Kevin into temptation. He can't resist a good witch hunt."

Betsy hugged me. "I'm glad you're okay, Dae. I was really worried. I'm sorry everybody thought you were a witch."

"Thanks. I'm so glad you came with Ann to save me. It's nice to know I have friends in faraway places."

"I could tell you weren't a witch right away," Betsy continued. "You were dirty but you sure weren't ugly or green."

"That's right. I wasn't ever green, was I?" I hugged her again and laughed. "Tell your mother hello for me. Do well in school. Maybe you can come back during the summer when the weather is nice."

"That would be fun. I'd like to go to the beach and look for pirate treasure."

"We might be able to find some too. There's some pirate gold in the museum next door. We'll go take a look at it next time you come."

The good-byes were said and Betsy was settled in the middle of the pickup seat between Kevin and Ann.

Ann squinted at me a little as she closed the truck door. She reminded me of Flourine. "Take care of yourself, unless you want me to make regular visits. You're a part of my soul now. You can't hide anything from me."

Maggie daringly switched places with me and giggled.

I held my breath and pushed her back. *What was she thinking?* I didn't want Ann to change her plans and join Shayla's efforts to out the witch. "Thanks, I think."

"That's the only reason I'm leaving so soon." Ann seemed not to even notice the switch. "I know I could feel if there was anything in you besides one hundred percent Dae O'Donnell. Good luck in the election, although I guess you don't really need it now."

Kevin waved to me as they started out toward the airport. "Sorry I have to go right away. I didn't know you were bringing the desk. Maybe you can come back later and we'll check out the best place for the desk with dinner."

"I have an appointment later. I know this was a surprise. We'll get to it when you can."

He closed the window and I watched the old pickup drive away. I took a deep breath when they were gone. That stunt of Shayla's last night with the mirror hadn't been anything. I was a little nervous that Ann was capable of so much more.

Still, she and Betsy had come to rescue me with my friends in Duck. How much better could things be than that?

"You took quite a chance back there," I warned Maggie. "This could be bad for both of us if we get caught."

"I'm sorry, Dae. But how could you stand her saying that to you when it is so untrue? I had to laugh at her."

"Well, pray thee do not do it again." I shook my head. "Just don't take those chances."

I got in the golf cart to drive it back home, humming some music and feeling happy with the day. I planned to drop off the cart for Gramps in case he needed it and then walk to the shop. I got a surprise when I found a strange car in the drive at home.

I knew most of Gramps's friends drove golf carts. I knew the vehicles of the few who didn't. It wasn't a police or sheriff's car, so there was no trouble. I parked the cart near the garage and went inside to see what was going on.

Gramps was pouring coffee and already had a few oatmeal cookies on the kitchen table. Laura Wilson—Mad Dog's wife—was there, smiling at him. Her eyes were red-rimmed with crying and her hand was unsteady as she took a mug from him.

"Hi, Mrs. Wilson." I took off my jacket and hoped she wasn't there to yell at me about finding the race car. "I'm so sorry about what's happened to Councilman Wilson."

Laura Wilson wasn't flashy or flamboyant like her husband. She looked like someone's grandmother, which she was, many times over. Her gray hair was nicely coiffed by Trudy every week, and her brown eyes were steady and calm. She'd worked for Dare County as a clerk for many years before retiring.

"Hello, Dae. I hope I'm not interrupting anything you and your grandfather had planned."

Gramps shrugged his shoulders under his red flannel shirt and black suspenders when I caught his eye. He was wearing his tall boots, so I knew he must've been on the way out when Mrs. Wilson stopped in.

"No, of course not." I sat down at the table with her. "Is there something we can do for you? I know this has to be a terrible time for you and your family."

I was still hoping she wasn't going to go off about the election and the murder investigation. I was cringing at the idea of handling that from her, especially at this moment. She was tortured, and I felt responsible in some ways, even though finding old number twelve hadn't been part of my plan. It couldn't lead to anything good.

Mrs. Wilson kept her composure. "I was wondering if

you could do me a favor, Dae. I know it's a lot to ask, but all of us—Randal's family and close friends—we believe he's innocent of this terrible crime. We can't think of any way to prove it."

Gramps sat down and ate some cookies, washing them down with a big swig of coffee. "What can we do, Laura? Of course we'd be glad to be of service."

Mrs. Wilson dabbed her eyes with a clean white handkerchief. "Well, we were wondering if Dae would be willing to drive down to Manteo and talk to Randal. You probably don't remember this, Dae, but I came to you once looking for an overdue library book that I'd lost. The fine was already quite high. You held my hands—you couldn't have been more than five or six at the time—and you found that book for me. I was so impressed with your gift. Your mother wouldn't let me give you any money, but I had a sucker in my pocketbook and she let me give you that."

She was right. I didn't remember. There had been many such incidents in my childhood. I understood what she was asking. She wanted me to use the same gift that had put her husband in jail to find him innocent of the crime.

Gramps nibbled on a cookie silently, letting me make that decision. I appreciated the gesture, but there was only one answer I could give her.

"Of course I'll talk to Councilman Wilson. I don't know for sure that I can help, but I'll be glad to try."

# Chapter 8

We worked out the arrangements to go to Manteo tomorrow. Mrs. Wilson insisted that she'd have someone drive me there and back and pay my expenses, but I'm not a professional psychic like Ann.

I agreed to let her son, Amos, drive me, since our old car didn't get out much and I would've had to line up a ride with someone there and back. I refused to take money for expenses from her. It was a deal-breaker if she wanted my help. She finally agreed.

I knew it wasn't my fault that the old race car was buried there. It would've been found later when they'd started drilling the new geothermal hole, no matter what.

Mad Dog and I had been fierce competitors during the last year. We'd both said some things that weren't very pleasant. It felt like an unfair way to win by contributing, no matter in how small a way, to my opponent going to jail. Even if he was found innocent in time for the elections, his reputation might be ruined.

Maybe I didn't feel guilty so much as responsible.

I would've helped the family even if the election hadn't happened. They were part of Duck. And like a lot of people in town, I didn't want to believe Mad Dog was guilty of killing Lightning Joe Walsh.

Gramps and Mrs. Wilson were still talking about the good old days when I said good-bye and left to go to Missing Pieces. I didn't take Treasure with me, since he was licking his lips and waiting patiently for a little cream from Gramps when he was finished with his coffee. For a man who'd never wanted a pet, Gramps had sure done a great job of spoiling the cat.

I left the golf cart at home and walked to the Duck Shoppes. A stiff wind had picked up, rattling the bushes and blowing trash along the road. I reminded myself to put in an order for the public works people to do some trash patrol. It was probably coming from people not putting the lids down tight on their trash cans.

The first thing I noticed as I walked into the parking lot was a TV news crew from Virginia Beach. A van was parked outside the coffee shop.

I saw Chris and Jamie talking to two people—one with a microphone and the other with a video camera. It seemed Duck was going to get some attention for the odd murder. The media usually wasn't interested in us, but I knew the businesses that were still open would be happy to have them there.

I avoided the news crew and scuttled up the stairs to the boardwalk. The freezing wind was fierce coming off the sound. I was glad to slam the shop door on it. I put on the kettle and put away my jacket and bag. It seemed unlikely that there would be any customers on a day like this, but there was always something to do.

La Donna Nelson found me there an hour later cleaning a set of 1886 silver I'd acquired a few weeks before. She was a member of the town council and Chief Michaels's sister. She and I had always gotten along, frequently agreeing on the issues we faced as a town.

"Just in time for tea." I put out another cup as she came in shivering. It was my third cup of the morning but who was counting?

The wind was whipping at her ankle-length brown skirt, coat and scarf. Her long grayish brown hair was pulled back from her face with a wide, knitted headband.

"I shouldn't have put this off for so long." She closed the door with an extra push. "The weather was better last week, but I was so busy with other things. I'll take that tea, Dae, thanks."

We both sat down on the burgundy brocade sofa, our hands wrapped around the warm mugs. I complimented her on the knitted headband. It had a few beads woven into it. She told me her granddaughter, who was taking textile design in college, had made them for a marketing project.

La Donna was there to scrounge up whatever I could spare for the St. Vincent's Church annual bazaar the following week. I told her I'd find some things for her and bring them over.

Talk, of course, led to Mad Dog and everything that had happened in the last few days.

"I still don't believe it." Her eyes were wide with disbelief. "Randal isn't a killer. It was so long ago—how will they ever be sure what really happened?"

"I don't know." I told her what little I knew about his arrest, excluding what I was supposed to keep to myself, according to Chief Michaels. He was her brother. Maybe he'd told her the rest. "I don't know if they *can* be sure. So far everything is circumstantial. Mad Dog and Joe argued. Mad Dog's car disappeared. Joe was found dead in Mad Dog's car. That's not much."

"They all like to close these old cases. I know Ronnie does. I'm sure your grandfather was the same. It's like birthday and Christmas rolled into one."

"It's so weird after hearing all those old stories about Mad Dog's racing career. It didn't seem real to me, I guess, because it happened before I was born. Looking down in that hole and seeing the number twelve car was like seeing a mermaid or something."

La Donna frowned. "You're making me feel really old. Stop now." She took a sip of tea and gazed across the store. "Lightning Joe Walsh has been a legend for the last forty years, and all this time he's been down there under the sand, dead."

We both shivered as the wind whistled by. It was a terrible thing to think he'd been down there with no one knowing.

"Did you ever meet him?" I sipped my tea, trying to get out of that weird, melancholy mood.

"That would be dating me, wouldn't it?" She smiled. "But yes, I met him. He was dashing and romantic. He'd race onto the track after Mad Dog had beaten all the other drivers. We'd watch for him and clap when we saw him. He was Elvis and all those other faraway celebrities to us."

"Did you know who he was? It sounded like no one knew his identity."

"After the first time he came out on the track, we all knew him, and loved him. I was president of his fan club for a while."

"Sounds to me like you were smitten," Maggie said with no warning that we were changing places.

I put my hand over my mouth. What would La Donna think?

"Yes, I was. What an odd way to say it, Dae. I think dealing with all these antiques is affecting you."

I sighed in relief. Another disaster avoided. What part of not making me blurt out her thoughts didn't Maggie understand?

The tea was gone and La Donna said she had to go too.

"I guess we would've found him eventually." She put on her coat and scarf. "What led you there, Dae? I know you have a gift for finding things. But what made you look there of all places?"

I was struggling with a suitable answer when the shop door burst open again. The two newspeople I'd seen at the coffee shop blew in with the cold breeze.

"We're looking for Mayor Dae O'Donnell," the first young man said. "Are either of you her?"

"Are either of you she," La Donna corrected with a frown. "Grammar, gentlemen, is the stage on which we communicate our lives."

"Are you . . . she then?" He rephrased his question.

"I'm sorry." La Donna turned to me. "I hate to leave you like this, but I have to visit five more businesses before I can go home. I'll see you later."

The reporter's feral eyes focused on me. "You must be the mayor."

"Or not." I smiled as I put our cups on the tiny counter beside the hot plate. It had to be an exasperating job trying to get reticent people to talk, but I played with them anyway. "That might have been her leaving."

"You're the mayor all right." He urged his partner with the camera forward. "I'm David Engel from Channel Two News. I'm here to talk with you about the race car you found buried underground. What made you dig there for it, Mayor O'Donnell? We understand that's the site of the new town hall building. How did you know the car would be there?"

The same question La Donna had asked. It was bound to come up. I could only avoid people for so long. Obviously

I needed a good stock answer that was general enough to make everybody happy without going into the real reason.

The Channel Two News team wasn't from Duck, so they didn't know anything about my gift. I told them I had heard something of historical value to the town might be buried there.

"I wanted to check before the town hall was built. As you can see, I'm very involved with history. I'm a member of the Duck Historical Museum too."

It was actually a good answer—boring enough to ensure outsiders wouldn't come to dig up the area, interesting enough to make the camera pan over the whole shop. Maybe enough to bring in a few new customers.

David feigned interest in the shop too. "So you're a collector and an antique dealer. That explains it." He nodded to the cameraman who'd stopped filming. "That's enough extra footage. I'd like to actually interview you, if that's okay."

I looked at the camera and the other young man who held it. I'd been on TV a few other times as mayor. It didn't bother me. "That's fine."

"Okay, Tonto." David laughed. "I'm the Lone Ranger." He held up his microphone. "We're ready."

Once the camera was rolling again, David smiled and explained the basic story of what had happened. "This is Mayor Dae O'Donnell, who was out looking for historical artifacts for her antique shop, Missing Pieces. She actually found what was left of a murder victim buried in an old race car. Did you know the dead man, Mayor?"

"No. Whatever happened to him was forty years ago, before I was born." I remembered not to look right at the camera, advice I'd been given years ago.

"Building has stopped on the new Duck town hall, Mayor O'Donnell. Still, you felt like it was important to get this car out of the ground. Why was that?"

It seemed obvious to me, but past experience had taught me that reporters many times asked questions with obvious answers. "Well, completing the new town hall couldn't take priority over the fact that a man had been buried at that site. His family has been looking for him for four decades."

"A Duck city council member is accused of murdering the man in the car, is that right?"

"Unfortunately, that's correct."

"And the accused, Councilman Randal 'Mad Dog' Wilson, is also your opponent in a close contest to be the next mayor of Duck. Is that also correct, Madam Mayor?"

I wasn't sure where he was going, but I had a bad feeling about it. "That's true but—"

"Finding the car opened the field for you in this election only a short time away. That didn't have anything to do with you looking for the car, did it?"

There it was. You had to be careful or an interview could bite you in the butt. If this man who wasn't even from Duck was thinking about me making the vote go in my favor, probably a lot of people in Duck were too.

"I don't want to win the election this way. Councilman Wilson has always worked hard for Duck. He's a good man."

"Still, the guilty must be punished." He looked at the camera. "There is no statute of limitations for murder, even in a small town that didn't notice it had happened for a lifetime. Reporting from Duck, NC, this is David Engel, Channel Two News on scene."

The interview was over and both men thanked me for my time. It was hollow praise since we all knew it had made me look bad.

Maggie's words spilled out of my mouth. "You two handsome gentlemen should stay for a nice warm cup of tea. And maybe we can find some other things to talk about."

David looked at his cameraman. "We have to be going now, Mayor. Thanks for the invitation."

I saw them out of the shop and closed the door behind them. "You know, we talked about this," I said to Maggie. "You can't start talking like that. I have to live here."

"You're too uppity," she chastised me. "It's a wonder you have a man at all. I hate to leave you in these poor circumstances."

"Yeah, well, quit trying to help."

I ignored her, hoping I would find time very soon to be rid of her. My life was complicated enough without a flirty, four-hundred-year-old tavern wench trying to hook up with every man we saw.

It was hard to believe everyone thought Mad Dog being accused of murder gave me some kind of edge in the election. They knew nothing about small-town politics. When word got around that I'd found the car, many people who had been planning to vote for me wouldn't, simply because they'd think it was an unfair advantage.

Part of me felt like I should bow out of the election. It was always going to feel uncomfortable. People would say I only won because Mad Dog was accused of murder. That felt difficult to bear for the next two years.

Mad Dog had used all his little tricks and some underhanded distractions to try to win the election, yet nothing he'd done had equaled this.

But there wasn't anyone else. The council would have to appoint someone, a person not chosen by the people of Duck, and wait for another election. I didn't like that idea either.

"Perhaps this is the very reason you should disprove this man's guilt, if you are able," Maggie reminded me.

I suppose I agreed. But what if Mad Dog was guilty of murder? What then?

# Chapter 9

I went through the clothes and household goods that were in the shop. I made a big pile of items that might be good for the bazaar and boxed them up. It helped keep my mind off of things I couldn't do anything about.

After lunch, with the sun warming the boardwalk, a few customers came in. One woman was looking for a fancy dress for her daughter in high school. We looked through the secondhand clothes and found a powder blue dress with silver sequins on it. I had a coupon for thirty percent off at Sunflower Fancy across the road that she could use for shoes.

It was lucky that Darcy, the shop's owner, stayed open until Christmas. It wasn't a big sale, but I could tell from the smile on the woman's face that it was an important one. I liked selling to people who enjoyed what they'd bought.

A man came in a little later looking for something with some pirate lore. He was in Sanderling for business, and the hotel clerk had recommended Missing Pieces as the place to go. I didn't know the young man from the hotel, but I planned to send him a thank-you card. Referrals were the best.

I'd found a very nice piece of scrimshaw that resembled a whale. It had a local background to it. Big Dan Russell was a privateer with a heart of gold, according to the stories. He was the Robin Hood of the Outer Banks, robbing wealthy merchants to distribute their gold to the less fortunate.

The little I could pick up from touching the scrimshaw made him feel like he was a real hero—and good-looking to boot.

It was valuable, but I also thought it might make an interesting gift. Looking up information on how sailors had carved walrus, narwhal and other bones would make a good project too. Because of its rarity, I couldn't let it go for a small amount of money.

Would this man pay what I was asking?

It was easier to tell with women. I usually knew instinctively by how they acted with something they were interested in. Men were harder to figure out. They didn't walk around the shop touching things then circle back when something took their fancy.

I looked at the smiling man in front of me. He was well dressed, well-groomed. He might be the right person for this find. Or it might be something he wouldn't appreciate.

"I might have something for you. How old is your son?"

"He's twelve. Danny is quite the pirate buff. I'm hoping to bring him down here over the summer."

*Danny.* That seemed like a good omen to me. I took out the scrimshaw and the box I'd found for it. The wood box I'd recovered it in had fallen apart, but the new one made a great presentation of it.

"Wow. It's scrimshaw, right?" He looked up at me. "And this really belonged to a pirate?"

"It belonged to Big Dan Russell, a well-known privateer. He was one of the most feared pirates of this area in the 1800s. The people who lived here loved him. The Spanish, French and even the American governments put a huge bounty on his head. He was never caught, and some people here claim him as a relative. Most of the people from Duck have pirates in their background."

"Are you sure you don't want to keep it?" He hadn't taken his eyes from it. "Doesn't it have sentimental meaning for you?"

I smiled when I thought of all the things I'd recovered that had belonged to interesting people. I would never sell any of them, but I had to pay rent and power on my shop too.

"I have sentimental feelings for a lot of things I've collected in here," I confessed. "My grandfather won't let me keep everything I find, so I have to part with some of it. A piece like this only goes to the right person."

"I'll take it." He took a credit card out of his wallet and put it on the counter. "Can you gift wrap it and give me some ideas for books where we could look things up?" He also took out his business card.

"I can definitely do that." I rang up the sale and he didn't even blink. He was the right person for the scrimshaw. I could almost hear Big Dan Russell chuckling about it. I gift wrapped the box and handed it to him. It was enough money to keep me and Missing Pieces going through the winter. I also sent him to the museum for research material.

Feeling celebratory, I closed early and hurried home through the late-afternoon sunshine while it lasted. It was going to be a cold night and I didn't want to be out walking after dark.

Besides, Jake was coming to pick me up for dinner and to check out his historical find. I was looking forward to being with him and the excitement of seeing something new that might not have been seen for hundreds of years.

I wasn't planning on dressing up or doing anything special besides trying to stay warm that night. I knew everyone would read something into whatever I did with Jake. I didn't see a problem with having dinner with him at his house, despite Nancy and Gramps believing he was romantically interested in me. I felt confident that Jake and I were just friends.

He was hot, no doubt about it. So were other men I knew. Kevin and I were together. That was enough for me.

I got home and the house was quiet. Gramps was playing bingo before the Lions Club meeting. He wouldn't be home until much later.

Treasure was walking around, complaining about being left alone for so long. He wasn't happy about it when he found out that I was leaving again right away.

I fed him and stroked his plush black fur while he ate. He stopped eating, and his huge green eyes looked up at me. It was as though he'd said out loud, *"Beautiful."*

I knew it wasn't possible, as I knew all those other thoughts I attributed to him weren't real. He was very human sometimes. I felt like I understood him.

He followed me upstairs and watched from the bed as I changed clothes. I put on jeans and a thick green sweater. My grandmother had knitted it for my mother, who'd passed it down to me. It was so soft and warm, the color of spring leaves. When I wore it, it made me feel the years of family love behind me.

I looked at myself in the mirror, my short sun-tipped brown hair messed up from putting on the sweater. My blue eyes were dark suddenly and I heard Maggie laughing.

"Faith, I cannot believe this is what you wish to wear when you go to see that handsome man tonight. You appear to me a boy in those trousers. Surely you have something more feminine."

"He's a friend, and I don't want him to think of me as being feminine." It was hard to explain to her. "This is how we dress today, especially when it's casual and you go out with a friend."

"I've seen the way he looks at you. He is not thinking of you as anything but a beauty to grace his bed. Exactly what a man should think when he looks at a woman. If my Thomas didn't look at me that way, I would find me another."

"Please stay out of this tonight." I remembered what she'd said the last time I saw Jake. "No sudden, impulsive words, if you don't mind. Could you move so I could do my hair?"

"Aye, I'll move. Remember, I wouldn't be here if you had already reunited me with my Thomas instead of all these other things you do. It is not as though I want to be here."

Treasure meowed loudly, hissed and ran out of the room. I looked at my face in the mirror. Maggie's reflection stared back at me. I tried to coax Treasure back, but he wouldn't listen.

When I turned back to the mirror again, I looked like myself.

A shiver of fear ran through me, colder than the night outside. I'd realized from the beginning that there was some danger involved in trying to help Maggie. I didn't have to be a witch to know that it was possible that I could be lost in one of those personality transfers. I might not be able to find my way back again through that portal that separated Maggie and me.

This was the only way to get her where she belonged. I took a deep breath and tried to steady my resolve to see it through.

There was a knock on the door downstairs. I switched off the light in the bedroom and went down to meet Jake.

"I hope your truck is running." I opened the front door. "I don't think I can ride a horse through all this cold."

Of course it was Kevin. I knew I had nothing to feel bad about, still I felt a little guilty anyway. Maybe I should have mentioned my dinner with Jake to Kevin. "Sorry. I was expecting someone else."

"I noticed. Someone with a horse. Still seeing the cowboy from Corolla?"

I didn't like the way he'd said *seeing*. Obviously, Nancy or Trudy or both had been talking. "He asked me if I'd come out and take a look at some artifacts he found on his property."

"I see." Kevin smiled. "I heard you were going to Manteo to interview Councilman Wilson tomorrow. I tried to call your cell phone and offer to take you out there. Maybe we could have lunch somewhere besides my place for a change."

"That sounds great, but I already promised Mrs. Wilson I'd let her son drive me there. She wanted to pay me. I couldn't accept that. I think she might be upset if I don't let Amos drive. I'm sorry."

"Well, I'd like your opinion on where I should put the desk you gave me—when you get a chance. Call me, Dae."

"Oh, don't worry, dearie," Maggie impulsively reassured him. I saw her smiling face in the tiny mirror near the door. "She'll be giving you a call."

Kevin lifted his left brow over a question that lurked in his gray blue eye. "Dae?"

"We'll do something tomorrow when I get back." I rushed past that instant when I didn't sound like myself.

Another pickup had pulled into the drive. I knew it was Jake. Talk about awkward moments.

"When you get to it," Kevin called back as he walked away. "Burleson."

Jake's low, sultry voice said, "Boyfriend," from the dark.

There definitely was a hint of strain in Kevin's voice, though not in Jake's. Did Kevin believe whatever Nancy and Trudy might have said? I hoped not. I planned to set him straight, as soon as I got back from Manteo tomorrow.

I closed the front door and walked out to Jake's truck. Maybe I should've offered to let Kevin come with us to look at the artifacts. I hadn't thought of it until it was too late.

"Evening, Miss Dae," Jake drawled when I was in the truck with him. "I should warn you that this truck doesn't have seat belts. I've got some nice hemp rope in the back I could tie you in with if that would make you feel safer."

Maggie was positively giddy. "Oh yes! I would feel ever so much safer if you tied me up with some good stout rope."

"Shh!" I warned her and smiled at Jake. "I mean, there's no need for rope. Thanks."

"Are you okay, Dae?" His gaze was curious.

"Fine. I'm fine. It's been a confusing day."

He let it go, thank goodness, and we settled in for the ride.

Jake's pickup was at least twenty years older than Kevin's, and Kevin's wasn't new. I was pretty sure I could see the driveway through some cracks in the floorboard, and most of the metal appeared to be rusting away. Still, it was better than a horse.

He laughed and started the old pickup after several tries. The engine kind of wheezed as it was going down the road, but it kept going.

"I've been working all day with these artifacts. I can't describe it exactly. I've never seen anything like it. I hope you'll know what they are and can give me some clues about what I should do."

He described a little about the project. It sounded like one of those old pottery finds that happened occasionally out here where a small settlement used to be. It seemed like every historical feature should have already been found on our island. There was only so much land between the Atlantic and the sounds that separated us from the mainland.

Yet there were always new finds—either above or below the water. There had been inhabitants on this hundred-mile stretch of land long before the white explorers had come. Between the natives, the pirates and the settlers, there were plenty of items to find.

I'd forgotten how dark Highway Twelve was after passing all of the stores and houses at that end of the island. I wasn't out there much at night. The high dunes seemed to close off the road from everything else. It was like being transported into another world.

I wouldn't have been able to find Jake's place in the dark. There were no lights at the house or on the driveway, nothing to say that there was anything back on the rutted, sandy road. The pickup headlights wavered and almost went dark a few times as the tires negotiated the curves.

"It gets dark out here." Jake kept his hands on the wheel. "Maybe I should think about putting in some lights. I run what I can from my generator. I don't like to waste the gasoline. But I know it doesn't look like much of a place to have company."

I'd been to Jake's house a few times in the day. He liked to live off the grid, as he called it. He made everything he could, including his own electricity, and grew most of his food. He bartered for what he and his horses needed. The Wild Horse Association paid him a stipend to care for sick and injured wild horses from the herds.

"It's too late to try and impress me," I said. "I've been here before."

He laughed and stopped the pickup as we reached the house that suddenly appeared in the headlights. I was afraid the pickup might not start again. It sounded like it had wheezed its last.

"I love your sense of humor," he fired back. "At least I *hope* you weren't serious."

Dinner turned out to be scrambled eggs we made in his tiny kitchen. The eggs were covered with chili and cheese. Jake loved things spicy. He'd almost emptied a bottle of Texas Pete at my house each time he'd had dinner there.

I wasn't much for spicy food and gasped when I tasted his chili.

"Here. Eat some cornbread. Drinking water won't help."

I enjoyed his company as we talked about the elections in Duck and the dead driver in the race car.

"You know I'm not political." He leaned back on two legs in his chair. "I'd vote for you if I lived in Duck. You're smart as a whip, twice as cute, and you find dead people. Perfect qualifications for a mayor in my book. Who wants all those dead people rotting away down there?"

"Great campaign slogan. Mind if I use it?"

"Go right ahead. Maybe you could put it up there with the big picture of your face on the water tower. What does it cost for something like that? Bet I could feed a lot of horses with it."

He joked around about my picture scaring seagulls off of the tower. Then he told me about his new horses. We got bundled up and went out to the barn to take a look at them. They were beautiful, one caramel colored and the other mahogany. They let me pet their noses while Jake put down some feed for them.

"Someone hit this one, probably with something smaller than a car." He pointed out the damage to the caramel colored one. "We'll never know if it was an accident. They left

97

him there, not able to get to his feet. I don't know what's wrong with people."

"What about this one?" I patted the dark brown horse's side. They were a little shaggier and smaller than most horses, possibly from spending their lives in the wild.

"She got tangled in some wire. People put it out to try and keep them off their property. She was all cut up when I got her, but she's healing nicely. I think both of them should be able to go back to the herd."

"Wouldn't it be better if they didn't? People put out the wire because there are so many wild horses. They eat all their plants and shrubs."

Jake smiled at me and pushed his cowboy hat back on his head. "The horses were here before the people, Dae. They have a right to live here in peace like God meant them to. It's bad enough we have to sell some of them every year to outsiders. If a few people had their way, there wouldn't be any more wild horses here."

It was a lot for him to say at one time. I knew he was passionate about the horses. It's what made him good at what he did and what made the wild horse protectors lucky to have him.

"You have my vote for wild horse protector of the year," I joked then shivered. "I'm not good for long in these colder temperatures. You'd better show me the artifacts before I freeze."

"I wouldn't want that to happen." He settled his jacket around my shoulders. "Come right this way."

Jake explained how he'd been looking for another well site when he'd found the homestead. His current well was going dry. "It's easy to use a hand auger to drill down and find water—it's only a few feet. I got to about twenty feet and hit something. This is what I found."

He picked up a tarp covering a hole in the sand. It was

right outside the barn. This was much deeper than twenty feet and had been dug out to a six-by-six area. He shined a flashlight into the pit. There were pieces of wood on the sides supporting the sand so it wouldn't cave in.

"After you." He shined the flashlight on a ladder going down into the hole.

I stared at him, wondering if I'd lost my mind or if he'd lost his. Why would he bring me out here at night to see this dig? Surely daytime would have been better.

It occurred to me that everyone might be right and that Jake was interested in me—besides being my friend. Men did some weird things sometimes to show you that they loved you. It seemed to start when they were kids and punched you in the arm.

"No way. I've seen too much nighttime excavation recently. You go down first. I hope you have a bigger light down there."

"Chicken." He laughed and turned on two floodlights that lit up the darkness.

"I can't believe you were trying to trick me into going down there in the dark. You're lucky I don't have secret service protection or something. I *am* a public official, you know."

"Okay. I'll go down first. And don't worry, I'll catch you if you fall."

*There it was.* My stomach started churning. I was going to have to tell Jake that I wasn't interested in him that way. I really hated to lose his friendship, but suddenly, I could hear that tone in his voice.

I watched him go down the metal ladder. It wasn't in good shape, all bent and rusted. When he got down there, I assumed it must be stronger than it appeared, and I followed him.

On the way down, I noticed all the large rocks embedded

into the side walls. It was unusual to see so much rock in one place. This even seemed to have patterns, as though someone had been trying to create an image of some kind.

At the bottom of the hole, there was barely enough room for both of us to move around. Jake reached around and found a wood box that was filled with strange artifacts—horses of all shapes and sizes made from shell, wood and stone. They appeared to be very old, possibly older than anything else that had ever been found on the island.

"What do you think?" He held one of the horses in his rough hands.

"I think you found something really important."

# Chapter 10

He picked up a few more horses from the box. "Do you want to hold one?"

I really wanted to, but I'd left my gloves at home. Jake didn't know about my gift, and I wasn't thrilled with the idea of what could happen if I picked up something that might be from the prehistory of the island. I didn't want to pass out or find myself in another time with Jake standing there wondering what was wrong with me.

On the other hand, he was bound to find out about me if we stayed friends. "Let me wear your gloves. I can't touch them with bare hands. No one should, really. I'm not an archaeologist, but I know it's bad to get the oils on artifacts."

He took off his gloves and gave them to me. "I haven't touched them with bare hands because I've been digging. I hope I haven't done any damage to them."

"They're probably fine, especially the stone ones." I picked up a gray stone pony whose tail was missing but otherwise was in perfect condition. "Again, I'm not an expert, but I think this goes back before the records we have from the native tribes that lived here."

The pony was beautiful with smooth flanks and muscular legs. I admired it, processing what it could be worth. My brain told me all of this should be in a museum.

To someone like Dillon, these little statues would be worth a lot of money. My hands inside the gloves itched to find out more about them, but I was chicken, as Jake had said, to try it.

"There's something else over here." Jake moved over a little so I could see what he was talking about. "I've only unearthed part of it."

We both knelt in the damp sand and he shined his flashlight on a lower part of the wall near the bottom. My heart pounded when I saw the beginning of a very large horse's head.

"The whole thing must be buried in there. Jake brushed a little more sand from the horse's face. "If the nose and mouth are this big, there's no telling how large the whole statue is."

"I've seen things like this in books." I carefully touched the horse's nose with my gloved hand. "I think there may have been a horse cult here. These statues are older than our stories about how the wild horses got here. This little hole could rewrite history for our part of the world. You have to tell an expert, someone who knows how to excavate this properly."

Even with the dim light at the bottom of the pit, I could see Jake's expression harden at the idea.

"That's not gonna happen. I don't want a bunch of government employees running around on my land. You know what I mean, Dae. They'd want to write about it in magazines, take millions of pictures and put the whole thing on the damned Internet. I'm not into that."

I knew he felt that way. Of course he didn't want strangers out here every day, possibly for years. "Maybe you can find one person who'd be an expert at this kind of thing and have access to the equipment you'd need to carbon-date the site."

"You and I both know we don't need all that rigmarole." His earnest face was very close to mine. "You can hold one or two of the horses, touch the big horse's nose and find out everything about them. I know we haven't talked about it, but I've heard the stories."

I didn't know what to say. Not that my gift was a secret. I didn't try to hide it. I was surprised that he hadn't said anything about it before. Most people talked to me about it right away.

Jake had saved my life. Asking me to do this wasn't anything in return for that. Of course I could do it—but not here. "I'll take a few home with me." I gave him back his gloves. "I can't touch them here. It's too dangerous."

"Dangerous? How so? Is there something I can do?"

I thought immediately of Kevin. I wouldn't want to try something like this without him. He'd pulled me back from other murky places I'd gone by touching objects I shouldn't have touched.

Jake didn't have that experience. He wouldn't know what to do.

"I have to be prepared for what might come to me." I knew it sounded ridiculous. "Something like this could be bad for someone like me. You never know what could happen."

"Okay. I understand. I'll bring a couple of horses up with me. You can take them home and see what happens."

"I don't know what to say about the big horse, Jake. I'll have to see what happens with the smaller ones first and we'll go from there."

I went up the ladder first, my cold hands finding that the ladder was old, made in Michigan about twenty years ago and sold at the hardware store in Corolla.

I'd learned to process the information I received from everything I touched like I would have noticed it was cold and made of metal. It was the other information—particularly held in older artifacts—that led me to trouble.

The amber necklace was like that, trapping me in the past, not really ever part of it, for a few days. It was the emotions in the objects I touched that brought disaster. While some were good memories held in love and hope, others were dark and terrifying. I'd once worn an old dress that a woman had drowned herself in.

I knew I had to be careful.

I waited while Jake climbed to the top after me. He pulled the two small horses out of his jacket pockets. I'd have to find a box or bag to take them home in.

The spotlights were still on, so the area was bright enough to see. I thought about what this end of the island was like when those horses were buried. Who had owned them and what were they used for?

I turned to start back to the house through the old, ramshackle barn where Jake kept his horses. Maggie chose that moment to flirt with him.

"Oh, come on now," she said to him with a wink. "Surely we aren't going home just yet."

"*Shh*," I cautioned her, but it was too late.

"Maybe we should go inside for a nightcap, if you know what I mean." She winked at Jake. "The night is young. We should take advantage of it."

Jake caught up with me and smiled as he put his arm

around my shoulders. "I've been waiting to hear you say something like that, sweetheart. I hoped you'd think about us being more than friends."

*Darn Maggie's mouth.*

"I only meant we could look at the horses inside before I go home." My hands were shaking as I moved away from him. I'd never meant to give him the wrong idea.

"Sure." He stepped back. "We can still have that nightcap too." His face was shadowed, but I could see the sincerity in his eyes. "Anytime the equation changes between you and Kevin, let me know. I think you and I could have something special."

I thought he was going to kiss me, and I tensed, trying to decide what to do. I don't know if it was Maggie's effect on me or what. I panicked. My heart was pounding and my mouth was dry. I could have moved away, but I didn't.

I focused hard on Kevin and how much he meant to me. The moment passed and the danger was over. I hadn't asked for this to happen, but at least while Maggie was inside me, I wouldn't be alone with Jake again.

He acted as though nothing had happened, or almost happened. His left arm was still draped across my shoulders as we walked inside. There was no more talk of anything personal. It was all about the horses and what information I thought he could look up to get an idea about what he'd found.

He wrapped the small horses carefully in pillowcases then put them both in a big tote bag. "I wish you'd tell me about this ability of yours." He handed me the bag. "What kind of bad things could happen from you touching something?"

I explained a little about my gift and how it worked. "I seem to absorb emotions, good and bad, when I touch things. When things are new, it's not a problem. I just see where they came from and a little of their history. Old things are different. I've had to give away some of my most prized possessions because of the emotions trapped in them."

He grinned and went to get a brown horse blanket. "Okay. Time to prove yourself. This is a new blanket. What can you tell me about it?"

I smiled and touched it. "It was actually made in this country, in New Mexico. You bought it, and a few more like it, because they had them on sale at the feed store last week. The store manager bought too many, so he needed to get rid of some."

"Well, I'll be. That's a neat parlor trick. You should've told me a long time ago. I would've been dragging out everything so you could tell me all that."

"That's okay. I only started touching things to understand them recently. Sometimes I'm not sure if I'm going to come back from the places they take me."

"You're a strong lady. I'm sure you'll always find your way back."

We had a drink for the road and Jake took me back home. The horses in the bag on my lap called to me, daring me to touch them without gloves. There were deep mysteries hidden in that place Jake had found. How long had those horses been there? Maybe more importantly, how would he handle the intervention that was bound to come as people found out about the discovery?

"Keep me in the loop about the horses." I needed to emotionally keep my distance, but I wanted to help with what he'd found.

"You know I will. Let me know what you find out when you touch them. I'm curious what might be attached to them. Be careful, darlin'. I wouldn't want to be the one who caused you pain."

Maggie rolled "our" eyes as she said, "Oh, for goodness' sake, give us a kiss, lad."

Jake's expression was confused but willing. I couldn't explain, so I kissed him quickly on the cheek and got out of the pickup.

"For luck." I smiled through my anger and hoped he didn't think I was a big flirt.

"Thanks." He didn't get out of the pickup, just waved and left the house.

"What about my relationship with Kevin don't you understand?" I raged at my alter ego when we were alone. "Here I am, looking for the spot where you can rest in peace because it's near your lover. Did Thomas know how amorous you are?"

"I have been alone for a very long time." Her voice was pitiful, on the verge of tears. "You can't image what it has been for me. Surely you could have given someone a little kiss or a hug."

I felt bad after she said it. I also realized I was standing in the front yard having a conversation with myself. She was right. I didn't know what she'd been through, how lonely she was. I wanted to help, but she couldn't go around throwing us at every man we met.

"I'm sorry, Maggie. The next time I see Kevin, we'll give him a big kiss. Okay?"

"Thank you, Dae. You are very kind to me."

I went inside quickly, worried about Old Man Sweeney next door calling Gramps and telling him I was crazy. He loved to snoop.

I was also worried about my relationship with Maggie. Was it my imagination, or were the changes coming too quickly, too easily, between us? I hoped this would end the way I'd thought it would when I first took on this burden.

A little voice whispered, *What if Maggie becomes me and I don't exist anymore?*

I wasn't sure whose voice that was. Not mine and not Maggie's. I had to get hold of myself. This was going to be okay.

Of course, the more we changed places, the easier it would get. I was letting all the witch talk color my judgment. I knew what I was doing.

I slept dreamlessly that night. There was a full moon shining in through the bedroom window, but it didn't keep me awake.

I woke early and took a quick shower, despite Maggie's longing for a bath. I went downstairs and started making pancakes for Gramps.

There was a knock on the back door and Kevin glanced inside. "I brought donuts if I can stay for breakfast."

"Too late. I made pancakes. You can stay anyway. What brings you out so early?"

"You." He shut the door and came inside. "I had a dream about you and horses. I don't know exactly what it was all about. You were scared. It was enough that it woke me up and I decided to come over."

I smiled and kissed him—extra long and hard for Maggie's benefit. I could feel her sigh.

"You don't have to worry about me and Jake. You know that, right?"

"This really didn't have anything to do with me being jealous of Jake." Kevin sat down at the table. "It's not the first time I've dreamed about you and it came true. I think I've lost my objectivity with the subject."

I put my arms around him. "Would that be me? If so, I don't like being called a subject."

"Is this your idea of love talk?" Maggie blurted out.

"Your words should be tender and gentle. Ask him to kiss us again. Mmm, it was *good*!"

Kevin frowned at Maggie's words. "What's going on, Dae?"

"Nothing. I got back late last night." I told him about the horses, hoping to distract him. This wasn't the same as fooling Jake. Kevin knew me so much better. Worse, he was still suspicious about what had happened to me.

"I guess that's why I had the dream about the horses. You didn't touch one, did you?"

"No. Of course not. I wanted you to be with me when I touched them."

"I'm sorry." He smiled and put pancakes on plates. "I know I can't be with you all the time, but you can't blame me for wanting to protect you from men who make me jealous."

"Really? You're jealous of Jake?"

He laughed. "I hope you'd be jealous too if I was having secret meetings with some cowboy who saved my life."

The conversation I didn't want to have with him seemed to have been averted. "I get it. I'm sorry. He really is just a friend. And we really did eat and look at prehistoric horses. Want to see them?"

"What about that romantic moment in the barn where he pledged his troth to us?" Maggie asked me with a sigh.

Kevin frowned again as I struggled to keep Maggie under control. He either had to think I was crazy, or that I was possessed by a witch, as Shayla had said. I was losing the battle. The separation between us was becoming thinner. I knew by the look on Kevin's face that my secret wasn't going to be a secret much longer.

Gramps saved the moment when he came out in his waders and heavy sweater.

"Dae, have you seen my yellow slicker? I can't find a thing since you cleaned the house. Shouldn't you be getting ready to go with Amos instead of canoodling with Kevin?"

"Your slicker is on the back porch, where it belongs. And I'm all ready to go. I got up early and made pancakes. What's canoodling? Sounds like a kind of pasta to me."

Gramps grinned and swatted at my butt as I walked by. "Always sassy. Good thing I lived with your grandmother all those years or I wouldn't know how to handle it. Can't stay for pancakes. I've got an early charter. I'll see both of you later. Take care you don't get in any more trouble today, Dae."

Kevin didn't say anything until Gramps was gone. Neither one of us ate much, and there was no conversation. Maggie stayed quiet.

"Do you want me to stay so you can look at those horses?" Kevin sipped his coffee as he studied my face.

"I really can't do that this morning." I smiled, glad I had a legitimate excuse to leave. "Maybe later. Amos Wilson should be here any minute."

"Okay. Call me when you get back and we'll set something up."

"I will."

"You know you can tell me anything, don't you? There isn't anything that could happen to you that I wouldn't want to hear, and help with."

"I know."

He took a deep breath before he got up, kissed my forehead and left. I waved to him from the door as he got back in his blue golf cart to leave.

I wanted to say something, find some way to explain about Maggie. The words wouldn't come. I wasn't afraid of his reaction. I was worried that he would try and stop me from what I needed to do.

Treasure yawned and turned away from the door. He clearly was bored with the situation once the pancakes were gone.

"I'll see you later." I ruffled his newly cleaned fur. I knew from the look he gave me it would take hours to reclean it. "If there's time, I'll pick you up before I go to the shop."

Amos, Mad Dog's son, was waiting for me when I stepped out the door. I didn't know him well. We saw each other at council meetings and other town events. He seemed to be a very serious man. He looked more like his mother than his father. He also seemed to have her quiet, nonflamboyant temperament.

I hurried out to the late-model Buick and got in the passenger door. "Thanks for waiting. Sorry it took so long."

He reversed the car out of the driveway. "It doesn't matter. It's not like I'm looking forward to spending all morning with the woman who ruined my father's life."

# Chapter 11

If I was looking for the hostility Laura Wilson was lacking, I found it in her son. I wished a hundred times on the way to Manteo that I'd driven there with Kevin.

"You've got a lot of nerve even pretending you want to help my father." Amos could barely look at me. "You may have convinced my mother that you're sincere, but I'm willing to bet you aren't going to find anything to help my father right before the election."

I had to answer back. I wished I could sit there and take it—everything I said was bound to make it worse. "What makes you think I knew that car was down there? I wasn't looking for it. It just happened."

"Everyone knows what you do. You find things other people can't find. Don't you think that's a little suspicious in this case? Don't bother trying to play innocent with me. Your guilt is written all over you."

"Look, I'd rather not win the election because your father has to go to prison. I don't even want to win because he was accused of killing Joe Walsh. That's not going to make my job—or my reputation—any better."

"That's right." He sneered at me. "And that's my only consolation. Everyone knows you dug this up to stop my father from being mayor. I'll make sure no one forgets it either."

I was so glad to see the county courthouse that I almost got out of the Buick while it was slowing down. I bit my lip as Amos parked the car then got out and walked as fast as I could up the courthouse steps without waiting to see if he was coming too.

Mad Dog's lawyer was a white-haired man from Nags Head who said he knew Gramps. He shook my hand and then we walked down the long, green hall that led to a small room where we waited for Mad Dog.

I was relieved when the lawyer told Amos that only one of us at a time could come back and talk to his father. Amos seemed to have lost all of his steam in the car yelling at me anyway. He sat down on a bench in the hall to wait without complaining. I didn't mind that at all. I knew facing Mad Dog was going to be hard all by itself.

The lawyer and I made polite conversation about the weather and how many large fish Gramps had caught recently. I looked around at the bleak room, the plain chairs and table, and felt bad for Mad Dog. I hoped he wasn't the killer. When I touched his hands, I wanted to find something inside of him that would show me that he didn't kill Joe Walsh.

Mad Dog was as feisty as ever when the jail guards finally walked him into the room. He was wearing an orange jumpsuit that didn't suit him like his normally flamboyant clothes.

He wasn't handcuffed, and that started me wondering why he was here at all. It seemed hard to believe that he hadn't been able to make bail. I knew he owned property, which was usually all it took.

"You know, Laura said you were coming today. I couldn't believe it." Mad Dog chuckled as he sat down. "Why are you here? We both know you have me right where you want me."

I looked across the table and felt even sorrier for him. "I know you think I did this on purpose, and I don't blame you. I'd probably think the same thing if I were you."

"Good. Then we're on the same page. You might as well leave." He looked away from me.

"Why are *you* here? Why aren't you out on bail?"

"I'm not giving the county my property to set me free when I haven't done anything wrong. Those jackals want what's mine. I won't give them that satisfaction."

I glanced at the lawyer, who shook his head and shrugged. I knew Mad Dog knew better. He understood how a bail bondsman worked. As long as he showed up for court, he wouldn't lose anything. As for calling government officials jackals, it was like referring to himself, since he was a councilman.

"I told you to leave." Mad Dog tapped his fingers impatiently on the table between us. "Why are you still here?"

"I may be the only one who can help you. I drove all the way out here with Amos calling me everything bad he could possibly think of. I don't want to win the election because you're too stubborn to let me help you. Put your hands over here so I can see what's going on."

I used the same voice I'd heard all my life from Gramps and my teachers in school. I assumed it was a parent's voice telling a child what they should do.

Would it work?

I wasn't sure.

What I did know was that, despite his bravado, Randal

"Mad Dog" Wilson was scared. Not only for his life but also for his reputation and standing with his friends and neighbors in Duck. He was desperate inside. I hoped I could use that to help him.

He stared at me like he'd never seen me before. His usually clean-shaven face was prickly with gray stubble. His hair was uncombed, and there was a spot of jelly near his lips. He was a man who was scrupulously careful with his appearance. Now that didn't matter.

"I *know*. I understand why you aren't letting yourself be released. You don't want people to see you this way. You don't want to see in their eyes that they might think you killed Lightning Joe. I don't have to touch you to see that."

It was exactly the right thing to say. Mad Dog started crying. I sat back in my chair, not sure what to say or do next. I hadn't thought he would break down that way. I'd wanted him to cooperate, not fall apart.

"You're right, Dae." He sniffled, using his lawyer's clean white handkerchief to wipe his nose and eyes. "I don't want anyone to see me this way. I've worked too hard all my life to have this happen. I swear I didn't know my old car was down there. I sure didn't know Joe was in it."

"Then let me try to help you. I can't promise anything, but it might work."

"Okay. I have nothing to lose." He smiled at me through his tears. "One time, Horace brought you over to my house. You were just a kid. You found a notebook for me. I'd lost it at the beach. It had all my insurance customer contacts. It wasn't like today where everyone makes copies of everything on their computer. You held my hand and told me where it was. You've always been a good girl, Dae. I know we don't always agree, but I'll always remember how you were that day at my house."

He held out his hands to me across the table. His blood-shot gaze was glued to mine. I held his hands and closed my eyes.

At first, being in someone else's head is like trying to sort through what's left after a hurricane. Everything is jumbled up, not necessarily where it should be. I have to find a point of reference to use or I get lost in all the confusion.

I thought the car could be that reference. "I need you to think about the last time you saw your number twelve car. It was lost for years. When was the last time that you drove it?"

"The last time was when I hurt my leg. I flipped the car going around a turn too fast. I thought I was a goner. I couldn't get out. I was pinned in."

I was beginning to get a clear image of the car Kevin and I had unearthed. It was damaged but shiny with new paint. A truck was coming for it.

"You got out. What happened next?"

"They took me to the hospital in Kill Devil Hills. The car was wrecked—so was I. They tried to operate on my leg and make it better. It didn't help much. When I got out of the hospital, my car was gone. A truck had come to get it and tow it off, but nobody knew whose truck it was. I never saw it again."

I tried to push him one step further. "And Joe? When was the last time you saw him?"

The image of the race car stayed clear in Mad Dog's mind. He loved that car. I saw hundreds of images of him painting it, changing the tires, working on the engine. He was devastated by its loss. It was a life-changing event for him. The one thing he'd loved in life was over. It was symbolic to him that the car that had made his reputation was gone too.

That was it. There was no image of Joe at all.

I let go of his hands and opened my eyes. He was still

staring at me like I was a life preserver in the middle of a storm.

"Well, Dae? What did you see?"

"I saw you when you were younger and I saw your car."

"That's a *big* help. Everyone knows that car was mine."

"True. I also know you lost the car right after the accident. You never saw it again. That means you weren't the one who put Joe in it."

He gave a little excited yell. "I guess that's better than nothing."

His lawyer intervened. "Of course, that won't help him in court."

"I know. It doesn't say anything about who *did* put Joe in the car after he was killed. But it's a start."

"Where do we go from here?" Mad Dog seemed happier with what I'd told him.

"I'm not sure. It seems like the next step might be for me to touch the car." After my recent experiences with touching things that had bad histories, I wasn't exactly eager to volunteer for that task. But there was no one else.

"I don't think that will be as easy as it sounds," the lawyer said. "That car is material evidence in a capital case. I don't know if being the retired sheriff's granddaughter will get you access. Let me know if you find any other leads."

I promised to keep both men up to date about what I found. I shook Mad Dog's hand and the guard came to take him away.

The lawyer and I parted company at the front lobby after he gave me his business card.

I took one look at Amos's angry face and decided there was no way I was riding back to Duck with him. I'd walk first.

"I promised my mother I'd bring you home," Amos argued as he walked beside me down the courthouse steps.

"I'll call her and explain. She'll be fine."

He stopped abruptly. "I don't know what you expected. He's my father. You ruined his life."

"Good-bye, Amos." I walked across the courthouse parking lot like someone was waiting on the other side to take me home. It was only a show for him. Nothing could've been further from the truth. I had no idea how I was going to get home without calling one of my friends to make the trip.

"Dae!" I heard a familiar voice shout my name.

I turned to look and saw La Donna Nelson in her green minivan. I walked to it with a big smile on my face. Providence had to be watching out for me.

"Hi! I'm really glad to see you! What brings you out here?"

"I brought my mother out to get some tax forms she needed. I don't understand why these things aren't available online by now. We shouldn't have to drive all the way out here to pick up paper copies. I know why *you're* here." She smiled.

"Probably you and most of Duck. Please tell me you're headed back to town. I lost my ride home."

"As soon as we get done with everything here—mother has to return some library books—we're going home. I'll be glad to take you. How did you lose your ride?"

I explained about Amos. She understood. "I'm surprised he brought you out here if he had those kinds of feelings about it. Although I can relate. If Randal was my father, I'd hate you too."

I got in the front seat of the minivan. "Not you too."

"I don't think you found that car on purpose, Dae. I'd hate the coincidence and the timing if I were Amos, wouldn't you?"

"I wish I could do it over."

"What would you do different?"

"I'd wait and do it after the election." It was a joke. Maybe I could've found some way to stop the geothermal drilling. I didn't realize it was going to be so hard to get Maggie's bones so she could be buried next to her boyfriend, Thomas, or that there would be a race car in the way.

"So you saw Randal." La Donna looked around at the people passing by. "Was he happy to see you? I've been wondering about that all morning. Did he *want* to see you, or was that Laura's idea?"

"You mean you don't know?" I grinned. "I thought everyone would know that too."

"Quit stalling and answer the question. What did Randal tell you?"

"He didn't tell me anything he hadn't already told everyone else. As far as picking something up from him, the only thing I got was that he truly didn't know what had happened to the car. I think that means he didn't bury it there. As his lawyer reminded me, no one cares what I think."

"So you think he's innocent?"

"It looked like it to me. I'm afraid I'm going to have to do something I'd rather not do—touch the car and see what's there."

"Can you do that?" La Donna looked shocked and a little fearful. "I knew you were doing some strange things recently. I didn't know you were doing things like that. Is that even possible?"

Before I could answer, La Donna's mother, Beverly Michaels, hobbled angrily up to the minivan. Beverly was in her early nineties, but she was like a force of nature. The woman did yoga in Duck Park and got through footraces every year during the Fourth of July celebrations.

"I don't know what's wrong with those people." She yanked open the minivan door and I almost fell out at her feet. "And you've picked up a hitchhiker. I can't believe you'd do such a thing with your brother as the chief of police. What do you think he's going to have to say about that?"

"She's not a hitchhiker, mother." La Donna reminded her that she knew me. "Even if she was, I'm old enough to make decisions about my life without Ronnie's help."

"Right. Because you made such wonderful decisions when you were growing up. Always hanging out with those fast boys."

La Donna had a pained look on her face. "Are you ready to go?"

Beverly only grunted and said, "She's sitting in my place. Can we go to the library now?"

"Sorry." I got out and climbed in back.

"Sorry, Dae," La Donna whispered as I changed seats.

"Don't worry about it. I'm glad to have the ride home."

Beverly kept up her harangue from the courthouse to the library. Twice La Donna tried to get her off on another subject—*Isn't the sky beautiful? The water is so calm today. Not so much traffic as the last time we were here.*

It didn't matter. Beverly kept on about La Donna's short-comings, the stupid county government and her son, Chief Michaels, not using his authority to do the things people needed, such as getting their tax papers.

By the time Beverly got out at the library, I was mentally exhausted. It was hard to say whether she was any better than Amos. At least it wasn't directed at me.

La Donna went in the library with her mother. I stayed in the quiet minivan, thinking about my options. I knew I should probably ask Chief Michaels if I could go into the impound lot and touch the car.

I wasn't sure whether or not that would work. Chief Michaels was more accommodating on some days than others. He was steadfast when it came to enforcing the law, but he was a little fickle when it came to using my gift.

If he wouldn't help me, my next angle would have to be getting in the lot without his help. Tim had always been very reliable at this type of thing. It didn't seem like it would be a problem. I hated to take advantage of him—he always wanted a favor in return that amounted to a quasi-date. Maybe not now, since he and Trudy seemed so close.

Scott Randall, the other full-time police officer who'd have access to the impound lot, was far too intense and worried about upholding the law. He was very sweet, but he'd never go along with it.

I could try and break into the lot by myself, and it might come down to that. One way or another, I was going to put my hands on old number twelve.

# Chapter 12

La Donna and Beverly came out of the library a few minutes later. Conversation was slow and intermittent during the ride back to Duck. I didn't mind. It was nice to look out of the window at the sky, the water and the dunes.

Traffic started backing up as we got into town. Something was up at either Duck Park or the construction site for the new town hall. Since I knew they weren't working on the town hall for a while, and it was a little cold for many people to be in the park, I was curious about what could be going on.

"I'll get out here, La Donna," I said. "Thanks for the ride back."

"Do you know what's going on, Dae?"

"I'll let you know when I find out." I smiled at her in the rearview mirror and got out of the minivan.

I walked along the side of the road. It didn't take long to see what the problem was. A large truck was picking up

Kevin's excavator. Two men were in the street stopping traffic both ways while the work was being done.

I saw Kevin near the excavator and walked quickly up to join him. "Finally getting to take it home, huh?"

"No. Sheriff Riley decided it was part of the investigation, since it dug up the car. He's having it taken to Manteo— unless Chief Michaels can persuade him to leave it at the Duck police impound lot."

I felt terrible again. Kevin looked angry about it too. "I'll go talk to them."

"I don't think that will help. We're lucky he isn't impounding *us* because we were there." He smiled and put his arm around me. "It doesn't matter. I'll dig the storm cellar later. They can have it for now, although I'd rather them keep it here."

"I'm sorry." I knew I'd already said it a few dozen times. There wasn't much else to say.

"Don't worry about it. Do you have time to come and look at the desk with me?"

I thought about my plan to open Missing Pieces for a while. It could wait, like Kevin's storm cellar. "Sure. Does lunch come with that?"

"Yes. My golf cart is right over there." He laughed. "Who thought I'd be saying that to someone?"

"Life changes, I guess." It was good to see he still had a sense of humor.

"I'll call Ronnie later to see where they've decided to put the excavator."

We walked around the crowd as everyone else watched what was going on. Kevin's phone rang. It was Chief Michaels.

Kevin talked to him for a few minutes. When he said thanks and hung up, I asked him what had happened.

"It's the endless tug-of-war between different law enforcement groups," he said. "Chief Michaels won on the race car staying here in Duck. Sheriff Riley gets the excavator."

"I'll pay to have it brought back to the Blue Whale when they're done." I'd hoped it would stay in Duck. That would have been cheaper.

"You don't have to do that, Dae." Kevin started the golf cart that had *The Blue Whale Inn* airbrushed on the side. Sometimes he used it to ferry guests down to the beach or to a local event—another part of Blue Whale service that people loved.

He continued, "I think the desk is enough. I know it's a bad situation. I guess we both should've known better."

This wasn't where I'd pictured being right before my first real election. When I became mayor the first time, Duck had just incorporated and no one had run against me. Mad Dog, La Donna and the other council members hadn't wanted to be mayor.

This election with Mad Dog had been a taste of the real thing. There had been too many angry words and careless accusations between us. That's what had made everyone suspect that I'd gone out of my way to find his old race car with Lightning Joe in it. They believed in my gift. Too bad they believed I'd do something so underhanded with it.

Kevin and I passed ten posters and three signs stuck in the ground campaigning for either Mad Dog or me. There were posters, signs and banners all over Duck for each of us. I cringed when I saw some of them, especially the ones that had been put up by Dillon's money.

The big banner that had been displayed at the history museum, next to the Blue Whale, still stung. It was one of the biggest and earliest in the campaign and was looking ragged after a year of being outside.

It was a big picture of Mad Dog smiling with the

quotation, "Vote for me. I won't fool around all Dae." The Duck Historical Society had decided to back him for mayor. I constantly asked myself why.

I had belonged to the historical society since I was eight. Mad Dog had never been interested in Duck history, as far as I knew. Did their endorsement of him mean they thought I was doing a bad job?

I hadn't been there for months because of it. I knew I wasn't supposed to take it personally. I did anyway.

I was feeling sorry for myself. It had been a long, strange night and a hard day. I probably should've gone home before it got worse.

But Kevin was excited about his desk, and that made me smile. He'd already moved it into his office and placed it in front of a window that overlooked the ocean. It was a nice, sunny location. He could work, or he could look out of the window and dream.

"This is great." I admired the location. "You need a better chair for it. I'm sure I have one."

He looked at the white plastic chair he'd drawn up to it. "I suppose so." He ran his hand over the desk's mellow wood. "I love it, Dae. I know you've either done your research or you've touched it. Tell me its history."

"It was made in England and shipped here for an accountant who was setting up a new practice. He was John Edgar Anthony, the third son of a duke. He lived to a ripe old age and was the father of twelve children. He died wealthy and happy. Doesn't that sound good?"

"That sounds like what I'd expect from you. It didn't actually cost you five thousand, did it? That would be too much."

I started to remind him that it was what I owed him after he'd been fined on my behalf. I knew that would only bring back a series of questions, so I kept my mouth closed.

It seemed fair in my mind to pay that much—better if he'd just let me give him the money. I knew Kevin too well to think he'd accept it.

"It was a really sweet deal." I winked and gave him what I hoped was a sly smile.

"Good. What do you suggest for a chair?"

I looked at the dark oak roll top, probably big enough for me to climb inside. It had dozens of slots for papers, some he'd already filled.

Maggie, who'd been silent all day, suddenly giggled as we traded places. "Why don't we just give it a try, eh? It looks like a good place to have some fun."

Kevin stared at me. "What did you say?"

"I said it should be this color." I hoped he'd let it go. There was nowhere to escape as I had that morning. "Maybe with a nice brown leather seat or a manly tapestry cover."

"That isn't what you said. What's wrong?"

"Nothing. I'm not feeling well. I should probably go home."

"You probably should, but not until I have some answers about what's wrong with you." His gaze seared into me. "Tell me what's up with the strange bursts of dialect. Should I call Shayla for help?"

"There's not really much to say." I decided to tell him the truth. "Shayla was sort of right about Maggie. Not completely. She's inside of me. But she's not a witch. What about lunch?"

Kevin took a deep breath. "I happen to have a new recipe for potato soup that I'm working on for dinner tonight. My guests tell me they both love potato soup. Want to be my guinea pig while you explain the whole thing about Maggie?"

"Can't we just eat?" Kevin is a great cook. I love everything he makes. "Really, explaining about Maggie is complicated."

He took my hand. "I'm a good listener."

We ended up having potato soup and fresh-baked bread with those cute little rosettes of butter he makes for his guests. He opened a bottle of white muscadine wine, which was excellent. This is the only type of wine native to the state. It has been made on the Outer Banks for hundreds of years.

Over lunch, Kevin asked again about Maggie.

I tried to divert his attention by telling him about my meeting with Mad Dog. I didn't mention my plan to touch the race car. I didn't want him to get into any trouble for me again.

He was too persistent to ignore.

"There really isn't much to say." I buttered my bread despite disliking the destruction of the rosette.

"Except that you have a four-hundred-year-old woman or witch, depending on who you ask, living inside of you."

"It happened when I put on the amber necklace." I hated to remind him of my careless mistake.

"So that part of the story is true."

"Yes. I don't know what else I could've done. Maggie's not a ghost. She's not a witch either. I'm trying to find where she belongs. In the meantime, she comes out—once in a while."

His blue gray gaze harpooned me across the table. "Comes out?"

"You've heard her. I know I haven't done a great job covering her up. She gets excited and talks through me. She's not easy to contain."

"I knew there was something more going on. I hope Shayla wasn't right about this. How can you know that

Maggie isn't making you do terrible things that you're not aware of?"

"I *know*. She's not like that, for one thing. And I can hear everything she says and does. She can hear me too. I don't think this is a classic form of possession. There's nothing to worry about."

Kevin sat back from the table. "That makes me more worried. Shayla and Ann might be right about Maggie."

"They aren't. How can I convince you?"

"I don't know. Even if Maggie is a saint, I'd worry about the two of you getting lost in each other's consciousness. It doesn't sound like you have any control over her. I know you're Dae right now, and not Maggie." He frowned. "Let's do Maggie for the sake of comparison."

"Okay." I closed my eyes—not necessary, but I felt weird about the whole thing.

"I'll be glad to talk to you, sir." Maggie's voice was distinctive. "I shall be happy to do whatever you like, and Dae won't mind either. That's the God's truth of it."

"All right. Thanks, Maggie." Kevin nodded. "Dae?"

"So now you know," I said.

"It's amazing. I wouldn't have believed it. Her voice, even her inflections, are different than yours. I never thought I'd say this, but it's kind of spooky thinking you have someone else inside of you."

"She's really very pleasant for a ditzy, lovesick tavern wench. Her ideas about men are a little crazy for me, but we're doing okay."

"I noticed her ideas are a little racy—I hope she didn't give Jake the wrong idea."

"There was a moment." I swallowed hard and admitted it. "I handled it. He knows how I feel about you. He probably thinks I'm crazy now anyway."

When we'd finished lunch, I convinced Kevin to walk

next door with me to the museum. I really needed help from the historical society to find Maggie's boyfriend's grave. Thomas Graham had died after Maggie and was buried somewhere on the island. Maggie wanted me to move her bones to lie beside Thomas's. While I hadn't been able to reach Maggie's bones yet, it was only a matter of time. It would be good to know where I was taking them.

I felt strange going there after the group's endorsement of Mad Dog for mayor, but I was going to have to get over it. They knew everything about the local graveyards and the old names of the original settlers.

I had to remember that the president of the Duck Historical Society, Mrs. Euly Stanley, was on my campaign committee. Not all of the group planned to vote for Mad Dog.

Lucky for me, several members of the historical society were present when we got there. Mark Samson from the Rib Shack, Barney Thompson from the Sand Dollar Jewelry Store and Miss Mildred Mason were all there, drinking tea and eating scones.

I wished Mrs. Stanley had been there to bolster my confidence, but she must have stayed home that day.

"Dae, it's good to see you." Miss Mildred was a vibrant ninety-two. Her cloud of white hair made her blue eyes stand out in her tanned face. "How's everything going?"

"Fine, thanks. I was wondering if I could ask you some questions about two people who lived in Duck in the late 1600s."

She looked at Mark and Barney. They nodded, always ready for a good historical debate, even if they didn't want me to be mayor for a second time.

"I'm looking for information on Maggie Madison. She was a tavern wench and had a small house where Duck Park is now. The second is a sea captain, Thomas Graham. That's all I know about him."

The three invited Kevin and me to have tea, which we declined since we'd recently eaten. Miss Mildred patted the chair next to her, inviting Kevin to sit down. I got no such invitation from Mark or Barney, but I sat down beside them anyway.

"I wish Euly were here." Miss Mildred smiled at Kevin. "At least for assistance with your sea captain. I think we all know the story of Maggie Madison. Dae, I'm sure you know it too."

"I know everyone thought she was a witch and ostracized her. She died during a big storm when she was eighteen. She worked as a barmaid at the local tavern. That's about all I know."

"That's about all any of us knows about her." Mark laughed. "Actually, I didn't know she was only eighteen. How did you find that out, Dae?"

"I received a necklace that belonged to her." I put all the pieces of amber I carried around with me on the table. "It had some information about her with it. She got the necklace from her lover, Thomas Graham."

All three history buffs marveled at the necklace. At least it got their attention.

"I've never heard of Graham," Barney said. "He had to be a pirate to purchase something of this quality. What makes you think she got the necklace from him and didn't steal it?"

It was all I could do to hold Maggie back.

"There was every indication that it was a gift and that the two were lovers." I managed to say it around her trying to take over my mouth. It came out sounding like I'd had a stroke, but I got the point across without Maggie's help.

"This will take some research." Mark rubbed his hands together gleefully. "What exactly are you looking for in regard to him?"

"I'm looking for his grave. It's purely curiosity on my part. After I read about him, I wanted to check it out."

"We'll send this out as an email to the other members of the group," Barney said. "I'm sure between us, we can find your sea captain. Could we keep the necklace here as an artifact?"

That was too much for Maggie. She wanted it buried with her bones next to her lover. "I see no reason for the likes of you to keep something personal from me. If you want some jewelry, you should go out and buy it for yourselves."

The words were out. I couldn't call them back. All three historical society members looked shocked and a little angry.

Kevin laughed uproariously and put his arms around me. "Was that great or what? Dae, you've nailed that accent down. I know you're going to be great in that upcoming play."

Miss Mildred blinked. "What play is that? I hadn't heard a historical play was coming."

Barney and Mark agreed, looking at us, eager to hear the news.

"It's a new play they'll be doing this summer in Manteo," Kevin began explaining as he walked us to the door. "Thanks for all the help. Come next door for tea when you can."

We walked outside quickly and headed toward the tree line that separated the museum from the Blue Whale.

"Are you all right, Dae?" Kevin carefully scanned my face.

"Fine. Sorry. I'm glad you were there to bail me out. Like I said, Maggie gets a little rowdy."

Maggie took issue with that. "They were calling me a witch and things good folk don't say. What was I supposed to do? They had no right to call me a thief."

"I can't blame you, Maggie," I said. "But I wish you'd let me handle it."

Kevin smiled. "Now I know how someone feels dating a person with a split personality."

We parted company after that. Kevin had to help unload a truck full of fresh vegetables being delivered. I still had time to go to Missing Pieces, collect the items for St. Vincent's and take them to the church.

Treasure wasn't going to like it that he got excluded from the trip, but I didn't want to walk home first.

I came across Trudy and Tim sitting close together on the boardwalk, feeding each other pieces of their sandwiches and laughing. I wouldn't have thought about the two of them getting together, but seeing it, they were a good match.

"Hi, Trudy. Hi, Tim." Neither one looked up or even noticed me. That was all right. I hoped they'd be happy together for a long time.

The boardwalk was crowded with people enjoying the nice weather. As I was picking up my donation to the church, Stan the UPS man stopped off with two packages. He wished me luck with the election, which would take place before he came back. Stan wasn't from Duck, but he said he'd vote for me if he could.

As soon as he was gone, I packed everything into my rolling carryall and walked down to St. Vincent's. It looked like the bazaar would be well stocked. There were cars, golf carts and walkers like me bringing in all kinds of clothes and household items. I knew I'd want to be there for the event in case something wonderful might have accidentally been given away. I'd found a few treasures at this event before.

I opened the door to the big community center and it felt like everyone stopped talking and looked at me.

There was hostility on some of their faces, pity on others.

I knew all of these people. I realized most of what I noticed came from the same feelings Amos was venting earlier.

I ignored it and wheeled my carryall toward La Donna. "I hope this helps."

"Thanks, Dae." She smiled and lowered her voice. "Don't worry. All of this will blow over. You know it's just talk right now. Randal is the underdog and everyone knows it."

"I guess that's what I get for being a great mayor, right?"

She squeezed my hand. "That's exactly right. And don't you forget it. Thanks for bringing all of this over. I would've come and picked it up."

"I needed the exercise anyway. I'll see you later."

I focused in on how much easier it was going to be to walk back to Missing Pieces without dragging everything behind me. I smiled at familiar faces. It was one of the first things I'd learned about being mayor—keep a big smile on your face no matter what. My friend Sandi Foxx, the mayor of Manteo, had taught me that. She knew her way around difficult situations.

As I walked out the door, I heard a woman mutter, "Witch!"

I looked back and saw Martha Segall, the town's resident complainer, staring back at me. Her white hair was wild and her clothes looked as though she'd just come from working in the yard. Martha loved to find ways to stop anything the town tried to do. Between that and trying to make money from things she felt like the town had done wrong, she wasn't the council's favorite person.

"You heard me." She raised her chin when I looked at her. "Call it what you will, but finding that old car right in time to ruin Mad Dog's chances at being mayor is plain witchcraft. Two hundred years ago, we would've burned you at the stake."

# Chapter 13

Reverend Lisa, a local minister, intervened. "Martha, that seems a little harsh. We all know Dae was born with a gift for finding things. I have a feeling she's helped you out when you were looking for something lost, like she's helped most of the people here. I'm sure she's found many things she wished she wouldn't have, including that old car."

Martha put down the sweater she was folding. "I admit it's a stretch. The timing was perfect."

"Dae has been a wonderful mayor." La Donna put her arm around me. "And she's a great friend."

"Well, I grew up with Randal." Martha wasn't giving it up. "He's a good friend and an asset to this community."

"Then you'll be glad to know Dae is trying to help him get out of this mess." La Donna kept trying to defend me. "We're stronger as a town having both Randal and Dae right here where they belong."

Martha sniffed. "I'm sorry, Dae. I get a mite riled sometimes. You know that."

"I do," I agreed. "Thanks."

"I'm voting for Randal though, whether the police think he killed Lightning Joe or not. He's the man for the job. And that's what we're missing. *A man.* A sturdy hand on the helm. No offense, you being a woman and all."

"None taken." I smiled at Lisa and La Donna, glad they were there. The witch term had hit a little too close to home for now.

"You know . . ." Martha came a little closer. She smelled strongly of garlic. "If you *really* want to catch Joe's killer, you should talk to some of those crazy girls who used to chase him around. They used to toss their panties at him when he did his victory lap. I suspect one or two of them might have been angry when he got married. Mind my words, girl."

*Married?* I hadn't heard anyone mention that Joe had a wife. Chief Michaels had talked about Joe's sister filing all the missing person's reports on him. Who was his wife?

I would've asked Martha—I'm sure she knew—but I didn't want to push my luck with her. Her earlier performance was about as friendly as she ever got.

La Donna might know. I asked her about Lightning Joe's wife.

"I never kept up with that stuff, Dae."

"I thought you were the president of his fan club?"

"It was a long time ago." She smiled and started folding clothes that had become rumpled in the buying spree. "I can't talk right now. Let's get together later, okay?"

Was it just me or did she seem evasive about it? Maybe she didn't like to think about those times. After all, she'd lived a whole, different life since then. Her mother's reminder of her poor choices might be more than she wanted to remember.

It started raining—cold, hard rain—as I stalked back to Missing Pieces pulling my empty carryall behind me. This just wasn't my day.

The whole thing at the church was exactly what I'd feared would happen. Everyone blamed me for Mad Dog probably being taken out of the election—like I couldn't have won even if we hadn't found the old race car. I'd been a good mayor. I cared about Duck. I didn't need to cheat.

I let myself into Missing Pieces and shut the door behind me. I was drenched and not sure if my old brown suit would survive the downpour. Freezing, I grabbed a shirt and pants from the clothing rack and ducked into the side storage room to change.

I managed to strip off my suit and step out of my soaked shoes before a large, heavy net descended on me from the ceiling. "What the—"

"Don't bother trying to get away." Shayla's voice came out of the dark. "The net is made of pure hemp that's been blessed and is soaked in camphor to boot. You're not going anywhere."

"Have you lost your mind?" I shivered in my wet bra and panties. "Get this thing off of me, Shayla, or I swear—"

"You don't scare me, witch. Go ahead, Gram. Do what you need to do."

Apparently burning feathers was a stronger treatment than shaking them around. Flourine lit dozens of them in the small storage room, enough to make me gag. My eyes were watering when I heard the little bell on the front door announce a customer.

In the light coming under the door from the shop, I could see Flourine and Shayla standing still, staring at each other, probably trying to decide what to do.

"Dae?" I heard Trudy's voice and grabbed it like a life preserver.

"In here," I yelled back. "Shayla has lost her mind."

The door opened and Trudy's perfectly coiffed head appeared around the corner of the doorway. "What's going on? Why is Dae in that net?"

"Best you leave now, girl." Flourine shook her feathers again. "We're driving the witch out of your little friend. Don't make us hurt you."

"Gram." Shayla pulled her grandmother back and approached Trudy. "Sorry. She gets a little carried away."

Trudy sneezed repeatedly, probably from the burned feather smell. "*She* gets carried away? Get Dae out of here before I call Tim. You have truly lost your mind, Shayla."

Shayla seemed a little apologetic. "I know it looks bad. But I'm telling you, something's not right. Gram and I have done a bunch of tests. We both think the witch is still in her."

"If you don't get her out of there, I'm calling for help. I don't care *what* you think is in her. Get that thing off of her. She's not even decent. What are you thinking?"

Gram nodded. "I can take the skinny one. You go ahead with the ceremony."

Shayla backed down. "No. Trudy's right. This is crazy. There has to be another way."

"You could force her to the crystal." Flourine's voice took on dark undertones like she was announcing for a horror show on TV. "That *always* shows the truth."

"Would you be willing to go and look in the crystal, Dae?" Shayla's tone was skeptical.

I coughed. "Anything is better than this."

"Fine." Trudy fumed. "You have to let her put some clothes on. And I'm going too so there's no funny stuff."

"Okay." Shayla gave in. "Let's go."

Trudy stayed in the storage room with me while I put on

the shirt and pants. Shayla insisted that I shouldn't be alone. She and Flourine went to her shop next door to get the crystal ready.

"What is her problem?" Trudy looked at an old clock as she fussed. "She's taking this way too far. Maybe you should get a restraining order. Tim would be glad to get it for you. He'd probably enforce it too."

I started looking for a pair of shoes that would fit. I usually kept an extra pair at the shop for emergencies. I remembered that I'd taken them to the Blue Whale to work on a project there and left them.

"I guess I wasn't imagining things about you and Tim being together." I tried on a pair of scuffed yellow leather dress shoes.

"No. You weren't. We've seen each other every day. We're perfect for each other. Tim is so considerate and eager to please me. I want to do everything I can to make him happy. And he's a really good kisser, Dae. Have you kissed him lately?"

The leather shoes were ugly, but they fit like they were made for me. "No. I haven't kissed him since high school. I've been trying to get him not to think of me like that. You know what I mean."

"Well, it's too late for you now. He's mine. I hope you won't regret giving him up." She smiled so brilliantly she appeared to be lit up from inside.

"I'm so happy for both of you." I hugged her. "I hope you'll be together forever."

"Thanks. That's what I came over to talk to you about when I found Shayla and her grandmother acting like weird people. Is this the kind of thing that goes on in New Orleans? I'm still not sure I shouldn't call Tim. He's on duty right now. He doesn't have a supper break until six. I know he'd come in a heartbeat if I called him."

"It sounds like you're looking for an excuse to call him." I found an old sweater I could wear too. I was still so cold.

"Not an excuse exactly. Chief Michaels complained that we were talking too much while Tim was on duty. It has to be something official. I think this might be official, don't you?"

I hated to take the sparkle from her eyes, but I didn't think it was a good time to call Tim. "I think I can handle this. I'm glad you came by, but you don't have to go any further with it."

Trudy was a little disappointed that she couldn't call, but she insisted on going with me to Shayla's shop next door. The cold rain had slowed to drizzle and a heavy mist as we left Missing Pieces. I wondered when my luck for that day was going to change.

Shayla's shop was darker than most. She had some rare and original artifacts—some that she'd brought with her and others from a woman who'd spent a little time in Duck a few years ago.

I'd just opened Missing Pieces when Mary Catherine Roberts opened her shop next to mine. She said she was a psychic and could talk to animals. She left her shop less than a year later. Mrs. Roberts, Spiritual Advisor was still set up as though she knew Shayla would move in a few weeks later.

I'd looked into Shayla's crystal ball before with mixed outcomes. She said she could see everything in it. She used it to help her clients find happiness—money, lovers and new jobs.

Sometimes when I looked in it, I saw things that shouldn't have been there, at least according to Shayla. Would I see Maggie in the crystal ball?

I wasn't sure what Shayla and Flourine would make of that, but I was willing to take my chances. Anything to get them off my back.

It wouldn't be long now before I could end my time with Maggie. The police were bound to be done with the crime scene now that the car and the excavator were gone. All I needed was help from the historical society to lay her to rest. I was looking forward to it being over.

"Sit down, Dae." Shayla pulled up a chair with an air of drama. "You know how this goes."

I sat at the rattan table where the large crystal ball was resting on a black cloth. It had a glow to it that I couldn't explain. I'd examined it several times. There were no batteries, nothing that should have made it light up.

Maybe it was magic, but I wasn't one hundred percent convinced.

"You don't have to look like you expect us to kill her or something," Shayla said to Trudy, who'd moved in closer to guard my back when I sat down.

"That's not what it looked like to me back there. I'll stay where I am—and skeptical—until this is over."

"Suit yourself." Shayla went to the other side of the table and sat down.

Out of the corner of my eye, I saw Flourine take up a sentinel post beside Trudy. It was definitely best to get this over before anyone became physical again.

The crystal ball was clear until I touched it. At first it grew hazy, as it always did, a little like it was trying to tune in to a TV station. Shayla and I both leaned over it, trying to see through the mist.

Almost immediately, Maggie appeared. I glanced at Shayla. She hadn't moved.

Maggie looked at me. "Dae? Is that you? Where are you?"

"Aha!" Shayla called out. "I knew it. There she is. Maggie Madison is still right there, under your skin. She's waiting to come out and take over."

Before I realized what she was doing, Shayla had laid a

silver mesh across the crystal. It was brightly polished—the light from the crystal flaring up inside of it—making it difficult to see.

She said a few words in a language I didn't understand, and the crystal went dark.

"You did it!" Flourine hopped around the room. "You trapped her and banished the witch. I knew it would work."

"What is she talking about?" My heart was beating quickly. Had they really gotten rid of Maggie?

"The witch showed up in the crystal, as we knew she would." Flourine gloated. "The silver trapped her and took her out of you. The spell will keep her away. She won't be back."

Shayla stared at me nose to nose. "How do you feel, Dae?"

"So much better. I feel just great. I'm going back to my shop now. Thanks so much."

I thought that would be it, but when I tried to stand up, Flourine put her hand on my shoulder. "Sit back down there. We have to make sure you're clean."

Trudy slapped at Flourine's hand until she moved it.

"Don't touch her," Shayla said. "This is *my* shop." She removed the silver mesh from the crystal. It stayed dark for a few seconds and then eerie light flickered and gleamed. "Okay. Now touch it and look again."

I did as she said, eager to get this over with. The light became hazy, as it had before. This time, all I saw reflected in the crystal was my face. Maggie was gone.

Flourine declared me free of the witch's influence. She and Shayla cried and hugged each other. Trudy and I slowly made our way toward the door.

"I'll see you later, Shayla." I wanted to get out before they changed their minds.

Trudy walked out with me. "Well?"

"I don't know. I know what it looked like, but it doesn't make any sense."

"Yeah. I know what you mean." She glanced down the boardwalk and her pretty face grew more animated. "Tim! Are you taking early dinner?"

He swung her into his arms and they kissed passionately, despite the mist and the drizzle. "I had to stop at town hall and pick up some paperwork for the chief. I was thinking I could at least see you for a few minutes before I have to go back to work."

"I'm so glad."

Tim glanced at me. "Hi, Dae. How's it going?"

"It's going fine. Great." I felt like crying about losing Maggie, if that was what had happened. I wasn't sure.

I thought about my need to touch the old number twelve car that was in the impound lot. I didn't feel so bad asking Tim for a favor since he was so wrapped up in Trudy, and he didn't seem to mind.

"Sure. I can help you with the car." He kissed Trudy's nose and she giggled. "When do you want to go?"

I told him I needed to call him since I wanted Kevin there too. He was fine with that.

"I'm going home now. You two enjoy your time together."

"We will." Trudy took his arm and led him into Curves and Curls, closing the door behind them.

Nancy stepped out of the town hall doorway, electric cigarette in her hand. "Ain't love grand?"

I changed my mind about going home right away. We sat in my office at town hall and talked for a while about everything that was going on. Nancy was usually a very laid-back kind of person where problems were concerned. She was a little worried about the election.

"The best thing you could do is resolve this race car

thing with Councilman Wilson," she advised. "I know that's asking for a lot in a short time, but it would go a long way in making people feel better about you finding that site."

"I know." I shrugged, feeling overwhelmed. "People think I found it on purpose, but I was looking for something else. I didn't know the car was there."

"Something like what?"

"Bones. There are remains of an old house from the 1600s. I was trying to get them out before the construction crew started drilling again."

She paused in mid–electronic puff then started laughing. "Oh, Dae, you're always into something surprising. How did you find out about the bones?"

I explained that it was a history thing and an important find for the town.

"I'm afraid you've run out of time. The police said the construction crew could start working over there again tomorrow. Good thing too. We'll lose our grant to pay for everything if they don't get started again soon. I'd hate to see Chris's face if we have to tell him that."

# Chapter 14

*Tomorrow!*

Another impossible deadline. How was I going to get the bones out of there by then? I didn't know if Maggie was gone or not, but I still felt committed to laying her to rest with her lover.

I couldn't ask for help again. That had created cataclysmic consequences. This was something I had to do on my own. The hole was already in the ground. It had to be wide and deep to have taken the race car out. Hopefully, Maggie wasn't too far down from there.

I didn't go back into Missing Pieces. It would be too easy to lose myself and let it all go. I brooded about it on the way home, trying to decide what to do and how to do it. I almost walked right into Jake. He'd come to visit, eager to talk about the horse site again.

We walked toward my house on Duck Road. "I wish you'd come out again," he said. "I could use a second opinion."

He was even talking about hiring two men to help him

work on it. They were members of the Wild Horse Society, but for him, even that was a reach.

"I'd love to come. I can't right now. I'm swamped with everything going on. Maybe after the election."

"Have you had a chance to hold one of the horses without gloves? Is there anything else you can tell me about the site?"

"No, I'm sorry. I've still got them in my bedroom. I promise I'll look at them."

"This is the find of a century, you know it? This is going to stand the whole historical world on its ear. You have to be involved. I need you to touch part of one of the horses, Dae. That could clear up everything. We'd know what was going on before those scientists even realize it."

"I know. I have a lot on my plate right now. I promise I'll do it as soon as the election is over. Okay?"

He studied my face. "I guess that'll have to do, won't it? We'll keep digging. Call me when you do it."

One of his real wild horses was tied to the old birdhouse pole in the yard. He climbed on and clicked his tongue at the horse and was gone.

"Nice horse," Gramps said from the front steps. We watched him canter away down Duck Road. "He seems like a nice person, Dae, but I think he's a little obsessed with this horse thing."

"Yeah. I know. He's excited. He wants this to be something big." I went inside and changed clothes. The second-hand pants and shirt weren't going to be warm enough for what I had planned tonight.

I went back downstairs where Gramps was making dinner for himself and his friends. It was his turn to host the pinochle game.

"Stay and watch us play pinochle." He tasted the fish stew he was making. He added salt, like always. "Or you could learn to play."

I ate a cheese sandwich and played with Treasure for a while. "Thanks but I have something I have to do."

"You seem a little preoccupied. What are you up to tonight?"

I wasn't going to explain to him about my mission to get the bones out of the ground before morning. I'd already filled a backpack with a lantern, gloves, two large trash bags and a bottle of water. I planned to collect a sturdier shovel from the toolshed before I left. One way or another, those bones were coming out tonight.

I couldn't get the words out. I knew he'd try to stop me.

"Lots of cleaning and redistributing at the shop." I didn't like lying to him. What choice did I have? "It might take me all night."

He grunted and changed the subject. "You know, Dae, honey, you've done a good job as mayor of Duck. Things change though. We should both be prepared. You could lose the election."

"I know."

I actually wasn't sure how that would work. Unless Mad Dog was proven innocent and released from jail, how would he be mayor? The town charter called for the next highest vote getter in an election to take the office. About the only way I could lose was if I helped him and proved he didn't kill Lightning Joe. Even then, he'd have to win the election.

Some people might not like it, but I was probably going to be the mayor again, until at least the next election.

Gramps hugged me. "There's been a lot of talk. I know it's not true, and so do your friends. I want you to be prepared for whatever happens."

"I am. Whatever happens, it will be okay."

"Good. I'm glad you feel that way." He turned off the pot on the stove that was beginning to smell really delicious. "Any luck with Mad Dog today? Did you see anything?"

"Not really—except that I don't think he killed anyone. I can't prove it yet. Gramps, did you know Lightning Joe was married?"

"That's news to me, but I suppose it's possible. I don't know a lot about the racing scene back then. I was raised with Randal, so I kept up with his exploits, but that's about all. Who was he married to?"

"I was hoping you could tell me so I wouldn't have to go through records at the county courthouse."

"Sorry. That was a long time ago. If I knew back then, I probably forgot. Want me to ask around?"

"Sure. I'll see what I can find too. We still have some time to get him back in the election."

I left the house soon after. Treasure had reminded me that I'd been gone all day and should have stayed home that night to be with him. I apologized and hoped he understood.

He had wonderful, expressive body language. It was as though he really knew what I was talking about.

*Or I was imagining it*

I'd never had a pet before. I'd heard Nancy talk about her bulldog like that. She said he always let her know what he did and didn't like and swore he had a different bark for each person who visited her.

Treasure held on to me with his claws until I had to disengage myself from him and hurry to close the door behind me. I hoped he didn't know something about going out there that I'd missed.

I waited until I got out on the back porch to put on a pair of tall fishing boots. I collected my shovel and backpack, ready to leave.

"Are we finally going to get my bones out then?" Maggie pushed forward. "I was wondering if *you* were trapped in the crystal ball."

*So much for Shayla's crazy magic ball.*

I promised her again that I was going to get her bones out of the ground. "I still haven't heard anything about Thomas's grave site. I might have to wait to rebury you."

"Well, let's not wait too much longer. Living in you is almost as bad as not living at all. How can you stand all this quiet and working all the time? Why don't you want to go out and have some fun?"

I felt a little like a mental patient, arguing with myself as I got everything together. I reminded Maggie that if I was a party person, I wouldn't go through all of this to help her. She subsided after that, and we were able to peacefully cohabit the same body again.

It was cold walking down Duck Road. The rain and wind had calmed down. No one else was out. I kept my head down, my hood pulled over my hair. It wasn't a long walk down to the site. I spent it going over everything that needed to be done.

I realized there were still things that could go wrong— like running into some other late-night walker or Tim being on patrol and wanting to talk about Trudy. I knew I would be lucky to find the bones by morning. There was no time to waste and a long night ahead.

I made it to the construction site in record time. The yellow tents were still up around the spots where they planned to start working again in the morning. That would be helpful. I glanced around before I went inside the tent where we'd found the car.

I turned on the lantern to get my bearings and was astonished at the size of the hole and how far it went down now. It was at least thirty feet down and another thirty around. I supposed it had to be to get the race car out of the sand. The hole was marked with yellow chalk and orange caution flags, probably to keep people from falling into it.

How was I going to get down there and back out again?

This made the dig at Jake's house look miniscule, and it had taken a ladder to get in and out of that hole. Maybe there was a ladder in one of the other tents. I hated to take the time to look for it but I had no choice.

A loud, metallic sound—like chains clanging together—made me jump. An emergency ladder rolled out at my feet. I gasped and turned around.

"Need some help?" Kevin stepped out of the shadows near the tent flap.

"What are you doing here?" I was happy—and upset—to see him. I couldn't stop a smile from stealing across my face even though I knew he shouldn't be there.

"I heard they were starting work on the project again tomorrow. You didn't find the bones yet, and you being you, it was easy to figure out where you'd be."

"Kevin—"

"Don't tell me you wouldn't be here for me if I needed you. You'd be here for all of your friends too. That's why they were all here for you digging up the car."

That warmed me inside despite the cold. "I don't want you to get in trouble again."

"Me either." He dropped one end of the ladder into the hole. "That's why we'd better get done fast and not get caught this time."

He was there. He had a ladder. What could I say?

I dropped my shovel down into the hole and began crawling down after it. My backpack held the lantern and trash bags to hold the bones we'd hopefully find this time.

Kevin had a shovel too, and we worked in companionable silence for a while. We both dug for a few minutes then had to take buckets of sand up to the top to keep the hole from filling up. Luckily, Kevin had thought of those too.

Maggie directed us to the remains of her house.

"It's like watching a puppet show." Kevin observed me. "Shayla called this afternoon and told me she'd taken care of the witch. I guess it's not that easy."

"I wasn't sure if Shayla had really done anything when I was at her shop. It looked impressive. Maggie vanished and didn't come back, but I could still feel her. We have some kind of bond. She's not a witch and she's not a ghost. She's trapped and she's alone. She had to wait all those years for the right person to put on the necklace. I understand why everyone was so thrown when they felt the power in it. It was Maggie's love for her young man that trapped those emotions in it. All I have to do is find the bones and then find Thomas's grave."

"But you have no idea where to look."

"No. She said there used to be a chapel that burned down. There are still members of her family buried there with some other Duck residents from that time."

"You know, I can speak for myself." Maggie came between Dae and Kevin. "I would know the spot if I saw it. I don't think I have seen it, but nothing looks the same."

Kevin laughed. "I suppose you'd have to expect a lot of change in four hundred years."

Maggie moved up close to him and put her (my) hand on his chest. "Some things never change, your lordship. You know what I mean?"

That was enough for me. We switched places in me. "Let's dig and get this over with."

"Fine with me, your ladyship." Kevin kept laughing as he dug.

"I'm glad you think this is funny. Wait until some four-hundred-year-old pirate takes over *your* body. I'll be laughing then."

"I don't think anything like that is going to happen to me." He grinned at me.

"I never thought it would happen to *me* either."

"Well, I surely never thought it would happen to me, ducks!" Maggie added.

The sand was dark and wet where we were digging. By that time, we had taken turns passing fifty buckets out of the hole, up and down the ladder.

I understood why they called those emergency ladders. They were difficult to climb and shouldn't be used unless there was no other choice. They twisted and turned as I climbed. Kevin had a ladder in each of the upper-floor rooms in case of fire. I hoped no one ever had to use one on the outside of the Blue Whale.

My back and legs were aching when my shovel hit something that sounded like metal. "I think I found something."

"Not another car, I hope." Kevin leaned on his shovel.

We dug the sand from around the heavy metal object. It was badly rusted, water and sand taking their toll on it.

"I think it's an old iron kettle. We must have found the house, Kevin."

Maggie's voice was choked with excitement. "You're very close now, Dae. Mayhap this will be the end of it. A maid can get overwrought waiting to be rescued."

"Don't worry," I told her. "We're going to get you this time."

We located a few more artifacts and carefully wrapped them in pieces of torn tarp as we took them to the surface. I felt terrible that we couldn't do a full excavation here, as should have been done, but Nancy had been right about the limited time frame. We had to continue working on the town hall project or lose the funding for it. I couldn't let that happen.

"Dae—"

I looked where Kevin was carefully digging only small amounts of sand at a time and saw some pathetic little pieces of bone, darkened and falling apart. It was all we could do to pick them up and get them into the trash bag.

Maggie was laughing and clapping. I asked if we had all the pieces. It was dark and I wanted to be sure. I didn't want to have to come down here again.

"You have most of them," she whispered. "God, who knew a person would come down to such a small amount."

Kevin carefully dug up a few more artifacts—a beautiful plate, a cooking pot and the swing arm that would've held it over the fire in the hearth.

"We must be near the fireplace." I hoped most of the items were salvageable as I wrapped them.

There was more here than I'd expected. It might be more than Kevin and I could carry away when we were finished. I hated not to keep everything we found, even though the items weren't worth much money. I knew time was against us. It was nearly two A.M.

We dug a few more shovels of sand before using our hands to drag out the rest. We had to be very careful of what was trapped in it.

Something hard was lodged in front of me and I pulled gently. The light from the lantern gleamed on a skeletal hand. There was a gold ring, the band heavy and wide, set with some jewel I couldn't identify.

Maggie was excited. "There it is! My wedding band. Well, it would have been if I had lived. Death has a way of changing things."

"This is an expensive ring." I examined it carefully. "Thomas must've been a very successful sea captain. Was he a pirate, Maggie?"

"I'll not be saying. My Thomas was a good man. He tried to take care of me. He was gone when the storm took me. I know it grieved him when he returned and found me gone. I've often wondered what happened to him. Did he meet his death at sea, as was his wont?"

I put the ring into the bag with her bones, glad I was wearing gloves. I didn't want to experience Maggie's death with her. It seemed like the best thing to do. I was sure she wanted to be buried with it.

My business sense told me the ring would bring a hefty price. Gold from that age was purer than in our own time, and that didn't take into consideration a collector who would love to have something with the background of this ring. I was pretty sure that big stone was a bloodred ruby too.

I wasn't a grave robber. Some things shouldn't be for sale.

The rest of her bones came easily. Most were in pieces and blackened with time and weather. Finally Maggie confirmed that all of her bones were out of the sand.

"I feel so light." She smiled brilliantly. "I am sure I could fly."

She pointed to the other side of the pit. "Look yonder to find something not belonging to me or mine that will aid you in your other endeavors."

Kevin was already making his way up the ladder with the last of the artifacts. I looked at the side of the pit where Maggie had pointed. I didn't really expect to find anything of use, maybe some trinket she thought would be valuable. I didn't want to hurt her feelings by not looking.

I saw something glint in the dim light about ten feet up from the bottom. I zipped up the backpack and put it on, grabbed the lantern and started up.

I picked at the metal with my fingers until it fell into my hand. It was a corroded Dare County Deputy Sheriff's badge.

# Chapter 15

I didn't really have time to think about what that might mean. I knew we had to get out of there. We couldn't be caught again.

Luckily, Kevin had also brought his golf cart. We loaded everything into it and got away from the site by four A.M. It was still dark, and raining again, but I was able to breathe a sigh of relief to have found the bones and gotten away cleanly.

Kevin sped toward the Blue Whale. My house might have been closer, but I knew this wasn't something Gramps should find out about. There wasn't enough time to have been out of trouble to be back in it again.

I wanted to feel as light as Maggie, knowing her bones were safe from the rest of the town hall construction. The sheriff deputy's badge in my pocket worried me. I had all those feelings of finding something important when I took it from the site—time felt slowed down and I was a little light-headed. This was something that mattered.

Of course anyone *could* have lost it. I knew that better than most people. I'd found some incredible things all over the Outer Banks since I was a child. A deputy sheriff could have lost his badge too.

*Except that it was at the site where we found Lightning Joe's remains.*

If the police had found it there, they wouldn't have thought it was a coincidence. Underneath my optimism, neither did I. This could put a whole different spin on what had happened to Joe.

I showed it to Kevin after we'd brought all the items from the cart and stashed them inside the Blue Whale. The rain started falling heavier, and I listened as the old inn creaked and groaned under its onslaught. So many lives had passed through these rooms in the more than one hundred years the inn had been open. Sometimes it was as though I could feel them all around me.

Kevin turned the badge over and examined it. "Let's get it cleaned up and have some breakfast before we jump into anything else. Have you touched it yet?"

"No." I still had my gloves on from the dig. "I didn't want to be at the site any longer than we had to be."

"Good thinking." He yawned. "I'll make a planner out of you yet."

He looked exhausted, probably a lot like me. There was sand in his hair, all over his face and on his clothes. Probably a lot like me too.

I knew the badge would wait to reveal its secrets for a little while longer. I quelled my impatience. I hoped it would lead me to some answers about Joe. Morning was coming, and I was no closer to solving that mystery before the election.

I showered and washed my hair until I thought the sand was gone. I found one of Kevin's shirts and some shorts I'd left there over the summer. My legs were chilly, but I planned to wash and dry my clothes before I left.

The TV was on with the morning news when I went into the kitchen where Kevin was making breakfast for us. The smell of coffee was like perfume. The weather forecast was over, and the news anchor from Portsmouth, Virginia, was talking about Duck.

"Forty years ago, stock car racer Lightning Joe Walsh disappeared. He was found recently in Duck, North Carolina, right before a combative election for mayor is about to end. One of the candidates, present mayor Dae O'Donnell, found the remains of Joe Walsh while the challenger, Councilman Randal 'Mad Dog' Wilson, has been charged with Walsh's murder."

"So that's what Lightning Joe looked like." I put orange juice and glasses on the table in the corner of the kitchen.

Kevin put two bagels in the toaster. "I guess I thought you knew all about Joe, since he's from around here."

There was a picture on the screen of a tall, thin, serious-looking young man with a head full of curly black hair. He was holding a trophy in one hand and had an arm around a pretty girl in red short-shorts.

"La Donna told me he was popular with the girls." I poured two cups of coffee and put out cream and sugar. "I've seen pictures of Mad Dog when he was young. He wasn't good-looking like Lightning Joe."

"Joe got a better nickname too."

I saw the picture of myself from the stunted interview at the shop. There was also a picture of my campaign ad on the water tower.

Kevin brought the two bagels over, open-faced and covered with a cheese and egg mixture. I got silverware and napkins, suddenly hungry when faced with food. The sun was coming in through the kitchen window as we sat down to eat.

"What's your next step on the Mad Dog thing?" Kevin asked as he cut his bagel. "Touching the race car, right?"

"I was thinking about that. The car is in the Duck impound lot. It won't be too hard to get in. I think Tim will help without expecting anything in return." I told him about Tim and Trudy.

"Sounds like a plan." Kevin sipped his coffee. "You know the thing I don't get—why did the killer put Joe in Mad Dog's car? Was that symbolic? And where's Joe's car?"

"I don't know. I can't imagine anyone around here killing someone in a symbolic way. It was probably an accident. Why put him in a car at all? It had to be hard to dig that hole and bury it. Easier to bury a body."

He smiled. "You should know. Maybe the killer was trying to keep the body from being found. The sand moves and drifts. Maybe the killer thought the car would keep that from happening with his victim. What was there before the park?"

"Nothing, as far as I know. I rode past there every day on my way to school. Someone said there was an old general store there once, maybe in the 1800s. I don't remember seeing pictures of it. We got the land for Duck Municipal Park really cheap because there was nothing there."

The eggs and bagels had looked good at first. I was too nervous, too worried to eat. I thought I'd be exhausted after being up all night digging sand. My shoulders and arms were sore and my blisters had blisters, but otherwise I felt wired to an electric current.

It was the sheriff's badge in my pocket. I had to force myself to look at Kevin as we talked. I kept stealing glances at my pocket. My fingers itched to touch the badge even though it scared me to consider it. I kept thinking about what Chief Michaels had said about Gramps signing off on those missing person's complaints from Joe's sister.

"You might as well go ahead and touch it." Kevin was prosaic about it. "Want me to clean it off a little first? I don't think we'll be ruining any fingerprints or DNA after all those years being buried in the sand."

I realized that I'd stopped looking at him altogether and was staring at the bulge in my pocket where the badge was.

"Sorry. I get a little obsessed."

"I know. You might see the crime when you touch it."

"In a way, that would be a relief."

"I suppose so." He took my hand and pulled me gently to my feet then wrapped his arms around me. "You should get some sleep before you do this. You could give yourself a chance to get over being possessed by a witch before you try to save Mad Dog."

"I wish I could." I took full advantage of his warm body against mine and held him tightly. "My time is running out for this too."

"Mad Dog isn't going anywhere, Dae." He kissed my ear and neck. "You have a lot of time before he even goes to trial."

"I don't have that much time to save my reputation and get him back into the race. I have to prove it wasn't him before the election. People already think I found the car on purpose to wreck Mad Dog's name. Who wants a mayor who would do something like that?"

"Dae." He kissed me for a long time then raised his head. "There might not be enough time. Mad Dog could be guilty. People in Duck love you. There may be a few who will think that you did it on purpose, but you won't be able to change their minds even if you prove he's innocent."

"Maybe. I have to try."

"Not right now, though." Maggie scooted in between us. "It's been such a long time since someone held me. Could we try the kiss again too?"

"That's enough, Maggie." I didn't want to share Kevin with her.

"This is really complicated." Kevin let me go. "I'll clean off the badge. You try to ground yourself, Dae."

I waited, trying not to be impatient, as he cleaned the badge. I took some deep breaths and tried to prepare for what I might see. The whole thing filled me with such dread, I wanted to bury the badge again and forget I'd found it. It was too late for regrets.

"Okay." Kevin dried the badge and put it in front of me on the table. "I can't make out the last number on it. The first three look like 111. I'm here if you need me."

I looked at the badge but couldn't tell what the last number was either. Gramps's deputy badge had started with 111, but so had many others, no doubt.

Gramps wouldn't have been sheriff yet when this badge was lost with the number twelve race car. A tidal wave of fear fell inside of me. Before I could drown in it, I grabbed the badge in my ungloved hands and closed my eyes.

*Instantly I was propelled into a warm summer evening. I could hear the frogs and the buzzing of the gnats flying around. From somewhere, water lapped against a shore.*

*It was that time of evening when it wasn't quite dark but the light was fading fast. I looked around for any clues to where I was. All I could see was a Pure gasoline sign and an old storefront with people going in and out.*

*A sheriff's car, large and brown, like Gramps and other deputies had driven during that time, was parked near the gas pumps. It was a Ford Galaxie with a large red light sitting squarely on top.*

*The car on the other side of the pump was black and had badly painted streaks of lightning on it. The number twenty-three was emblazoned beside a name and slogan—* Lightning Joe Walsh—faster than lightning.

*I recognized Joe from his pictures on TV. He was standing with a streetlamp shining into his face. He was filling the car with gas as he waved at people who hailed him.*

*I heard a car door slam and saw the deputy get out of the car. Where the streetlamp illuminated Joe's face, it hid the deputy's. I could only see him from an angle as he walked up to Joe and said, "I won't tell you again to leave her alone, son."*

*"Good. Don't bother. There's nothing you can do about it, old man."*

*A quick move brought the deputy's fist into Joe's jaw. The race driver hit the ground and the gas nozzle fell beside him, gas flowing everywhere. The odor of it was pungent in the night air.*

*"Leave her alone, Joe. You've got plenty of others. Don't bother her again, you hear me?"*

*Joe got up right away and put the nozzle back on the pump. Even in the dim light, I could see a large bruise forming on his jaw.*

I took a deep breath and I was back in Kevin's kitchen. His gray blue gaze was fastened worriedly on my face.

I felt cold all over. My hands were shaking. "I saw a Dare County sheriff's deputy fighting with Lightning Joe. I couldn't tell who he was, but he was angry enough to kill Joe."

# Chapter 16

"Don't be so quick to judge." Kevin chafed my hands to warm them. "There's probably a simple explanation. People get mad and fight all the time. It doesn't mean one will kill the other."

"This was more than that. I could *feel* how angry he was. I'm not judging. I'm worried that Gramps may be involved. What if he knew who killed Lightning Joe and that's why he didn't pay attention to the reports? I can't save Mad Dog and hurt Gramps."

"You said yourself that you couldn't see the deputy's face. Just because Horace signed off on some missing person's reports doesn't mean anything."

"You're right." I put my hands to my head where it had begun to pound. "I don't have enough information yet to make a decision. I need to touch the race car."

"I think you're asking for an overload, Dac. You've been up all night. You need some rest before you use your abilities again. If nothing else, stretch out on the sofa in my office for a while. Things will look better."

He knew I loved that old sofa. It was a vintage piece, left there from the 1930s when the Blue Whale was in its heyday. The red velvet was so thick and rich, it was like sinking into a cloud. Its memories held only intimate moments and afternoon teas.

"What about you?"

"I'll set the alarm and we'll both get some sleep. The world isn't going to stop turning because Dae O'Donnell takes a break for a couple of hours."

He convinced me. I lay down on the elegant old sofa, and Kevin put a blanket over me then kissed me good night. It would be easy to get used to him always doing that, I thought. My eyes closed and I fell asleep.

I was dreaming about my mother and the terrible fight we'd had before her car went off the bridge on the way back to Duck. It had been about my bad grades in college and a boy I was dating that she didn't like.

*Stupid kid stuff. If I had it to do over again—if I only had it to do over again.*

It had always bothered me that her body and the car had never been found. I'd lost track of how many dreams I'd had about her still sitting in the driver's seat at the bottom of the sound.

I saw her again that way in this dream. She still looked as she had that day at school. Her hair, so like mine, floated around her face. She seemed frozen in time, her body not violated by the water and the more than thirteen years since she'd died.

I reached to touch her, something new for the dream, thinking I could finally learn exactly what had happened to her.

Before I could make contact, her blue eyes opened wide, staring at me. Her lips moved. "Find the black wardrobe."

I woke up, gasping, hearing Kevin's alarm clock in the next room as it switched on and started playing a Weird Al song. I didn't even know Kevin liked Weird Al.

I pushed off the blanket and the dream about my mother and went into his bedroom.

He was still asleep, his eyelashes dark against his cheeks. He'd pulled the blinds down at the windows to keep out the morning sun. I gently touched his face and hair, waiting for the smile to slowly creep across his lips.

"Do you feel better?" he asked sleepily.

"Yes. You?"

He pulled me down into the bed with him. "I do now."

I put on my newly washed and dried clothes from last night and ran a comb through my hair. I was still tired, but I felt refreshed by the short rest.

"I'm bringing some wire cutters in case that old fence around the impound lot needs cutting." Kevin was packed and ready.

"I don't think you'll need those. I'm going to call Tim. I think he'll let us in."

"Be prepared. Did I tell you I used to be a Boy Scout? I made Eagle when I was in high school."

"I believe you've mentioned it a few times." I looked at all the breaking-and-entering paraphernalia he'd assembled and laughed. "We could get into Fort Knox with all this stuff."

He zipped the duffel bag closed. "Let's get going. I have to make lunch alone today. I gave my helpers the day off. I need them this weekend for a big birthday party."

"You don't have to go."

He frowned at me. "Who's got the bag full of useful tools? Let's go."

The Duck impound lot was a scrap piece of land behind the fire and police department building. It wasn't fit to build on since it was too small even for a parking lot. Some tall shrubs hid it from the view of people going in and out each day.

Weeds and grass had grown up along the wire fence that surrounded it. The whole place looked like a junkyard instead of town property. This was probably because it was so well hidden from plain sight.

I made a mental note to get the public works men down there and get the place cleaned up. It definitely needed new fencing, maybe even some pavement.

That was if I was reelected mayor. I was so used to noticing these things—I realized I might have to become one of those dreadful Duck citizens who came to complain at every town meeting.

Some of the cars and trucks in the lot looked like they'd been there for twenty years or more. Vehicles were rusting apart, and others had flat tires. A few didn't look like they'd ever move again. There had to be a better way to do this.

That was the mayor in me talking. The scared woman in the pickup with Kevin was glad the place was mostly undisturbed and ignored. It meant not answering any questions about why I wanted to look at a car that had probably been involved in a murder.

We pulled right up to the gate. It was unlocked, only a metal bar keeping it shut.

"Okay." Kevin looked at me. "This is it."

As if on cue, Tim's police car crept up next to us.

"Morning, Kevin." He nodded. "Dae."

"Hi, Tim." I glanced around. "Do you have a key?"

"Of course. Every officer is issued a key to the impound lot. Why do you want to go in there?"

"I told you—I want to touch number twelve so I can see if Mad Dog put Lightning Joe in it."

"Really? I thought you were kidding." Tim looked at Kevin, who shook his head. "Come on, Dae. That's evidence from a murder scene."

"I only want to touch it. I promise not to spoil anything."

Tim looked at the key and then at Dae. "All right. But I can't stay. It would be a violation of my duty to watch you. Give the key to Trudy when you're done."

"Thanks." I smiled at him. It felt so weird not having him profess his love for me or telling me that I owed him dinner and a movie. It was a relief, of course, but also the end of an era of sorts. I hoped.

When Tim had driven away, Kevin and I crept into the fenced area toward the still colorfully painted race car. I thought about all the pictures I'd seen of the number twelve car at the Duck Historical Museum. Between the years under the sand and the damage that must've been done the last time Mad Dog had raced, it hardly looked like the same vehicle. Only the big number twelve and Mad Dog's name on the side door were there to confirm it.

Kevin surveyed the area, making sure we were alone. I could imagine him doing the same thing in his dark FBI suit and sunglasses. Only now, he was wearing jeans and a blue T-shirt. I never expected to meet a man like him, much less fall in love with him, but I was glad I did.

I took a deep breath and cleared my thoughts. The breeze from the sea made the shrubs shake around us and whistled through the empty old cars. I closed my eyes and touched the race car.

*And there was dust flying around the track, making it difficult to see. He gripped the wheel tightly, forced to go faster because Joe was hot on his heels. His foot slammed down on the gas pedal. He could feel rocks and sand hitting the bottom of the car. He wished he could go faster. He wished he could beat Joe once and for all. Maybe then Joe wouldn't come back again.*

*He'd been king of the track before Joe started showing up each time when the race was almost over. He'd drive the other racers out of the competition. Then the black car would show up. It wasn't fair and it wasn't right. But the people loved him. She loved him. If he could, he would—*

*He lost control of the car. It was flipping over and over again. The metal screamed and bunched around him. The windows burst out, spraying him with glass. He couldn't hold it. The side panel next to him pushed in and ripped into his leg. Hot blood ran down into his boot. He lost consciousness.*

I opened my eyes on the clear, sunny morning in the impound lot. Kevin was still standing beside me. The island breeze raced across again, flying from the Atlantic Ocean to the Currituck Sound.

It was hard to get my thoughts together and pry them away from the wreck that had happened forty years ago. It was as though I had been in Mad Dog's body for those critical few moments. I could still feel the violent movements of the car and the pain from his injured leg—the leg he still favored today.

"Are you all right?"

"Yes. I think so. It's hard to pull back."

"We should go."

"I know." I took several deep breaths and tried to think about everything that was important and real in my life. Gramps. Kevin. Treasure. Missing Pieces. The smell of the water. The moon riding high in the clouds on a soft summer night.

"What was that?" Maggie's voice was slurred. "What manner of contraption was that?"

"Dae." Kevin called me back. "Snap out of it."

I looked at him and nodded. "Okay. Let's go."

I heard the footstep behind us in the sand before I heard the man who'd joined us.

"Mayor O'Donnell. Mr. Brickman." It was Officer Scott Randall. "I don't know if you'd call this trespassing, but the town frowns on people visiting the impound lot without permission. Do you have permission?"

Scott was such a serious young man—respectful and careful of his job. Finding us there after the other night at the new town hall couldn't have been pleasant for him. He was as humble as Tim was brash. We'd received dozens of letters from people he'd stopped for speeding, all telling us what a nice young man he was.

I liked him and I hated that he'd been the one involved in my crazy life the last few days. But this problem was much easier to solve than the one at the construction site.

"The museum sent us out to take some pictures of old number twelve for the collection. After all, this is history too."

Of course the situation wasn't as bad either. Technically, there was no fine or even an ordinance to cover unlawful visitation of the impound lot. I'd thought ahead about this explanation. I knew it would be something easy for him to understand.

I didn't want to show him Tim's key and get him in trouble. My explanation was going to have to be convincing.

"Of course, ma'am." He looked down at my hands. "Did you lose your camera?"

He was *almost* too quick for me. I brought out my cell phone, with camera, and smiled. "You know, no one uses plain cameras anymore. We can download these pictures into the computer at the museum. All our new records are kept that way."

Of course nothing could have been further from the truth. Most members of the historical society still did everything the old-fashioned way. They could barely use a computer.

Scott didn't know that.

"That's fine, ma'am. Just be careful out here. I wouldn't want you to get hurt on all this rusted metal. Have a nice day."

"Thanks, Scott."

"You're welcome, Mayor." He turned to Kevin. "I'm sorry about you having to pay that fine, Mr. Brickman. I hope you know I was only doing what the town requires of me. Sorry about your excavating equipment too. The chief tried to get them to leave it here in our impound lot, but the sheriff had it taken to Manteo, to the county impound."

I sighed. The ghost of my misdeeds haunted me too.

"Aye," Maggie whispered. "I know the feeling."

Scott walked us back to the pickup at the gate as Kevin reassured him that he understood about the excavator.

"I think I can get someone to bring that back from Manteo for a good price," I said when we were in the pickup.

"Thanks. Don't worry about it." Kevin started the truck and backed out of the area. "What did you see from the car?"

I went back over it again in my mind before I answered. It was easy now that I'd distanced myself from it.

"I only saw Mad Dog's last wreck in it. There was something repetitive from the vision I got from the badge."

"What was that?"

"The deputy in my vision wanted Joe to leave some woman alone. Mad Dog was thinking about a woman he wanted who was in love with Joe. Seems like a coincidence, doesn't it?"

"Are you going for some mystery woman killing Joe and stuffing his body into the race car?"

"I don't know what I'm looking at. Joe was in love with some woman. The mystery deputy might have been in love with her too."

He laughed. "That's some theory."

"It doesn't help when the visions aren't clear."

"Nothing about the murder itself?"

"Not a thing. Although I understand why Mad Dog grimaces when he has to walk. His leg must've been a mess after the wreck."

"It might be interesting to find out how the police are dealing with that fact. It seems to me that being injured in the wreck would be the perfect alibi. Not many people with a torn-up leg could kill a man and stuff him into a car."

I glanced at the police building. "There's an easy way to find out, since we're right here. We can ask Chief Michaels. Sometimes he can be pretty chatty. Or he'll throw us out."

"I could help you," Maggie volunteered. "There were seamen who would do much only to watch the swing of my hips as I set down their ale."

"Let's try doing this without seduction." I hoped I wouldn't be sorry I was going in with her. What if she asked Chief Michaels for a kiss?

Kevin swung the pickup into a parking place. We got out and went inside, but Chief Michaels wasn't in one of his chatty moods. He was bent over his desk, his graying brown flattop making him look like an older drill sergeant. His black uniform was immaculate with perfect creases, and his patent leather shoes gleamed.

"Haven't you two done enough damage to this case already?" He actually got up from his desk to yell at us.

"There's no telling how many facts were lost by you ruining the crime scene."

I could tell Kevin was taken aback by the chief's tone. Chief Michaels was never rude or angry with him like he was with me.

"We both know there wasn't much of a crime scene left after forty years, Ronnie," Kevin argued. "And what there was would be in worse shape now if that geothermal work would've gone through it instead of Dae finding it. Almost all of your evidence is going to be anecdotal after all this time."

"Look, Brickman," the chief snarled. "You and Dae are lucky you aren't facing charges. Leave this alone. Go back to the inn and let the professionals do it. You aren't in that league anymore."

I thought that was a little harsh, even for the chief. He and Kevin always seemed to be friends, or at least friendly. The chief had asked for Kevin's help on cases before because of his work with the FBI. I told Kevin as much in the truck.

Kevin said, "He's frustrated by the whole thing. Ronnie's caught between a rock and Sheriff Riley. Not a good place to be. I'm sure he'd also rather not try to build a murder case against one of his old friends."

"Maybe I should have told him about the badge. I'd like to be a little more sure about Gramps first."

"You should ask him. Just face him with it. Let him tell you what happened."

"That's what they always told us at church," Maggie recounted. "Tell the truth. Shame the devil."

I didn't know if I could do that. Not that I didn't think he'd tell me the truth—good or bad. Except for a few instances, he and I had a good relationship. Gramps would tell me the truth. I believed that.

I just wasn't sure if I was ready for it.

# Chapter 17

Kevin dropped me off at home on his way back to the Blue Whale. Gramps pulled up in his golf cart as Kevin was backing out of the drive. I watched as they talked for a few minutes before Gramps came inside with two cloth bags full of food and other necessities.

"Hello, stranger." He grinned as he put down the bags. "Have I got news for you. You're looking at a man in the pinochle tournament next week. I clobbered Mark Samson last night like he wasn't even playing. He might as well have stayed home. I think I might be in line for that trophy this year."

"That's great. For you, anyway. I don't know about Mark. We might not be able to eat there anymore." Mark owned the Rib Shack, one of the few restaurants in town that stayed open during the winter.

"We'll survive. Think how good that trophy will look on the mantel."

I stroked Treasure then went to help Gramps put the

groceries away. It was probably the best time I'd ever have to ask him about the deputy's badge.

I couldn't make myself take it out of my pocket.

I wasn't sure where to find the words to ask what I needed to know. Despite my fears about him, I couldn't imagine him hurting anyone.

And what woman would he have been threatening Joe over? It seemed to me that my mother could have been the right age to get in trouble with the racing crowd, but I'd never heard anyone mention it. Surely it wouldn't have been my grandmother.

"I heard some news about the state's case against Mad Dog today." He handed me spinach to put in the fridge.

"What was that?"

"The ME doesn't think Joe was dead when he was buried in the car. Of course with bones, it's harder to tell. He'll have to send the remains to Raleigh for a conclusive report. There was no skull trauma. No fractures or breaks. There was dried blood and sand caked under the fingernails. He thinks that's a pretty good indication that Joe tried to get out of the car."

"That's awful." I was glad I didn't pick that up from the race car. I really didn't want to know what that looked and felt like.

I recalled how Joe's arm had been sticking out of the car window when we'd dug him up. Poor man.

"And some bad news for Mad Dog's case. They said the old records show that he was brought to the hospital by an ambulance after his wreck at the track, but he left before he could be examined by a doctor or treated."

"What does that mean?"

"Ronnie said it probably means that Mad Dog's last hope of not being found guilty of this terrible crime is gone. His lawyer was hoping to prove he was too badly injured that night to be able to kill Joe and bury his body. It seems to me we may never know the truth. Ronnie is plenty agitated about that."

I guessed that was why Chief Michaels was in such a bad mood at the station. He couldn't find anything to keep his friend from going to prison. I knew he was supposed to be looking for things to prove Mad Dog was guilty. I had a feeling it didn't always work that way with friends.

I knew the truth about Mad Dog's injury after experiencing the wreck with him. That wouldn't help him in court. It was frustrating that my visions wouldn't mean anything to the case—they never did unless I could convince Chief Michaels to look into something I'd seen.

I was more and more convinced that Mad Dog was innocent, but where was the proof I needed?

"You're very quiet." Gramps sat down when we were finished with the groceries. "Something on your mind?"

How could I say it? How could I even ask?

I sat down at the same table I'd eaten at since I was able to sit up. Gramps sat opposite me. He was the man who'd helped me learn to feed myself, walk, and nursed me through colds and the knee I'd dislocated when I was surfing. He was always there for me.

I couldn't say it. Maggie was the one who took out the badge, wrapped in one of Kevin's clean white handkerchiefs, and put it on the table. "I found this, Grandfather. I had hopes you might explain."

He picked it up, after looking at me as though I'd lost my mind, and examined it.

I cleared my throat and followed through. "At the construction site, close to where I found the car."

"You should give it to Ronnie, honey. It might be something important to the case."

I got up and took the little glass picture frame from off

the wall. Inside was his old deputy's badge. I put it on the table next to the badge I'd found and sat down again.

I stared into his blue eyes that could be stern or twinkling with laughter. I didn't say anything.

"Now I see." He looked at the partial number on the recovered badge. "You think I was there when Joe was killed?"

"No. Not exactly. Gramps—"

"Maybe we could do some kind of memory transfer. Maybe if I hold the badge in one hand and you take my other hand, you won't need to ask."

"I already held the badge."

He put it back down on the table. "And what did you see?"

I described the scene for him, waiting for his reaction.

He got up from the table and paced around the room with his hands behind his back and his head down. "Dae, honey, I am so sorry."

My heart felt cold like ice in the winter. What did he mean?

"Gramps? Are you saying—"

"I'm sorry I brought you to this place where you'd think I could be capable of something of this nature. I'm not responsible for Joe's death. The fact that you'd think of it tells me what a mistake I made carrying on with your mother's lie about your father. You don't trust me anymore. I blame myself. I should've sat you down when she died and told you that your father was still alive."

I actually hadn't thought about it that way. It was true that my mother had lied to me about my father and Gramps had continued to lie until I found out my father was living in Duck again. I had been very angry at the time, but I'd put it behind me. To me, this was different and had nothing to do with the other matter.

"I know I made your mother's life miserable because I believed your father wasn't good enough for her. I know I was wrong to stand in judgment of him. I would *never* have killed him. I would never kill anyone, Dae." He closed his eyes and buried his face in his hands.

I didn't know if I should apologize or keep still. I let him keep talking.

"I have always tried to live my life in an honorable way so that my family and friends would be proud of me. So I would never have to see anyone look at me the way you just did."

"I'm sorry, Gramps. You always taught me that everyone makes mistakes. That was why you said people deserved trials when they'd done something bad."

"That's true." He looked at me again. "And what have I always told you? What have I always tried to do, and told *you* to do, to keep faith with yourself?"

"Own up to my mistakes." I repeated his words that I'd heard so many times growing up. "Apologize, acknowledge what you've done and take your punishment."

"That's right. It's what I did when you told me you knew about your father. I knew I was wrong. I'm not a saint. But I've always owned up to my mistakes."

It was a good answer. An answer that made my heart swell with love and pride. Gramps wouldn't have buried someone alive, waiting for them to be found forty years later.

*Who would?*

We ate lunch together and talked the whole time. We walked down to Missing Pieces. Gramps said it wouldn't be that hard to find out whose badge had been buried with the race car. There were only ten possibilities, including his number.

"I could get you a list of those people and you could look

through them to see if anyone jumps out at you from what you know already. I could tell you about a few of them—Blackie Rogers is dead. Marvin Taylor moved away."

"That would be a big help. Thanks."

"At the same time, I can check on how many of those deputies lost a badge and had to order a new one."

"Maybe one of those things, linked with the woman everyone wanted, will help me clear Mad Dog's name."

"Let me help with this, Dae." We'd stopped to talk in the Duck Shoppes parking lot. "I know I'm retired, but I can be a valuable asset. We used to talk all the time. I know you share a lot with Kevin now, but don't forget about me. You're all I have in this world."

I hugged him. "I'm sorry. I love you, Gramps. I'll try harder to keep you in the loop."

The boardwalk was busy when I opened the shop. Gramps had gone on to his meeting with a few other volunteer firemen. He'd been a volunteer for as long as I could remember. The group of close to one hundred was essential to getting the town back on its feet after every storm that swept over us. They fought fires too, and handled many emergencies that we couldn't have paid personnel for.

Gramps had given me a lot to think about. Once he got the information about the badge holders, I could make a list of them and crossmatch those names with the badges that had been lost. It seemed that could be the answer I was looking for. I hoped he could have them by dinner.

I wasn't planning on spending all day at the store. I wanted to interview Joe's sister, Pam, at some point. If anyone knew what girl he was interested in, it would be her.

Thanks to the town's newfound popularity—mostly due to the election-murder scandal all over TV—stores and restaurants in Duck were crowded. I couldn't afford not to take advantage of all the potential customers who were waiting to get into Missing Pieces. That interview with David Engel didn't seem so bad now.

Most of the shoppers were from Newport News, Portsmouth, and the Virginia Beach area. One woman wanted to have her picture taken with me. That was fine. The crowd bought a lot of cheap souvenirs like T-shirts, postcards and maps. They wanted me to make a red X on the maps where I'd found the car.

A few were more serious shoppers. They were at Missing Pieces because they were looking for a special piece to add to a collection. I had that too.

For instance, I'd recently received an old cashbox used by Lucian Smith, one of the first merchants in the area to actually open a permanent store. Lucian Smith was interesting because he was educated to be an engineer. He went to school in England then settled on the Outer Banks. He was one of the first people to think about building a bridge from the mainland. He may have been the first to draw up blueprints for it. That was in the early 1800s.

I'd been given a whole group of his belongings when his great-great-granddaughter, Alice, had died. I donated a lot of the items to the Duck Historical Museum and gave the old Duck bridge blueprints to Chris, our town manager.

I thought Chris would appreciate them more than anyone else. He was the town's liaison with the state in our battle to have another bridge built to the mainland. It wouldn't happen anytime soon, but another bridge would ease the summer congestion when crowds swelled the island from a few thousand to over a hundred thousand.

Lucian Smith's cashbox was a prize even without knowing who he was and what he did. It was made of brass and had lovely detail put into it. All the intricate scrollwork was done by hand. It wasn't only a box to hold money, as some cashboxes were. It was a work of art that showed how important the details were to him.

I knew from touching the box that Lucian was indeed the good, decent man we'd learned he was from our forefathers. He was a man who worked hard and tried to help his neighbors in the struggling Banker community at that time.

So when a customer, an older woman with gray hair wearing a nice black suit and expensive shoes, picked it up and looked at it, I was happy. When she put it down only to circle back and look at it again, I was thrilled. I hoped she'd be willing to pay my price for it.

She finally brought it up to the counter where I patiently waited. I knew she was coming my way.

"I love this piece." She put it on the counter. "What can you tell me about it?"

I told her Lucian's story and showed her pictures I'd taken of the blueprints I'd given Chris. She and I talked about Duck's past and the people like Lucian who'd helped the area to grow.

"My great-great-granduncle was a pirate who supposedly visited this area. He sailed around the Graveyard of the Atlantic, looking for prey." She smiled. "At least that's what my grandmother always told us when we were kids. I grew up in Portsmouth. I guess I'll never know if it was true."

"What was his name?" I was always eager to learn new legends.

"She called him Sam Spit." She laughed self-consciously. "I can't imagine a person really having a name like that, can you?"

"I knew Sam Spit!" Maggie jumped in with all the eagerness of a child waiting to be acknowledged by her teacher. "He was a vile, filthy creature. No woman would spend time with him unless he paid her in gold first!"

"You mean you know of him?" My customer tried to understand what I was talking about.

"Pirates were usually running from something." I squared my shoulders and continued as if Maggie hadn't spoken through me. "Most didn't use their family names. They had all kinds of crazy nicknames. Most of those came from something they did, treasure they'd found or unique physical characteristics. I know of pirates named Bowlegs, One Eye, Fairweather and Topsail. One of my friends has a pirate ancestor named One Eye Tom."

"Aye," Maggie added defiantly. "You can imagine what his gift was! The man could spew twenty paces into a spittoon."

"So they called him Sam Spit. That makes sense." The customer seemed satisfied with Maggie's answer.

"We can only guess at why they called him that. That doesn't mean he wasn't a pirate. Not everyone was a famous captain. Each ship had dozens of pirates onboard. Your ancestor may well have been here."

"Oh yes, he was certainly a pirate," Maggie confirmed. "One of the lowest."

I gave up trying to explain why this was happening. Maggie refused to back down, since it was a subject she knew about and could understand.

"It's fascinating thinking about it." My customer admitted it as though it were a guilty pleasure. "I'm a little too old for pirate stories, I suppose, but I still love them."

"Around here most people have pirates in their family trees. Those who say they don't probably just won't admit it. I recently learned that I have a pirate ancestor."

"Lucky you. I hope he had a better name than Sam Spit."

"Mine was Rafe Masterson, the scourge of Duck. You should go by the history museum. They have a lot of pirate lore there." I drew her a little map of how to get there.

"I've heard tell of Rafe Masterson!" Maggie was delighted with her contribution.

Thank you so much." My customer shook my hand. I got a quick overview of everything from her new perfume to her teenage granddaughter—who was in trouble for something every time I came in physical contact with her grandmother. "It was delightful talking to you."

Usually that meant there was no sale involved. I quelled my disappointment by reminding myself that she might come back and buy something later, when Maggie had been laid to rest. Talking to customers and making a connection with them was good for future sales. I'd learned that at a conference I went to after opening Missing Pieces.

Barbara Reece, my chatty customer, surprised me when she took everything I had that belonged to Lucian Smith. She never even asked the price—my favorite kind of customer. She told me to wrap it all up and she'd take it home with her.

I thanked her repeatedly—it was a hefty sale—and helped her take everything to her car. Trudy wasn't busy, so she watched the shop for me while I carried the boxes out.

It was easy to smile through the process. A sale like this one was what kept Missing Pieces open and helped me do what I loved.

The last trip out, I thanked her one last time. She told me she was going to the museum to take a look around then asked about the news report on TV.

It was difficult to explain to someone not from Duck why I'd be out digging around in the middle of the night. I did the best I could by way of explanation without going into too much detail.

"You know, my grandmother was like you," Barbara said. "She found things too. It didn't matter what it was. If it was lost, she could find it. Do you find people too? Is that why you found Joe?"

"Not really. Once in a while people happen to be where I'm looking for other things." I laughed. "I don't know about your grandmother, but my finding comes with its own set of rules."

We parted company on good terms, and I watched her drive her late-model BMW out of the Duck Shoppes parking lot. I had the oddest feeling that this woman might be important to me in some way. Not now, but in the future.

# Chapter 18

"I can see you made some money." Trudy was filing her nails when I got back to the shop. "I wish I'd found a dead man in a car so I'd be busy. Even though I'm right next door, I don't get many drop-ins. People go to the same hairdresser all the time."

"Sorry. I'll be happy to keep my eye out for anyone who needs some time in a tanning bed or could use a massage."

We both laughed and she hugged me.

"You're a good friend, Dae. You always have been." She drew a deep breath. "I hope you'll be my maid of honor when Tim and I get married."

*What?* "That was fast. Are you really making plans to marry Tim?"

"No reason to drag my feet. When it's right, it's right. Don't you think?"

I glanced at her slender fingers. There was no ring. "Maybe you should have a nice long engagement and bask in the glory of getting married before me. Remember how we made that bet when we were kids? Whoever got married first won?"

"We'll see." She hugged me again. "I have to run back next door. I'm thinking peach for the bridesmaids' dresses, if we can wait until spring. If we can't, do you think tan would be too plain?"

She left before I could even think what to answer. Trudy and Tim, married? I was having a hard time wrapping my mind around that. It was only last week that Tim had asked *me* out.

"A wedding?" Maggie chirruped, at least waiting until Trudy was gone. "I haven't been to a wedding in a very long time. May I stay for it, Dae? What is a bridesmaid's dress?"

I ignored Maggie, speechless with surprise at Trudy's news. Trudy and Tim had barely noticed each other since high school.

The afternoon continued to be busy until the sun began to set. Maggie kept asking questions about weddings and talking about pirates she'd known. I made it through her talking around me and smiled at the customers who looked at me like I was crazy.

The boardwalk was suddenly empty, as though the waning light had been a warning for everyone to go home.

It wasn't how I'd envisioned my day going, but a woman had to make a living too. Who knew when the next time would be that I'd make another big sale? I'd been fortunate recently, but there were usually months that I had to survive on selling T-shirts and souvenirs.

I tried to get back on track with finding Joe's killer by calling Gramps, anxious for information on the badges. He didn't pick up. He rarely did, mostly forgetting he had a cell phone on his belt.

I started to call Kevin, whose luncheon was long over.

Before I could dial out, the group of ladies who made up my reelection committee trooped into the store.

It impressed me that I had a reelection committee at all. I thought it would be me and Gramps and the occasional schoolkid who put up posters, like last time. Of course I didn't expect Dillon Guthrie to lend a hand either. Life was full of surprises.

Cailey Fargo, our fire chief, had become the self-appointed head of my campaign. Mrs. Euly Stanley was a powerhouse when it came to getting things done. Shayla was there, even though she wasn't a political person, and Marjory Michaels, Chief Michaels's wife, had agreed to help out, despite his misgivings on her taking sides.

The appearance of favoring one person over another was what had kept La Donna from being part of the group. She'd contributed to my campaign but had stayed in the background.

"Good evening, ladies," I greeted them at the door. "Can I get anyone some tea? I'm out of cookies, although I could run next door and see if they have some at the general store."

I could tell at once that these were not the usual happy, determined ladies who'd worked so hard to raise funds for me and spent hours making buttons and posters. Something was wrong.

"Dae, you could've given us a heads-up on the new ads." Cailey, who was also my fifth-grade teacher, sounded hurt and angry. "People have been calling me all day. I didn't know what to say."

I didn't know what to say either, since I had no idea what she was talking about.

"I thought putting up Randal's banner on the museum was a bad idea, but Mark is in charge of that kind of thing and that's what he wanted to do," Mrs. Stanley said. "I thought your original ad on the water tower was a little ostentatious—what did I know? You've gone too far, young woman. What will people think?"

"I'm sorry, but I've been here all day. I don't know about any new ads."

"Well, let's step out on the boardwalk and you'll see why we're concerned." Marjory opened the door.

We all went out on the chilly boardwalk and looked toward the water tower. The lights had come on for the night. Replacing my face up there was now an awful picture of Mad Dog behind bars. The caption read, "Vote Dae O'Donnell. Keep the Mad Dog behind Bars."

I knew who was responsible, of course. Dillon had changed up his attack strategy for my election, even though I had asked him to stop. It was a terrible ad, one that made me wince to see it there with my name on it.

"Ronnie is telling me I can't help you anymore because of this." Marjory clasped her hands together. "Not that what he has to say bothers me, Dae, but we need to get on the same page with our strategy. Do you want this on all the new flyers?"

"No!" I shuddered at the idea. "I'm so sorry." I explained that a well-meaning but tasteless donor was funding the ads. "I don't have any control over him."

"He must not be from Duck," Mrs. Stanley observed. "Anyone born hereabouts would have better sense. It's not Kevin, is it? He doesn't seem to be that kind of person, even though he is an outsider."

"It's not Kevin. And I'll take care of it. The ad will be gone tomorrow."

All the ladies gave a sigh of relief, except for Shayla.

"You don't have long to set this right. I know you don't want to be the mayor who won this way."

I apologized again. The ad was already up. All I could do was call the ad agency and tell them to get it down right away. Of course that meant getting in touch with Dillon again. He'd invaded my life a little more than I'd bargained for, and now I owed him five thousand dollars too.

It occurred to me that the money I'd made that day on the Lucian Smith sale could rid me of that unwelcome debt, even though he'd promised to wait for the sale of the bells. It would probably be worth a little insecurity in the future not to owe him money.

The ladies of my campaign were happy again, satisfied with my answer. I was embarrassed that they had to point it out to me and ask me to fix it. I'd heard of presidents and senators having Super PAC donors they couldn't control. Who'd believe a mayor of a small town like Duck would have that problem?

Once the ladies were gone, I sent an email to Dillon and left a message on the voice mail of the public relations firm handling the ads he paid for. I closed up shop and headed home. It had been a tiring but exciting day. Now all I had to do was set it all right.

"Think you I should have given back my lover's ring, Dae O'Donnell?" Maggie asked as we walked down Duck Road.

It was too weird talking to her out in the open with cars whizzing by. I turned my back to the road and faced the bushes on the side. "No. Why would you ask that?"

"You desire to give back the gold your lover has given you for your campaign. Why would you not keep it?"

"Dillon isn't my lover. It's hard to explain, but he's only a friend. Kevin is my, well, lover."

"And you have only the one? The others want you too. Why not see what happens with them?"

"We don't do that today. We stay faithful to only one man."

Her voice was disappointed when she said, "I thought as much. There were women like you during my time too. They called them nuns."

I refused to answer any more questions until we got home. I didn't need anyone to see me talking to bushes. They had to think I was acting crazy enough already.

Treasure was glad to see me when I got back. He purred and tried to climb up on me before I sat down to look at the mail. Gramps had left a note on the kitchen table that he would be out late and that he hadn't heard back about the badges yet.

That was a disappointment. It was possible with that information that the whole thing with Mad Dog could be over and all I'd have to worry about was the next terrible ad that Dillon had put up before the election.

I looked at the old badge I'd found while I ate some leftover vegetable soup for supper. I had Treasure in my lap and was also watching the nightly news.

I heard them talking about Mad Dog and looked up to see Lightning Joe's sister standing in front of the Dare County Courthouse, surrounded by reporters. She had plenty to say about what had happened to her brother.

"After all these years, they finally found my brother, Joe." She held up a picture of him that the cameras zoomed in on. "Why aren't they moving forward with putting the man behind bars who killed him? Joe and Mad Dog were bitter rivals. It ended with Joe's death. I've known about this and tried to get the police to act on it for forty years. My brother deserves justice and an end to his suffering."

Lightning Joe's sister cried through the entire statement, the wind blowing her hair wildly around her reddened face.

I could understand her need for justice and revenge. I wondered if there was something, besides the surface tensions of competition between Joe and Mad Dog, that made her so sure that Joe had been murdered by his opponent on the track.

Someone knocked at the front door. I put Treasure down and turned off the TV. It was probably someone else complaining about the ad on the water tower. I'd already fielded three calls since I'd been home.

I opened the door and was surprised to find the woman I'd just seen on TV standing on the doorstep.

"Are you Dae O'Donnell?"

I recovered as quickly as I could. It was a little disconcerting to see her. I realized the press conference must have been prerecorded, of course. It was just an odd sensation.

"Yes. You're Pam Walsh, Joe's sister. Would you like to come in?"

She came in and I took her coat. We sat down at the kitchen table after I'd put on some coffee. We were completely out of anything resembling pastries, but I offered her a marshmallow treat.

She declined and came right to the point. "I want to thank you for finding my brother. I never guessed what happened to him. All those years, while Mad Dog Wilson was living his life, raising his family, Joe was buried right here."

"I know. I'm so sorry. I don't have any siblings, but I can imagine how hard and frustrating the whole thing has been for you."

Her eyes welled with tears. She wasn't a pretty crier. Her face was blotchy and her nose was red. She had Joe's abundance of black curly hair, although hers was streaked with gray.

"I fought as hard as I could to get the sheriff's office interested in finding him. I've gone through three disinterested sheriffs, including your grandfather. They all acted like Joe was wild and crazy, like he'd simply taken off for parts unknown."

She smiled a little as she sniffed into a tissue. "Don't get me wrong. Joe *was* wild and crazy, but he loved his family. When he disappeared, my mother and father were still alive. They sold everything they had and hired private investigators to look for him. No one ever had a clue what happened."

I poured us both a cup of coffee and put out cream and sugar. Pam stirred hers for a long time, staring down into the creamy circles in the dark brew.

"When did you first think it was Mad Dog who killed your brother?"

"When didn't I think it? They had that stupid game they played with each other. I was surprised both of them weren't killed on the track. I know a lot of it was Joe wanting to show off. There was no way to stop him. After that last night when Mad Dog was injured, Joe never came home. I knew right then that Mad Dog killed my brother because he ended his driving career."

"Was there ever any real evidence?" I tried to put it as delicately as I could. If she got angry at me, I wouldn't get answers from the source and it would take longer to work around her. Besides, the woman had been through years of torture looking for her loved one.

"The sheriffs didn't seem to think so. They questioned a few people—even Mad Dog—but there were no answers. Joe was just gone."

"What happened to his car? I've seen pictures of it. It was very distinctive. It seems to me that people would have noticed it."

She shrugged. "Gone with him. My parents and I followed that lead for a long time. I remember sitting in our old station wagon while my father went from house to house, store to store, looking for Joe's car. He talked to every mechanic on the Outer Banks, even crossed the bridge and asked around on the mainland."

I sipped my coffee and considered her words. "I'll bet you were surprised that we dug up Mad Dog's car instead of Joe's."

"You better believe it. The first report I heard about it, I thought they got it wrong. If Joe was found dead in a race car, why was it Mad Dog's? It doesn't make any sense."

"So where is Joe's car?"

"Exactly. I know from years of looking for him that it's not in a scrapyard or in the back of some mechanic's car lot. If Joe died here, he didn't take it to the mainland either. I think that means it's still here somewhere. Maybe someone found it and kept it as a souvenir."

"That's a really big souvenir."

"You don't realize how popular racing was back then. Hundreds of people from all over the state would show up every Friday night. I barely remember it because I was a kid. I wanted to be a stock car racer. I wanted people to love me like they did Joe. I have a whole room at home full of his memorabilia. After that night when Mad Dog quit and Joe disappeared, it was over."

"I've heard that women really liked them too."

"Oh yeah. Half of the pictures I have of Joe include his track bunnies, as he called them. They were all ages too. Grandmas, little kids, wives. No one was immune. They showed up all hours of the day and night at the house. It drove Mom and Daddy crazy. They finally set rules." She laughed. "No girls before eight in the morning or after ten at night. Mom said they had to be dressed decent too."

I laughed with her about that. I could only imagine what that had been like.

"He was married when he died, right? Who did he settle on?"

"Joe? Joe never married anyone. He always played the field. He was only eighteen when he went missing. He never even had a steady girlfriend. I guess there were too many to choose from."

Maybe I had my information wrong. Surely Pam would know if Joe had been married. He'd still lived at home when he died. Unless he hid it from his parents, it would've been common knowledge.

"I wish there was something more I could do to help. I'm glad we found your brother. I wish your parents had been alive to see it."

"So do I." She started crying again. "They were so convinced they'd find him. You know, they thought maybe he'd run off with a girl. They were strict on him for the kind of life he led on the track. They always blamed themselves for him leaving."

I gave her a few more tissues and we talked awhile longer before she went home. Before she left, she invited me to come and look at her brother's souvenir room. I told her I'd like that.

All the time I was thinking about Joe's car. Where could it possibly be? Was there some significance to putting him in Mad Dog's car? Like his rumored wife, either of those mysteries could lead to his killer.

# Chapter 19

Gramps woke me the next morning with a list of the ten deputies whose badge numbers fit the sequence. Unfortunately, all of them, including Gramps, had at least one replacement badge for one they had lost or destroyed.

"I remember this now." He chuckled, sitting on the side of my bed in his fishing gear. "Your grandmother, bless her soul, accidentally sent it to the dry cleaner's in the pocket of my uniform. The dry cleaner's were sorry that the badge was ruined by the process. They reimbursed me for the damages—you had to buy the second badge. I'd totally forgotten about it. It was a long time ago."

Treasure was snuggled up next to me on the bed. I was glad Gramps and I had reached an understanding about him not being guilty before he remembered that his badge was partially destroyed. It could've sounded like an excuse.

I was past that. I took the list from him and looked at it. "I didn't know Barney Thompson was a deputy. So was August Grandin."

"Well, you have to remember that the population was even smaller forty years ago. We had to recruit whoever we could find to be a deputy. August and Barney found out it wasn't for them."

I yawned at the same time Treasure yawned and stretched. "Good thing. It looks like Barney was only a deputy for six months but he lost three badges."

"They're only stuck on, you know. There were a few times a drunk would snatch off a deputy's badge. This one time, I was trying to break up a fight and a man ripped my whole shirt apart by grabbing my badge."

I realized as we were talking that there were three deputies from Duck on the list, all important figures in the community today. Barney and August, and of course, Chief Michaels.

In the back of my mind, I knew he'd have to be in the group. He and Gramps came up together as deputies. He and Tuck Riley ran for sheriff when Gramps retired. Tuck won the election. Chief Michaels took over our brand-new Duck police force.

"What about these other men on the list?" The only other name I recognized was Walt Peabody, the police chief in Corolla. He and I had never gotten along since he'd given me my first speeding ticket. There was also some kind of old rivalry between him and Gramps.

Gramps took the list back from me. "I told you I think Blackie Rogers is dead. We'll have to check to make sure. Not that being dead means he's innocent of the crime. There's no statute of limitations on murder, you know."

I laughed. I knew it was a serious subject, especially to him. I'd heard him say that phrase so many times in my life that it had become humorous to me.

"Sorry," I apologized. "Go on."

"You know men have been convicted of murder and other crimes *after* they were dead."

"I know, Gramps. Really. It's just that I've heard you say that so often that it's kind of like 'pass the sugar' in a normal family." I tried to make him understand.

His blue eyes got stern and he raised one outraged brow. "Are you saying our family wasn't *normal*?"

"Kids at school never seemed to think so. That's why I hated it when you took me to school. It reminded everyone again that you were the sheriff."

He cleared his throat and moved on. "Then there was Marvin Taylor. He moved away when he met that woman from Boston, I think. Somewhere up north. She was down here on vacation. She had the skimpiest bathing suit any of us had ever seen and a hot little Mustang. I would've gone with her—if I wasn't already married to your grandmother, of course."

"What about Russ Vidler? I've never heard of him."

"You've met him. He was the Hatteras lightkeeper for many years. We went to his birthday party at the retirement home a few weeks ago."

I remembered the short, rather portly, older man who had a constant squint and wore an 1800s sea captain's uniform when schoolkids went to visit the old lighthouse.

"And Brandon Hall." Gramps laughed again. "I haven't thought of old Brandy in ages. He lost his badge permanently because he couldn't stop drinking. I think he still owns a little bar in Nags Head. I'm not sure about that, but it would be easy to look up."

"Only one more I don't recognize—Wally Newcastle. Who's he?"

"I think he and his family still run that place that rents canoes and sailboats in Kitty Hawk. He bought the place when he retired, and his son and daughter went in on it with him later. He's pretty successful down there."

"Okay. All we have to do now is figure out if one of

them had a grudge against Joe because he was dating their sister, wife, niece or mother."

He patted my leg, still under the blanket, as he got up. "I'll make some pancakes and we'll come up with a suspect board, just like in the old days. It'll be fun."

I groaned. "That's what Kevin always wants to do. He even did it for a missing barrel of whiskey. What is it you lawmen like about that?"

"It organizes the thoughts so you aren't running around in a circle like a chicken with its head cut off."

"*Eww.* And now I'm supposed to eat?"

"Don't make me tell you about my mother keeping chickens when I was growing up and how they ended up in the pot."

I showered and dressed, making sure I wore my good jeans and a nice blue sweater. It was shaping up to be a long day. I wanted to be comfortable and warm through it.

Treasure watched me walk back and forth as I got dressed. He played with the pillows and sheets as I made the bed. He finally perched silently on the edge of the bed, like an Egyptian statue. His green eyes were fixed on me.

For a breathless instant, it was as though he and I became one. I felt merged with him as I looked into his eyes. I couldn't see anything different, but I felt *him*— every perfect muscle poised for action. It was incredible. I reached out a hand to touch his silky fur.

He jumped off the bed and ran down the stairs to see what scraps he could get from Gramps while he made breakfast. I guess the moment wasn't as incredible for him as it was for me.

I glanced at my wayward hair in the mirror one last time. Maggie's face and form appeared instead of mine.

"Are we going to have some fun today for a change?"

It was weird watching both of our mouths moving. No

wonder Kevin had been scared away when Maggie started talking.

"If it sounds like fun looking for the person who killed Joe."

Her lips turned down. "Ye can always look for this killer. I've only a few days at best to go out, dance, drink and have a handsome lad hold me in his arms. Can't it wait?"

"No. Not really. I'll give the historical society a call today and see if they've had any luck locating Thomas's grave."

"I guess that's all the fun I'll be having in this sorry life."

"I'm sorry. I have to get this done before the election."

I was happy and surprised to see that Kevin was there for breakfast—until I saw the pad of large sticky notes and several colored markers.

He kissed me and smiled. Maggie grabbed him like her arms were octopus tentacles. She was all over him, not letting him go for an instant, with me along for the ride.

"That's enough." I finally managed to get her off of him.

"Good morning to both of you." Kevin had a humorous touch to his voice. "Horace called and was telling me how much you needed to create a suspect board to continue your investigation. I couldn't bring my whiteboard since it was being used in the kitchen. These should be fine. We can make a sticky note for each person."

I shook my head. "I can't believe it. There must be something else that brought you over here this early."

"I wanted to see you, of course. And Horace said there were pancakes. How could I resist?"

Gramps winked before he turned back to flip another pancake. "I knew we needed help with so many suspects. Who better than the FBI? Or at least, the former FBI."

Kevin was busy tearing off the large yellow sheets and putting one on each cabinet door, two on the refrigerator and one on the front of the stove. I added a name to each sheet from the list. By the time the pancakes were done cooking, we were ready to get started.

"Okay, let's start with Rogers, since Horace thinks he's deceased," Kevin said. "It shouldn't be hard to get that information from the courthouse."

"I'll do that." I volunteered, since I had to go to Manteo to see Mad Dog again. "I can check for a marriage license in Joe's name at the same time."

Kevin put my name on that sheet of paper. "Since your strength is in finding things, that's a perfect job for you."

"I'll talk to Ronnie, although it seems a little pointless." Gramps grinned. "Ronnie's no more a killer than I am. I don't think he'd tolerate either of you asking him questions about his past."

"He *does* have a sister who was crazy for race car drivers," I pointed out, though I agreed with him about Chief Michaels. "La Donna confessed her weakness to me."

"Probably most of the women of a certain age around here would have to admit to that," Gramps said. "What about you, Kevin? How are we going to put that FBI training to work?"

"I'll look up Marvin Taylor, since he isn't local as far as you know. I have a friend in the Boston area who could help me with that."

"Gramps, you're going to have to talk to Chief Peabody in Corolla. He really doesn't like me."

"He likes you a lot more than he likes me, honey. Believe me. Take Kevin with you. He'll respect his FBI background, if nothing else."

I grumbled, but Kevin said he didn't mind, so our names went on the yellow sheet with Chief Peabody.

We divided up the rest of the names as we did the pancakes. As we ate, I told them about the surprise visit from Pam Walsh last night.

"The way she talked, Joe's parents were strict with him, so his marriage might have been a secret," I explained. "Joe lived at home, but Pam said she didn't know anything about a wedding."

Kevin sipped his coffee between bites of pancake. "Or she was lying. You always have to take that into consideration."

"Why would she lie about that?"

"You never know," Gramps agreed with Kevin. "I've had people lie about the dumbest things, things that didn't even make any difference."

I didn't necessarily agree with that. I felt like Pam was being truthful about not knowing if her brother was married. I suppose I trusted people more than Gramps or Kevin did, but I was good at reading people too. I thought if Pam had been lying, I'd know.

"Joe's car is perplexing to me." Gramps changed the subject. "It was a highly visible vehicle. Most people around here would've recognized it if they saw it. It couldn't just vanish. It makes me wonder if a fan might have found it and kept it all these years. I'm going to run that by Ronnie when I see him."

Kevin brought up another point. "The car could also have been purposely stolen by the killer because there's evidence in or on it."

"That's true." Gramps nodded as he finished his pancakes.

As we all finished eating, we sat looking at the list of names on the giant sticky notes all over the kitchen. I wondered how we'd make a meal in here again until they were gone.

"Gramps, what are you going to say to Chief Michaels about the badge I found? For that matter, what am I going to say to the people on my list? I can't walk around accusing people of killing Joe and demanding their alibis."

"You have to be subtle." He warmed to his subject, leaning his forearms on the table. "Interrogation is more an art than a confrontation. Kevin will know what to say when you go out to Corolla. Follow his lead. You can ask—Did they know Joe? Did they have any contact with him? Do they recall seeing his car after that last race?"

"Did any of them have a female member of their family? Would they rather have killed Joe than let her be with him?"

Gramps and Kevin exchanged glances.

"Don't worry, honey. You'll pick it up as you go along." Gramps looked at his pocket watch. "I've got to get moving if I'm going to see Ronnie before I take my charter out at ten. I'll see you later. Remember, you have to log in your findings here. You know, I haven't had this much fun in years. Sometimes I miss the old days."

When Gramps had stowed his gear on his golf cart and taken off for the marina, Kevin asked, "Need a ride to Manteo?"

"I thought we were supposed to start questioning suspects in Corolla. I'm supposed to learn from your masterful technique."

"I'd like to oblige Horace on that, but I need to pick up some flowers in Manteo this morning. I thought we could combine the trips and save gas."

I'd had an email from Dillon saying that he'd meet me at Missing Pieces at three. I could open the shop later when we got back from Manteo. The chances were, if the boardwalk was going to be crowded, it would be in the warmer afternoon.

"Sounds great. As long as we're breaking the rules, maybe we should stop at the boat rental place in Kitty Hawk on the way back and question Wally Newcastle."

"One thing they teach you in FBI training is to be flexible. I'd say that covers this operation. Let's go."

The sun was warm enough that we rode with the windows open in the truck. We passed the town hall construction site and I remembered to call the museum. No one was there yet and the call went to the answering machine. No one ever checked messages. I'd have to try again later.

The land where Duck Municipal Park had been, where Maggie had lived and died, was changing again. The park would still be there, but it would be smaller as it shared space with the town hall.

I felt her staring there, through me.

"It's like the seashore changing each morn," she said, a wistful note in her voice. "The land will be different again in another hundred years."

"It will." I could feel her melancholy. "Life goes on."

"Without me." She sighed.

"Are you okay?" Kevin asked.

"It's probably only the vapors." Maggie cheered up right away. "Who could feel sad when gazing upon a grand-looking fellow like yourself?"

Kevin cleared his throat. "Dae, I assume you spoke with Horace last night. Everything must be okay."

"Only at my instigation," Maggie answered. "The lass is good-hearted, Kevin, but a mite shy and awkward. They had a long talk and came to an understanding. She knows now that he could never have killed Lightning Joe. What an odd name. I wonder what he did to deserve it."

"Maggie, could I speak to Dae, please?"

"What? Oh, certainly, Kevin. Anything for *you*." She gave him a big kiss as he drove.

"Do we have any news about the boyfriend's grave yet?" Kevin glanced at me as I shook my head to clear it. "Dae?"

"Sorry. What were we talking about?" I felt like I'd been asleep. It was scary. Where had I gone? Usually, I could hear the conversation.

"You confronted your grandfather and everything is okay between you."

"Yes. I kind of felt like an idiot being suspicious of him."

He stared at me when we stopped for a red light. "Are you okay? Do you need help with Maggie?"

I smiled and leaned across the seat to kiss him, making sure he knew it was me and not Maggie. I didn't want him to worry. "I'm fine. I'm waiting to hear from the historical society. It always takes them a while to get information."

He pulled me close and said, "I don't like what's happening with you and Maggie, Dae. You have to put an end to it soon."

"I know. It can't be much longer."

We parked in a lot near the courthouse and Kevin's flower distributor. The jail was right next door to the courthouse.

"I'm going over to pick up my flowers. Call me if you decide to leave the jail right away and go to the courthouse before I get back." He kissed me again. His eyes were intent on mine. "I know you don't want to ask for help on this, Dae, but you might need someone else before this is over. Don't let it go on too long."

# Chapter 20

I got out of the pickup and went up the stairs to the jail entrance. I was surprised to see Laura Wilson sitting on a bench outside the door. Her eyes were red from crying, and her expression was one of hopelessness.

"Dae. I didn't expect to see you here today. Is Randal's lawyer here with you?"

"No. I needed to talk to him about a few things that have come up. Is everything okay?"

She shook her head. "I'm afraid not. Randal has mild emphysema. Probably from all those cigarettes he smoked when he was a kid. He had to be taken to the infirmary last night because he had a hard time breathing. I've all but begged him to let me talk to the bail bondsman and get him out of here. I don't care what anyone thinks. He should be home now."

Laura started crying again, and I put my arm around her. "I'm so sorry you have to go through this. I wish I had better news, but there are more questions than answers right now."

"I appreciate your help, Dae. I know it must be hard on you with all the fuss Randal has made for the last year while he's run for mayor. I don't know what got into him in the first place. He's been happy on the council. I don't know why he didn't stay there, old fool."

"It's been hard for both of us. I never intended for the race to get so hostile. There are some people contributing money to my campaign who don't seem to know when enough is enough."

She patted my arm. "Not from Duck, huh? Well, don't worry about it. I'd say your title as mayor is safe with all this going on. Not that I'm at all sure Randal could beat you. People in Duck love you, Dae. We've all seen you grow up. I would've voted for you, if it wasn't for my husband running too."

A guard came out and told us we could see Mad Dog in the infirmary. He wasn't sure about me, since I wasn't family, strictly speaking, but Laura said I could go in, and he held the door for us.

It always seems like government facilities have such long hallways. There never appear to be enough doors for the floor space. We walked and walked until we finally reached the yellow infirmary door. The guard unlocked it for us and held it open.

"I can't give you more than ten minutes."

Laura thanked him, and we walked into a large room that contained several men in hospital beds. She located Mad Dog like she had radar to find him. We both walked quickly to his side.

He was hooked up to different equipment with a needle and an IV bag on each side.

"Laura. I'm so glad to see you."

I thought he was going to cry too, but he held it back, sniffling a few times and lips quivering, no matter how hard he pressed them together.

She hugged him and didn't mind that she cried. "Will you let me take you home now? I don't care if you're prideful. You don't belong here. You need your own doctor."

Mad Dog fixed on me. "Let's hear what my heroine has to say. If it's bad news, I might as well get used to life behind bars."

There was no point getting his hopes up with promises I didn't know if I could keep. "I have two questions that might be important."

"All right. Ask."

"First, why didn't you stay at the hospital after you were hurt in that last race? I put my hands on your race car. I know how badly you were hurt. Why didn't you get treatment?"

He smiled a little. "You'll have to chalk that up to being young and stupid. You're right. My leg was torn up. I had to wrap it with old shirts and tape to keep it from bleeding. I wanted to get back out there. I told them that all the way to the hospital in the ambulance. They wouldn't listen."

Laura smoothed his hair. "And now they're holding it against you, saying you weren't hurt that badly. The DA said you were capable of killing Joe and burying the car."

He snorted. "Yeah, right. I wasn't even capable of getting back to the track that night. Besides, if I was gonna bury Joe in a car, it damn sure would've been his and not mine."

Laura laughed and kissed him. "That sounds more like you. That's why they called you Mad Dog."

"And the woman you were thinking about when the car was flipping over, the woman you thought Joe might try to take away from you. Who was that?"

"My God!" Randal caught his breath. "You could see all *that* from laying hands on number twelve? Dae, you are a talented young woman—more than I ever dreamed possible. You should take that talent to Vegas and get rich."

"Nice try. It doesn't work like that."

"And we're glad it doesn't." Laura squeezed my hand.

"The woman?" I reminded Mad Dog.

"Just so you know," he smiled slyly, "this was way before I met you, Laura. Her name was Rosie. Her father drove down from Virginia every weekend to race. He was good but he was older. At least what we thought was older—probably forty. It doesn't seem so old now. Amos is older than that."

He stared off into the room for a moment, probably thinking about those days. "Rosie was beautiful. She wore these tight short-shorts all the time. She knew everything about cars, even helped her dad work on his. At that point in my life, she was like a goddess."

"I think that will do," Laura complained. "I am standing right here."

"Sorry, dear. Childish memories." He took her hand but focused on me. "Rosie never belonged to any of us. We all wanted her, but none of us were ever quite good enough, not even Joe."

"I guess I can cross that off my list as far as a motive for you to kill Joe."

"I think so. Have you found anything else?"

I told him about hitting a dead end researching Joe's wife. I also told him about my vision with Joe and the deputy.

"Those sheriff's deputies hated us." His forehead furrowed. "Probably with good reason. We raced up and down every road we came to, didn't care that we were endangering people's lives. We were out of control, egged on by our fans. We thought no one could touch us."

"Was there anyone in particular who gave you a hard time?" I didn't tell him about the badge I'd found. I didn't think it would serve any useful function.

"No one that I can think of—except maybe Horace, because he was always bucking to be sheriff. He had to be better than anyone else. Ronnie kind of let us slide. So did a few of the other deputies. If Joe had a problem with any of them more than another, I didn't know about it."

"I'm sorry." I hated to let them down. "That's all I have."

"Don't apologize," Laura said. "If Randal had been minding his driving instead of thinking about that little hussy, you might have a clear answer today."

Mad Dog chuckled. "Oh, come on, dear, you know I've never looked at another woman since we met. You're the only woman in my mind now."

"If that's the truth, then let me take you home. The people who loved you before this started still love you. The rest, who cares? You need to sleep in your own bed tonight."

He kissed her. "All right, Laura. Set it up. I'll come home for as long as I can."

The guard came to get us. Laura jumped on her phone as soon as we got out of the jail. "I'm sorry to be so rude, Dae. If I don't get this process started, Randal will still spend tonight here."

"Don't worry. I'm meeting Kevin Brickman at the courthouse anyway. I'll let you know if I find out anything else."

"Thank you." The lawyer must have picked up at the other end. She started talking to him about getting Mad Dog released, and I walked quickly down the stairs to the sidewalk.

I took out my cell phone to let Kevin know where I was going, but he was waiting on the sidewalk when I got there.

"Good timing." I shut down my phone. "Did they have the flowers?"

"Not as many as I ordered but we'll make do. How's Mad Dog doing?"

I told him about Mad Dog's health problem and that he'd finally agreed to let Laura arrange for bail. "I'm sure it will be better for him to be home."

"No doubt. That's a powerful amount of pride that can make a man stay in jail when he doesn't have to be there."

"I really hope I'm right and he's innocent. After seeing him this way, I'd like to get to know him better. I always saw him as an old pain in the butt, especially for the last year. He's really a nice, funny man."

"They say situations like this bring out either the best or the worst in a person. I guess you're seeing him at his best."

We walked up another large flight of stairs to get to the courthouse. We had to go through a metal detector. Luckily Kevin had left his gun home that day. I knew he carried one sometimes.

We followed the signs to the register of deeds office. A tiny man with a face like a cherub told us it would cost ten dollars for each copy of a marriage license or death certificate. I produced my twenty dollars and wrote down Joe's name for his marriage license and Blackie Rogers's name for the death certificate.

The tiny man disappeared behind a mountain of shelves with thousands of files on them. I'd expected to get an electronic copy, but apparently most of the certificates weren't in the computer as yet. He had to make a paper copy of them.

"Do you think Blackie was his real name?" Kevin asked.

"I don't know. It was listed with the sheriff's office that way. I think it must be."

We stood around and waited about twenty minutes before

the man behind the counter returned. Both of the certificates were neatly folded and put into register of deeds envelopes.

He smiled. "Is that all?"

"Yes, thanks." I was surprised and pleased by his friendly attitude.

"You're that woman from Duck, aren't you?" He squinted at me. "The woman who found the dead man in the car. Are you doing research for a book or something?"

"No. Just personal. Thanks."

I walked quickly out the door and Kevin was right behind me.

"You've become famous overnight. Maybe you should run for governor or something. You may never be this famous again."

"Very funny. I'm not even sure about being mayor again, much less governor. They'd want me to live in Raleigh all the time if I were governor."

"Maybe you could move the state capital to Duck." He put his arm around me as we reached the bottom of the stairs again. "That would be something."

"Never mind." I ripped open the envelope the clerk had given me. "Well, it looks like Mad Dog was wrong about his fantasy woman only being a fantasy to all the drivers." I explained about the gorgeous woman who hung out at the track with a winning combination of tight shorts and a way with a ratchet.

"Joe Walsh made Barbara Rose Carpenter his bride two days before he died."

"Sounds like yet another reason for murder to me. That couldn't have been popular with all those other girls."

"And Gramps was right." I kept reading. "Blackie Rogers is dead. He had plenty of time to kill Joe—he's only been dead for twelve years."

"That makes all the difference."

I sighed. "How will we know if Blackie killed Joe? How do you prove a dead person is guilty?"

"With the amount of time that's gone by on this, it may come down to a process of elimination. At least we can put him on the bottom of the list until we question the others or find corroborating evidence that continues to show us that he could be a principal in the event."

"I love it when you speak law enforcement." I laughed. "In other words, we have to hope we can find something he left behind that will give him away. Or I touch something else that gives us another clue."

"Facts, Dae. Police officers all over the world rely on facts, even for cold cases this old. They have since before you and I were born. We can figure this out by following the trail of bread crumbs."

"You're right." I was actually happy to hear him say this. It wasn't easy touching things that still held the death throes of another human being. "Should we stop after lunch and still see Wally Newcastle?"

"It can't hurt."

We stopped at one of the few restaurants still open in Kitty Hawk and had huge bowls of chili with homemade oyster crackers. We ate outside on the patio even though the wind was cold.

I loved Kitty Hawk with its tall sand dunes standing guard like mountains over the town. Gramps brought me here for the first time when I was about five. We climbed the dunes and visited the Wright Brothers National Memorial. I remembered being fascinated by the whole idea that people could fly with nothing more than a kite.

Now people came from all over the country to take big, multicolored kites and jump off the dunes with them, hurling themselves into the air currents.

Not me. I've always been more at home in and on the water. I've never tried jumping off of anything that high, or getting in a plane. At least water cradles you when you're in it. There's not much support to air.

Kevin laughed at my feelings about the air. He'd flown many times and even used hang gliders. He'd never surfed though, and I could laugh at him for that.

Wally Newcastle's son, Miller, met us at the front door to their recreational rental shop, Away We Go. He told us that his father was confined to a wheelchair but still worked every day.

It was a large store with high ceilings. Various types of boats, hang gliders and other outdoor equipment hung from the ceiling above us. It wasn't very busy at this time of year, but Miller said they still did well enough to keep the place open.

We walked all the way through the store and exited through the back door. Wally was giving classes on how to paddle a canoe in a small pond behind the store. Even though he wasn't in the canoe with them, the students seemed to be getting the idea.

Miller told his father we were there to see him then left us. Wally grinned and shook hands with Kevin. "What can I do you for?"

"I'm Dae O'Donnell." I shook his hand too.

"Horace's girl? Wow! You've grown. I haven't seen you for a long time. Is Kevin your husband?"

"No, sir." Kevin kept his professional stance. "Dae is the mayor of Duck now and I run the Blue Whale Inn."

"Right. I knew about Dae. And I heard about that old place reopening. Some FBI—" His eyes widened and his voice dropped. "Are you here on federal business?"

Kevin smiled what I'd come to think of as his Fed smile.

"No. Dae and I are here looking into the death of Joe Walsh."

Wally made a disparaging face. "That boy. I heard they'd found him. He was nothing but trouble. I hate to speak ill of the dead, but it's true. Fast cars. Smoking. Alcohol. Women. There was no way he was going to end up right."

I defended Joe. "He was only a kid. Lots of people get in trouble when they're kids and turn out fine."

"He was a no-good kid who took advantage of everyone he knew. I busted him a few times, but his parents always bailed him out. It took everything they had to keep him out of jail and racing that hot rod. I felt sorry for them, you know?" He glanced at Kevin. "Why is the FBI involved in a local matter?"

"I'm retired, Mr. Newcastle. I'm doing a little favor for local law enforcement. There is some evidence that someone in the sheriff's department has information about Walsh's death. It could be someone who was a deputy during that time."

"Well, don't look at me. My daughter was born the night he disappeared. I was with my wife all night. You want to talk to Mad Dog Wilson. I thought he was already in jail for the crime."

Kevin lowered his voice, moved a little closer to Wally and kept his eyes focused on Wally's face. "We have *specific* evidence that ties a Dare County deputy to Walsh's death."

Wally swallowed hard. His eyes never left Kevin's. "I understand." He appeared to think hard for a moment or two. "Blackie Rogers had a few run-ins with the kid back then. He might be the one you're looking for, even though he's dead now."

"Did those run-ins include a woman?" I lowered my voice like Kevin and stared hard at Wally.

"A woman?" He frowned. "It was a long time ago but—oh, you mean Rosie Carpenter. I don't think she was involved with any deputy, if that's what you mean. She was gone on the race car drivers. Although, Blackie did ask her out once. She shut him down faster than the revenue men could shut down a still."

"Do you know what happened to her?" Kevin asked.

"Not really. When they stopped racing after Joe disappeared and Mad Dog couldn't drive, she stopped coming down with her dad. He ran a big car dealership in Portsmouth or Newport News, if memory serves me right. You might want to check there."

Wally was no help after that. Kevin and I left a few minutes later. I learned a lot from watching Kevin question him, as Gramps had said I would.

My cell phone was ringing when we got to the truck. I'd decided not to bring it in so we wouldn't be interrupted.

Gramps asked, "Where are you, Dae?"

"In Kitty Hawk. We just finished talking to Wally Newcastle and he—"

"Never mind. Come home. I'm with Ronnie at Mad Dog's place. We found Lightning Joe's car."

# Chapter 21

Kevin and I talked all the way back to Duck about what this could mean. He dropped me off at the Wilsons' big house on Racing Snail Drive. He wanted to stay, but he had to get the flowers he'd picked up back to the Blue Whale.

The Wilsons had been in Duck for many generations, like my family. Unlike my family, Mad Dog had used his local fame to promote his business building engines for stock cars and had become quite wealthy. They'd bought several pieces of land that had adjoined theirs so that he would have a place to work.

There were storage buildings and garages behind the brown clapboard, two-story house. All of the action seemed to be taking place at one of the garages. The police had already barricaded the concrete drive that led there, so I could only stand in front and watch. Finally Gramps saw me (he never answers his cell phone) and walked back toward the house to fill me in.

"They're still looking things over, Dae. Let's come over here and talk."

Chief Michaels had received an anonymous tip that car number twenty-three might be at Mad Dog's house. Gramps had been there at the time, talking to his old friend about his lost badge and asking uncomfortable questions about Joe's death.

"I didn't get many answers once this came up," Gramps said. "I don't mind telling you how hard it was to even ask Ronnie those things."

"I know." I smiled at him. "It was hard for me too."

"Well, the tip was right. Joe's car was in the back garage hidden under a tarp. It's in perfect condition. Probably like he left it the night he was killed. They think it's been here all these years."

"Who would know about that to call in a tip?"

"Could be one of the mechanics who used to work for Mad Dog. He might've thought about it with everything going on. That's what Ronnie thinks."

I thought about Laura trying to get her husband released from jail. What a homecoming this would be. Further proof, no doubt, that Mad Dog was guilty of killing Joe.

Sheriff Riley and one of his men pulled in behind us, blocking the way into the drive. "Horace." Tuck nodded to Gramps. "Mayor O'Donnell. I always love these down-home crime scenes that happen out in the county. Everyone in town is welcome to attend and give their opinion on what's going on. It's kind of like a county fair, without the bread-and-butter pickles."

Tuck laughed—obviously he found his words amusing. Gramps frowned but let it go.

Sheriff Riley left right away as a deputy waved him farther into the crime scene.

"I don't think any investigation of ours is going to help

Mad Dog at this point," he said after Tuck was gone. "It's gonna take a lot to dig him out of this hole."

DA Luke Helms showed up next. He smiled and nodded at both of us, asking after our health, then went to join the others at the garage.

"I wish I could get in there and touch it." I said it even though it wasn't really true. I wanted to find something that would help Mad Dog, but I didn't want the repercussions that would go along with it.

"That's not going to happen today. They're sending a crime scene team from Manteo to go over the whole thing. Maybe after that, you might be able to get your wish. I think Ronnie will want that badge you found, Dae. It's part of the investigation. We shouldn't have messed with it. I don't know what I was thinking."

I told him about our interview with Wally and the information I got from the courthouse. "Wally kind of implicated Blackie. He definitely had *his* alibi ready to go."

He looked at the marriage license. "We can probably find Joe's wife with this." He folded it up and handed it back to me. "But we're not going to. Any other ideas have to go through Ronnie first. It's bad enough I accused him of killing Joe because he has a sister who was interested in race car drivers. I'm not speculating on what happened anymore. I'd rather you didn't either."

I put the marriage license in my pocket. I respected both Gramps and Chief Michaels, but I was convinced from my visions that Mad Dog was innocent. I knew I couldn't use that information to make Chief Michaels believe me. I couldn't stop looking though, having seen that other side of Mad Dog.

Gramps had ridden down there with Chief Michaels, so neither one of us had a ride home. Lucky for us, Luke left almost as soon as he got there. He offered to drive us where we wanted to go.

"This is some bad stuff." Luke talked to Gramps, who was in the front seat with him. "Mr. Wilson's case seems to be going under. I'm afraid his wife may have only saved him a few weeks in jail."

"So he's getting out on bond?" Gramps asked. I hadn't had a chance to tell him.

"Yes. He should be home later today."

"Are you going to ask for a higher bond since you have new evidence?"

Luke shook his head. "I don't think so. Mr. Wilson doesn't strike me as a bail jumper. His wife is using their home as collateral. I don't see him endangering her home, do you?"

Gramps agreed with him. "I also don't see him as a killer, Luke. I know this is your job, but there may be compelling evidence that another person was involved."

He went on to tell Luke about the badge I'd found. It made me uncomfortable. Luke wasn't from Duck and he always seemed a little skittish about my gift.

"I hope Chief Michaels has that evidence." Luke glanced at me in the rearview mirror.

"He doesn't yet. He will soon enough."

Luke was a nice man. He took himself a little too seriously for me, but he'd been a big asset to Duck in the short time he'd lived there. Gramps said it was prestigious to have the Dare County DA living in Duck. I agreed with him. I wished he was on Mad Dog's side instead of prosecuting him.

Luke dropped Gramps off first at home even though it meant he had to come back to the Duck Shoppes to drop me off. There was this awkward moment right before I got out of the car when he tried to ask me exactly what I'd seen from holding the badge.

"It wasn't much." I described the scene. "I think the

deputy this badge belonged to had something to do with Lightning Joe's death."

He smiled and looked away as though he were searching for the right words. "Dae, I know people value your gift, but you can't take evidence from the scene of a crime."

"Even if I'm the one who found the crime in the first place?"

"Make sure the badge gets into the proper hands by morning. And stay away from that site. Let us figure out what happened. Be sure to tell Kevin the same thing for me. He's not in the FBI anymore. He shouldn't go around representing himself as an agent."

I started to argue with him. Kevin had clearly told Wally he was retired. I wanted to ask Luke what he was afraid of—did he think I'd solve the case without him?

I didn't say anything. Unfortunately, Maggie was too near an attractive man to let him go.

"Let's not argue anymore, good sir. There are far better things we could do with our time."

Before I could take over again, she'd leaned in close and given him a big kiss right on the mouth.

I looked at him in the instant that ensued. I was pretty sure I looked horrified.

Luke was calm about the whole thing. "It's okay, Dae. I know people tend to get emotional over this kind of thing. We'll talk later."

He kind of awkwardly patted my arm, and I got out of the car. It was too late to feel embarrassed, since it was already over.

Maggie was angry at what she took to be Luke's dismissal of her charms. "That man has no heart. If he ever comes to court you, Dae, steer clear."

I tried calling the historical society again. I was beginning to get desperate to find Thomas's grave, even though I was still a little sketchy about exactly how we were going to get Maggie in the ground beside him. When we buried her bones, would that be it?

I had an hour before I was going to meet Dillon at the shop, but I decided it would be nice to have some time to relax and enjoy a cup of tea before he got there. Not to mention issuing a severe warning to Maggie—for all the good that would do.

I said hello to Nancy as I went by town hall where the big election posters were up telling everyone that we voted at Duck Elementary School. Trudy was busy with Mrs. Johansen's hair as I walked by her windows. I waved but didn't interrupt.

I let myself into Missing Pieces and slumped against the closed door. "What were you doing back there, Maggie?"

"Nothing, it seems. You have no heart for romance. Neither did he. All I'm asking is for a little time being human again. A stout pair of arms around me would warm me through the chill to come. You ruin everything. You *are* more like a nun than a flesh-and-blood woman."

I made myself some tea and sat on the burgundy brocade sofa for a few minutes. I had to get myself together before I spoke with Dillon. He was sharp and eager to be part of my life. I knew repaying the money he'd loaned me needed to be the end of our relationship. I could see that it would be asking for trouble to continue being involved with him. I didn't need Maggie's "sight" to know that.

The front door opened, and two men in wildly flowered shirts and jeans came in. They were both wearing the same kind of fishing hat, and both of the hats looked brand-new. There was something odd about their shirts and jeans too. They were ironed, with neat creases in them. Gramps never went fishing looking that way. Neither did anyone else I knew.

They were probably from the mainland and thought they

looked like they fit in with the locals. If they wanted to buy something, I didn't care what they wore.

"Hello," the first man said. "I'm looking for an antique for my wife. She's not happy when I come home from fishing without a gift."

"Same for me," the other man said with a big, crazy grin. "Show us something nice."

I wasn't sure what that was, but I was happy to oblige.

We walked all over the store together looking at jewelry, vases, anything I could imagine that would interest any woman who might be married to these goofy-acting fishermen.

They had no idea what they were looking for, and I was about to send them to the Duck General Store when the first man said, "What's in here?" and stepped into the storage area.

"Nothing in there is for sale." I started to follow him.

The man behind me put his hand across my mouth and bodily moved me into the storage room with his friend. He pulled the curtain closed behind us.

"We need a few minutes of your time, Mayor O'Donnell." The first man flashed a badge and ID.

"We're with the ATF." The second man took out his badge too. I saw his gun at the same time. "Please stay calm. This room is the only one in your store that hasn't been bugged by Dillon Guthrie."

I relaxed, at least outwardly, and he released me. I wasn't sure I believed their story, even after I got a closer look at one of their badges. It did serve as a wake-up call on how easily something like this could happen.

"You can buy badges that look exactly like this online. How do I know you are who you say you are?"

The first man made a snorting noise. "Who else would come in this way?"

"Some kind of rival smuggling gang. Or people who want to kill Dillon."

The two men looked at each other. The first man shrugged.

"Those things could be possible," he agreed. "But we really are with the ATF, and we need your help. We're trying to build a case against Guthrie. We know you're in contact with him. We're here because we read your email about meeting him here today."

"Of course, anyone could have hacked into Dillon's email. I'm sorry. I'm not convinced. Do you have some other proof?"

The second man took out a pair of handcuffs and snarled, "How about if we arrest you for doing business with a man wanted for drug and gun smuggling? If we fly you to DC and put you in a federal lockup, would that make you feel better?"

"Easy, Bob," the first man said. "The mayor has a valid point. She's the granddaughter of a sheriff and the girlfriend of an ex–FBI agent. What did you expect?"

"I have a way to resolve this. Let me hold one of those badges. It won't take long."

They exchanged looks again, but the first man handed me his badge.

Lucky for me, there weren't a lot of bad emotions tied to it. I saw pieces of his life, including his wife and the swearing-in ceremony where he'd received the badge from ATF officials.

I handed it back. "How can I help you, Agent Moore?"

He raised his eyebrows. "I read your file. You're good. How come you aren't working for the government?"

"Yeah," Agent Bob Jablonski added. "Instead of hanging out with a sleazy dirtbag like Guthrie?"

"I'm sure you know becoming involved with Dillon

Guthrie wasn't exactly my doing. He came here with another man I was doing business with, Port Tymov. I didn't ask him to come back. He keeps following me around."

Agent Allen Moore nodded as he took off his fishing hat. "It starts out that way. It *always* starts out that way. No one made you borrow money from him, did they?"

They knew more than I thought they knew. I never said anything about the money in an email or a phone call. "How do you know that?"

Jablonski snickered. "What? You think Guthrie is the only one with listening devices? Look, you're in with him up to your eyeballs. You help us, we make that go away. You could be exactly what we need to bring Guthrie in."

"I plan on paying him back the money I owe him today. That's why I set up the meeting. He won't be doing any more advertising for my mayoral campaign. You do what you want with him. I'm cutting my ties."

Agent Moore shook his head. "We have something else in mind, Mayor. We want you to continue your relationship with Guthrie. We need information to stop the flow of illegal weapons coming in through this area of the country."

"Guthrie doesn't make contact with little people like you who don't play his game," Jablonski said. "I don't know why he's taken a shine to you, but it's good for us."

Their plan didn't sound like a healthy idea to me. I wasn't going into witness protection in Idaho when it was over. I knew I'd made some mistakes, but I wasn't willing to jeopardize my life, or Gramps's life, for them.

"I'm sorry. You'll have to arrest me. I'm not playing games with Dillon for your sake. I'll be glad to hold one of the illegal weapons, as long as it's new. I can give you all the information you need."

"Is that a joke?" Jablonski laughed. "You get lucky one time with the badge and that makes you a psychic?"

I snatched his hat off of his head and concentrated. "This was made in China, of course, in a small shop out in the country. You bought it, and Agent Moore's hat, at a convenience store in Morehead City as you were on your way here. You spilled your strawberry Slushie on it, a little on the left side. You don't really like strawberry, but they were out of blueberry."

"That's impressive," Moore said. "Unfortunately, we can't use that in a court of law. We have to follow procedure if we want our conviction to stick."

"What about if I find out where the weapons are being brought in and you can call it an anonymous tip? I know you people use that all the time."

Jablonski looked uncertain. "We've worked for two years on this case. Any whiff of crazy stuff could get the whole thing thrown out."

I shrugged. "That's the best I can offer. If you arrest me, you lose the whole thing."

My heart was pounding even though I sounded rational and calm. I wasn't sure how far these two were willing to go. I didn't want to go to prison, but that might be preferable to being dead.

"We'll have to clear it with our superiors." Agent Moore put away his badge. "In the meantime, don't burn any bridges with Guthrie when he gets here today."

"I won't." *I can always do that later.*

"We'll be listening," Jablonski reminded me.

# Chapter 22

Moore put his hat back on, and the two of them slipped out of the shop. I hoped Dillon wasn't watching Missing Pieces. If I'd noticed something off about the men, he'd probably pick them out as government agents right away.

I walked around inside the shop, trying to calm down. It was a strange feeling knowing someone, or several someones, were listening to everything that went on here.

What was Dillon listening for? Was he worried I might not sell him the third bell when it came in, or did he always listen in on the people he knew?

It didn't surprise me that Dillon might be smuggling guns into the country. I had an idea of what he did, if not exact knowledge. He scared me, but he was like a sand flea—hard to shake off. I knew I needed to cut all ties to him. Once I'd paid him off, that should be it, at least until the third bell came into my possession.

I realized I was standing in front of some old formal gowns when Maggie surged excitedly to the front.

"These are so lovely." She touched them carefully. "Could we try just one on? I never wore anything like this in my life. Please, Dae? Then you can go back to all the killing and killers in your life."

"All right." I gave in, distracted. "Let's do it."

I let her take over while I stayed in the background, worrying about Dillon and the ATF. I was determined not to get involved in that investigation. No good could come of it, like Gramps always said.

It didn't take Maggie long to take everything off and put on a lovely pink gown with plenty of silver sequins. She made *ooh*ing and *aah*ing noises as she found some matching shoes and even an old rhinestone tiara. She started dancing around the shop, making sure she watched at herself in every mirror she passed.

It was a very odd feeling to let it go on that long. The short spurts where she'd surged in before were so brief, they were hardly noticeable—except for the aftermath.

This was like being swallowed by life—a life that wasn't mine. I knew I could step forward at any time, so I didn't panic. Otherwise, I was sure I'd be trying to claw my way out of that prison.

The front door opened at exactly three P.M., and Maggie turned to face Dillon.

For a few moments, we couldn't switch places. I tried to push forward. Maggie was still in control. She panicked too, not sure what to say or do.

Finally she fell back on what she knew best. She curtseyed and smiled. "Hello, sir. Welcome to my fine establishment. I am certain you will find many wondrous things here. I am Dae O'Donnell, and I will be happy to serve you in any way."

"Dae." He nodded, glancing around the shop. Two of his men came in with him. They stayed by the door, looking out at the Currituck Sound. "How's it going? I like the dress. It suits you."

Maggie warmed to him like a flower turning toward the sun. "Thank you, kind sir. I am happy you find me appealing. May I fetch tea for you?"

Dillon got a look on his face that told me he'd begun thinking of other things besides business. This wasn't good.

"You know, I've always found you attractive." He trailed one finger down Maggie's arm. "I kind of hoped you might feel the same about me."

At that awkward juncture, I was able to replace Maggie as the primary resident of my body. "Thanks for coming."

"Of course." He sat back in his chair and pulled himself together. "Is there something I can do for you?"

I made tea, and Dillon took off his coat. Of course, I was trapped in the pretty pink gown. I ignored it and tried to act like I always did around him. I hoped it would throw him off on Maggie's performance and keep him from figuring out that the ATF was listening.

We chatted about my sale of the Lucian Smith estate articles. It was as though we were good friends or longtime business associates. Dillon might be a smuggler and a killer, but most of the time, he seemed like everyone else.

"I want to give you this from the sale." I handed him the envelope with five thousand dollars in it to repay the loan he'd given me. I wasn't sure how that was playing on the ATF listening devices, but I believed the only way not to act suspicious about them being there was to be myself.

"You didn't have to do that yet." He still looked in the envelope anyway and handed it to one of the men he'd brought with him. "You know you didn't have to pay me back at all. I know what it's like to be a struggling business owner. You should let me help you out."

"I appreciate it, but I'm not made that way. You should know that about me by now."

He smiled. "As a matter of fact, it's one of the things I admire most about you. You have integrity in a world where that doesn't exist much anymore. If you're comfortable paying me back after your big sale, I'm good with that. Just know that I'm here to help if you need me again."

When I talked to him, it was hard to imagine him being the monster I knew he was. He was very good at saying all the right things, and he was so smooth. We also shared a love of history and antiques. It was something I'd never been able to share with anyone else.

I listened as he told me what he'd been doing the last few days. His handsome face was so alive and charismatic. I felt sorry for him and wished I could tell him about the ATF. I knew it was the wrong way to feel about him. I couldn't help it.

"There's one more thing we need to talk about, Dillon. You have to stop running those ads. You don't understand that this is a very small town. People might not like what they think Mad Dog did, but that ad on the water tower is over the top. I think there may be some voters who won't vote for me because of it."

"I'm sorry. I haven't even seen it."

I pointed him in the right direction on the boardwalk so he could see it. His face got angry. "I didn't tell that moron at the ad agency to do anything like this, Dae. I'll take care of it. Don't worry. I'm sure you'll be fine in the election anyway. Most people don't vote for a man in jail."

I thanked him and didn't mention that Mad Dog was out, at least for the time being. I'd learned the hard way that telling him anything made him get involved. While I wouldn't go out of my way to end our relationship, as I'd promised the ATF agents, I didn't want to add to it either.

We went back inside, sat down on the burgundy brocade sofa and finished our tea. Dillon told me he had a surprise for me too and beckoned to one of the men by the door to bring it over.

"I'm not going to tell you what it is." He smiled as I took the package. "You're good at guessing. Tell me what you think."

I opened the box carefully and looked inside. It was a very old pocket watch, which I could see was no longer working. I put on a pair of white gloves to examine it.

"It looks like it's had some saltwater damage but it's been restored." I turned it over and peered into the inner workings. "The hands are stopped at eleven forty-three. Good craftsmanship. Silver, I think."

"Yes?"

I couldn't help the swell of excitement that swept through me when I realized what I was holding. I didn't need to touch it without my gloves to know its history or value.

"It's from Jamestown, isn't it? I've read about it, of course, and seen pictures of it. It stopped exactly when the earthquake hit that swallowed the town in the 1600s. Then it was washed underwater for years until divers found it. How in the world did you get it?"

The city of Jamestown, near what is now Guadeloupe, had been a pirate's den for many years. It was known as the wickedest city in the world, until the day it was swallowed by a strong earthquake followed by a tidal wave. The whole place was all but destroyed in a single day.

"I knew you'd appreciate it. I'm financing some under-water excavation down there off the coast. You know, millions of dollars in pirate treasure was either washed away or buried in the sand that day in 1620."

"That's awesome." I could barely keep my voice from squeaking with excitement. This was the find of a lifetime. I envied him at that moment.

He sat forward and took my hands in his. "Come down there. You can keep whatever you find. I'll pay for everything. I want someone to share this with. You might be surprised by how many people don't even know about Jamestown."

I was tempted. I even thought about the ATF listening in. They'd probably like it if I went with him. I could only imagine all the remarkable things he'd find. I wanted to see them all. I didn't even care about bringing them home with me.

Shayla told me once that the devil comes in all types of disguises. Surely Dillon was the devil tempting me almost beyond my capacity to say no. What harm could there be in going down there with him for a week or two? I could come back and live my life normally after it was over, except that I would have had this extraordinary experience.

"I'd like that." I sighed. "But I can't. You'll have to bring some pieces back to show me."

"Why not?" His grip on my hands tightened. "You and I are two of a kind when it comes to finding lost treasures, Dae. We could have a great time and we'd be able to talk for years about the experience. I want you to come with me. We'd be good for each other. Let me show you."

I knew he was too close when I could see the tiny flecks of brown in his blue eyes. Dillon was an attractive man who understood my weakness for finding lost things. He leaned forward and carefully kissed me in much the same way that I had opened the box with the watch in it—not sure what to expect.

It wasn't romantic so much as something emotional he could do to seal the bargain. I certainly didn't think I was his usual type of woman, but he was excited about looking for treasure with me.

At least that's how I rationalized it.

"Come on, Dae. You can close up the shop for a few months. Hell, bring your grandfather if you need to. There's good fishing, and I have a boat down there."

"I can't, Dillon. I have the election coming up, and the shop. I can't leave. I have responsibilities. I guess it goes along with who I am."

I purposely didn't mention Kevin. I wouldn't want Dillon to consider him an obstacle, especially one he should get rid of. It seemed likely Dillon might know about Kevin, since he liked to figure out things about my life. I wasn't going to make him think my feelings for Kevin would hold me back.

He sat back and let go of my hands. I could see he didn't take rejection well. I might have ruined our relationship by not agreeing to go with him.

"Don't say no right now. Think about it. We'll talk again. It will take years to find everything. Even if you can't do it right away, I can wait for the time to be right."

I was surprised and flattered by both his proposal and the fact that he didn't get angry and storm out of the shop. I wished he wasn't a killer and a smuggler. He was an interesting man. We could have been good friends.

"I'll think about it," I promised with a smile. "Thanks for asking me anyway."

He got up and put on his coat. "Keep the watch. I'll update you on our progress with Jamestown. I probably won't see you again before the election. Good luck. Let me know how it turns out."

I told him I would and watched as one of the men went out on the boardwalk and looked both ways before Dillon set foot outside the shop. The second man followed him out of the door, repeating the same watchful movements.

It was a reminder to me that Dillon and I might have a love of history in common but our lives were very different. I knew the ATF agents had heard everything. Maybe they'd even figure out some way to use what they'd heard to trap him.

It was out of my hands. Dillon had chosen this life for himself.

The shop door opened again a few moments after they'd gone. It was Kevin. "Was that who I think it was?"

"It was Dillon Guthrie, if that's who you mean. I'm really hungry. Are you hungry? Let's go down to Wild Stallions and eat."

"It's too early for dinner, and I'm more interested in what Guthrie was doing here."

"I think we should go. We'll get a better table."

"Like that?" His gaze went up and down on my pink ball gown.

"It'll only take me a minute to change." I ran back and put my street clothes on in the storage room while he waited. I looked at myself in the mirror, and Maggie smiled back at me.

"You are a fortunate woman, Dae. So many people love you."

I was terrified that Kevin would say something that would make the ATF come down on him too. I ignored Maggie and grabbed my pocketbook as I propelled us out of the door. "Let's go over there anyway. I'm *really* hungry."

We sat in Wild Stallions, and I explained why we had to leave Missing Pieces to talk and why Dillon was there—except for the part about me owing him money. I still thought Kevin wasn't ready to know about that.

"Dae, you should have untangled yourself from him a long time ago." Kevin's tone was low and angry. "I'm not surprised the ATF wants to use you to pull him in. You'd be very attractive bait."

"I didn't agree to what they wanted, but I offered to touch one of the guns he's smuggling."

*"What?"*

"Only one of the new ones. You know where this leads if I have to testify against Dillon. Or if I do *anything* they want me to. I'm not leaving Duck, Kevin. I don't care."

Neither one of us felt like eating. We huddled in the booth farthest from the door and tried to decide what to do next.

"You're going to have to work with them," Kevin said. "I know you're looking for a safe way to do it. One way or another, once they target you, you have no choice."

"There has to be some way to help them without ruining my life."

"Let me make some phone calls. I might be able to find out exactly what's going on and what they want from you."

"Thanks. I'm sorry I had anything to do with Dillon now. I like talking to him, even though I know he's dangerous. He understands about finding lost things."

He took my hand. "We'll figure something out. In the meantime, let's go back to your house and see where we are with our murder investigation."

We took his pickup to the house and sat in the kitchen for a while, not speaking. He excused himself and went outside to make a phone call. I could tell he was angry from the thin line his mouth had become as he had considered what to do. I didn't want to cause him any trouble. I only wanted my shop back again.

For the first time since I'd opened Missing Pieces, I didn't feel comfortable there. That was as much a loss to me as finding out the ATF had devised a scheme to use me to trap Dillon.

I missed my burgundy brocade sofa and my view of the Currituck Sound. I hoped when I got to the other side of this, I could go back and not think about it again.

Kevin came back in a few minutes later. He didn't say anything about Dillon.

"I called my friend in Boston earlier today." Kevin wrote on the big sticky note sheets Gramps and I had moved to the wall by the refrigerator. "Marvin Taylor has been dead for only the past six months. He could've been responsible for Joe's death too, just like Blackie Rogers."

"Not to mention Gramps and Chief Michaels, for that matter. Wally is the only one with a real alibi for that night."

"Right now, anyway. We still have other badge holders to interview."

"Wally said Rosie's father owned a car dealership." I wrote the information on a big sticky note. "Maybe we can find a Carpenter Ford dealership or something."

"That was a long time ago, and we don't know if the dealership had his name or was called something like Bayview Ford. Or for that matter, what kind of cars he sold. It could've been used cars."

"I know. I'm sure it's important to find her. She's the key."

He sat back in his chair and studied the sheets with information on them. "We're going to have to find something really convincing for anyone to look at it after they found Joe's car at Mad Dog's house."

I knew Luke would certainly agree with that. "We have to keep looking."

"I guess that means we keep going through the badges. I know you have a town meeting tonight. Do you think there's time to head out to Corolla before that?"

"Sure." I frowned. "I'm really not looking forward to confronting Chief Peabody."

"I'm not either. We might as well get it over with."

It had started raining lightly while we'd been in the house. It continued all the way out to Corolla. Darkness had settled in early with the clouds. We only passed one other car all the way down from Duck.

We didn't talk about Dillon, but I felt it was weighing heavily between us. Kevin was a very good person with a single-minded ideal of good and bad. Gramps was the same way. I understood them.

For me, good and bad weren't so clear all the time. I felt a kinship with Dillon, even though I knew he'd led a life that would someday see him dead or in prison. Maybe it came from actually seeing inside of things where most people couldn't see.

I felt like I understood Dillon too. Maybe that was wrong, but it was true.

The Corolla Police Department was part of the city hall building. It was easy to find Chief Peabody. He was the only one with his own office.

"Are you actually questioning me about what I was doing the night Joe Walsh died?" Chief Peabody asked angrily. "You both have a lot of nerve coming out here."

"We mean no disrespect, Chief." Kevin tried to put a different spin on our request. "We're trying to find out if anyone in the sheriff's department at that time knew anything about what happened to Joe."

"I think you all should be in Duck talking to Mad Dog. I heard they found Joe's car at his house. I'd say that fries his bacon."

"Mad Dog was never a sheriff's deputy." I entered the fray. "I found a deputy's badge at the site where Joe was killed. There are only ten of you the badge could've belonged to."

The chief shot to his feet. "And you think I was involved? What possible reason could I have had to kill him?"

"Maybe a woman you were both in love with," I suggested. "Maybe Rosie Carpenter. Did you know her?"

"I saw her around. Everyone did back then. What does she have to do with Joe?"

"They were married two days before he was killed." I watched his face, but his expression never changed.

"Married, huh? All I can say is that she was lucky he disappeared before she was stuck with him. He wouldn't take care of anyone—including himself. All he and Mad Dog knew was cars. People didn't matter to them. And as for what I was doing the night Joe was killed, how do you know *when* he died after all these years?"

"He was never seen again after the race between him and Mad Dog. The police think—"

"I know what they think. I know what they all think. They're wrong. Lightning Joe was still alive after that night. I gave him a speeding ticket for going eighty miles per hour on Highway Twelve a week later in that old hunk-of-junk car of his. You'd better get your timeline straight before you go around asking people what they were doing when Joe was killed."

"Have you shared this with Chief Michaels or Sheriff Riley?" Kevin seemed surprised to hear that information. "I'm sure they'd like to hear it."

Chief Peabody looked a little shamefaced. "I've been busy. You know we have stuff going on out here too. I plan to tell them what I know as soon as I can."

"I'll tell Chief Michaels to expect your call in the morning." Kevin nodded to him, but they didn't shake hands. He started walking toward the door, and I followed him, knowing he had to be angry to ignore a social courtesy.

I felt a little raw too when we went back out into the cold, wet night. "Well, that was a surprise. Do you think he's lying about giving Joe a ticket after everyone else said he'd disappeared?"

"Dae?" Maggie tried to get into the conversation.

"Not now," I whispered.

"It's possible." Kevin opened the door for me then went around to the other side of the pickup. "It would be hard to prove—one way or another. Nothing was computerized back then like it is today. Those records may exist or they may not. It would be his word against what could be called mythology since no one knew what happened to Joe until now."

"Dae, please!"

"Maggie, tell me later!"

Kevin smiled at me. "Everything all right?"

"Ignore my discussions with myself, please."

"Okay."

I returned to our conversation. "No one except Joe's sister and parents, who said he never came home again after the race."

"You have proof Joe secretly married Rosie Carpenter before the last race. This speeding ticket could be the only proof that Joe didn't die that night."

"I guess this would be bad for Mad Dog if Chief Peabody has any kind of proof that Joe didn't die that night. The only real thing Mad Dog had going for him is people saying he was too banged up from the wreck to kill Joe."

"That's true. We still have some other badges to go through. Maybe someone else will have another take on it."

I groaned a little. "I wish I could hold their hands and

know if they did it. This can't go on much longer with Mad Dog. The election is closing in on us."

Everything seemed to be stacking up against Mad Dog. I wasn't sure if we were going to be able to keep him out of prison. I felt so certain that he hadn't killed Joe. I wished I could show everyone what I'd seen to convince them.

I was relieved to see the terrible ad on the water tower was gone as we passed it going back home. I was definitely going to propose a new ordinance that absolutely no advertising could be put up there. I was sure, after seeing my ads up there, the council would agree with me.

Kevin dropped me off at the house, and I went in to change clothes and get ready for the council meeting. Gramps was home, and we talked over a quick dinner, with Treasure begging for table scraps. I told him what Chief Peabody had said about the speeding ticket.

"He said he'll contact Chief Michaels or Sheriff Riley tomorrow morning."

"I hope that makes a difference. A few days don't really matter so much here. I don't want to think Mad Dog is guilty of this any more than you do, honey," Gramps said. "But you have to admit the evidence is overwhelming, whether Joe was killed the night Mad Dog was injured or a week later. Why else would he have Joe's car at his house?"

"Has anyone asked him?"

"I talked to Ronnie a little while ago. He questioned Mad Dog when he and Laura got home from jail. Mad Dog told him he didn't know about the car. He said the garage was empty the last time he was out there."

"Maybe he's telling the truth."

"Maybe—but how else would the car get out there, Dae? It might have been there since Joe died. I'm afraid it makes a terrible kind of sense."

I put on my raincoat and boots. I needed some time to

be alone and clear my thoughts. This was a good opportunity. "I'll see you later. Are you coming to the town council meeting?"

"I wouldn't miss it. I'm going to try putting the new plastic sides on the golf cart to keep the rain out. I can drive you down there if you want to wait a few minutes."

"No, thanks." I smiled as I edged toward the door. Gramps's driving was a little scary sometimes. "See you there."

My walk in the quiet rain between my house and the town hall wasn't nearly long enough to solve all the problems running through my mind or answer all the questions. But it lightened my heart and made me feel as though it would somehow all work out. I didn't understand how yet, but I held on to my faith.

The Duck Shoppes parking lot was full, a tribute to everything that had happened recently. People were bound to have a lot of questions, and Duck residents tended to be very vocal about their concerns. It was going to be an interesting council meeting.

# Chapter 23

As I'd thought, the council room was packed. Besides having bigger offices in the new town hall, there would also be a larger public meeting room. It was going to be a worthwhile project for the future of Duck.

Everyone in the meeting room was talking to their neighbors, expressing their concerns about Mad Dog, as well as traffic speeding down Duck Road and sand erosion.

At least ten people had signed up to speak during the public forum. Two of them wanted to talk about banning advertising on the water tower. Five wanted to talk about crime. The other three had random concerns about everything from the new boardwalk to taxes.

"Big crowd." La Donna took her place at the council table next to me. "I wish they would've all stayed home tonight. I really don't want to be here."

"I know what you mean." I took a good look at her. She had dark circles under her eyes and had forgotten to wear her lipstick. She seemed depressed and worried. "Is everything okay?"

La Donna was someone I'd always looked up to. I'd never seen her less than prepared and enthusiastic about a meeting.

"Is there anything I can do to help?"

She stopped biting her lip, but her hands still trembled. "I don't think so, Dae, but thanks for offering. I think I'm the only one who can handle this."

Chris Slayton, the town manager, came up to shake hands with all the council members. He seemed a little off too. I began to think maybe it was just me.

"I have a few resolutions you need to sign, Mayor." He put the documents in front of me and handed me a pen. "I thought you'd like to know that construction is back on track at the town hall. We're still looking at a July opening. I hope it will be before the parade."

"That's great, Chris. Thanks for telling me. I'm sorry for the delay."

"Not a problem, ma'am. Maybe next time you could use your finding powers to do this kind of thing *before* the construction begins."

"I'll try to get it set up that way." I wished it were that easy.

I waved to Gramps, who was standing in the back of the room with Chief Michaels. I was making sure my nameplate wasn't upside down, as happened sometimes, when a hush fell over the council room. I looked up in time to see Mad Dog standing in the doorway, leaning heavily on his cane.

He looked uncertain, as though he might turn around and walk back out. He finally squared his shoulders, puffed out his chest and strode into the room. He glared at each person he passed until he reached the council table.

Everyone was silent, watching him. I could tell he'd lost a little weight with everything he'd been through. His gray sport coat fit him a little looser.

Laura and Amos came in after him. They found seats at the back and kept their eyes glued on him. Once he'd reached his place at the table, talk in the room began again. It was plain from the conversations that many people felt as though he shouldn't be there. Loud whispers and rude remarks followed as he sat down.

The other council members shook hands with him. Chris did the same. There were no ordinances or any other kind of rule about a person accused of a crime sitting on the council. Mad Dog was within his rights to be there—at least until he was convicted.

The buzz in the room continued until I banged my gavel at seven P.M. and called the meeting to order. Kevin sneaked in through the door and managed to find a seat in the back. I nodded to Nancy, and she turned on the tape recorder.

"Welcome, everyone, to the Duck town council meeting," I said as I always did. "We have a full agenda tonight, so please keep your remarks brief when you stand to be heard during the public forum. And don't forget to give your name and address."

We all stood for the Pledge of Allegiance. We'd barely sat down again when August Grandin said from the audience, "What's *he* doing here? Are we going to allow criminals on the council now?"

I brought my gavel down again. "You're out of order, Mr. Grandin. You know we don't allow shouting from the audience during the meeting. Just to clarify for everyone, Councilman Wilson is still a member of this governing body. He may be accused of a crime, but town statutes say that he can keep his seat until he is convicted of that crime.

Everyone in this country is innocent until proven guilty, I think."

There were a few people who applauded but as many who booed. I tried to get the room back in order so we could continue with the town's business. People kept talking, but they were more subdued. I called Chris to present our first issue on the agenda.

"A businessman has submitted a proposal for a floating casino," Chris said. "You'll see the specifics in your packets. Mr. Hughes is here from Elizabeth City tonight to address the council regarding this matter."

Hughes nodded to the council as he got to his feet. He was a tall, smooth-looking black man in an expensive gray suit.

I knew that name. He was the publicist Dillon had hired to do the advertising work for my campaign. I glanced quickly at the proposal for the floating casino. I felt convinced Dillon was behind it, using Carlton Hughes as a front person so he wouldn't have to be out in the open.

Mr. Hughes was explaining all about the benefits of Duck allowing the casino to be berthed here. The casino, which would resemble an old Spanish galleon, would travel each day to the twelve-mile limit for passengers to gamble and then return.

"Why come to us with this?" La Donna asked. "It seems like one of the bigger towns would be better for this enterprise."

Mr. Hughes smiled suavely. "We like Duck and would like to help the town become more prosperous."

"Have you been turned down by the other towns?" I questioned him.

"No, Mayor. We started with Duck. We can go somewhere else, if you like. This would potentially mean millions of dollars in taxes for your town, not to mention more tourists coming for the casino."

The council read through their packets again then talked a little about the enterprise.

"I'd like to make a motion that we wait until the next meeting to get a better idea of what's going on with this," Mad Dog said. "I'm all for enterprise, but I'd like to understand what the downside to this is."

I was glad he made that motion, because it would give me a chance to contact Dillon and find out what was going on. Why hadn't he mentioned to me that he had this project in mind?

The other council members agreed unanimously with Mad Dog, and the motion to wait for more information was passed.

I hadn't even noticed Pam Walsh in the crowd until she suddenly shot to her feet. "Are you going to let this killer tell you all what to do?"

Councilman Dab Efird groaned and muttered, "Here we go again."

Pam searched the faces around her. "He killed my brother. I know I'm not from here, but that should still mean something."

"Please take your seat, Ms. Walsh." I brought the gavel down. "If you don't, we'll have to ask you to leave."

I glanced across the room at Chief Michaels, who nodded in understanding. We didn't have many times when it was necessary to have the chief or one of his officers at a town hall meeting. This was certainly one of them.

Pam glared at me but finally sat down again.

It was too late. Two more residents began yelling. Amos, Mad Dog's son, shot to his feet and started yelling back. Laura cried silently. It only took another moment before more people joined in.

The room was completely out of control. I'm ashamed to admit that nothing I said or did had any effect on the chaos. I gave up trying to bang my gavel and be heard above the racket.

Councilman Efird was arguing with Elmore Dickie. James Millford was shouting back at Councilman Rick Treyburn. La Donna stared at the mess in front of us. She looked like she was hypnotized by it, not looking away at all but focused on the scene.

Chief Michaels put in a call on his radio then began wading through the large group to get to the front of the room. I wasn't sure if he could handle everything by himself before people came to blows. I saw Gramps and Kevin move to help him by taking similar positions in other parts of the room, trying to get people to take their seats.

If it finally quieted down, I planned to call for a suspension of the meeting, tabling it for another time when, hopefully, things would be calmer.

La Donna stood slowly. Her hands were clenched into fists. She looked angry. I was hoping she wasn't preparing to jump out into the crowd too.

"Quiet!" She started saying the word too softly for anyone else to hear. Then she started yelling, "Quiet!" at the top of her lungs. She was screaming so loud that her voice was raw and her face was dark red.

"Sit down," I urged her with my arm around her back. "Let the chief take care of it. It'll be okay."

Clearly she was a woman who'd been pushed to the edge. I couldn't stop her from climbing up on the council table. The other council members were too busy yelling at their constituents to even notice. I looked for help, but everyone who could help was otherwise engaged trying to restore order.

She kept yelling at the top of her voice until I thought

she might have a stroke. I didn't know what to do to help her.

"None of you understand. I killed Joe Walsh! Do you hear me? I killed him."

I heard her, and attributed what she was saying to extreme stress. After a few moments, the people arguing in the audience heard her too. They calmed down to listen and stared at her.

Chief Michaels finally made it to her side. He pulled La Donna down and held her in his arms until she stopped screaming. The room got very quiet until only her sobbing voice could be heard from the floor in front of the council table.

"I did it. I killed Joe. I killed him."

It couldn't be true. I'd known La Donna all of my life. She couldn't kill anyone. She was hysterical and only said whatever she thought was going to close down the argument that was ruining the council meeting.

Chief Michaels scooped his nearly incoherent sister into his arms and strode out of the meeting room with her. No one got up or said anything after that, including Pam, who had a look of total bewilderment on her face.

I asked Councilman Efird to make a motion to continue the meeting at another time. Nancy asked for a date, and I glared at her. "We'll announce that later, thanks."

I knew she liked to have everything neat and tidy for her records, but I didn't think this was the time to worry about it. It was all I could do not to run out after the chief and La Donna to try and protect her from the things she'd said.

She didn't mean it. She was overwrought by all the anxiety. She couldn't kill anyone. We'd find out what she was talking about as soon as we could get out of the meeting room. It would all be explained.

I dismissed the meeting and headed for the door, feeling

like a porpoise leaping and diving over the slower-moving people in front of me. A few of those people tried to stop me and talk. My focus went past them, ignoring them, until I found myself outside in the parking lot.

I saw the chief get into his SUV, La Donna in the passenger side. The door closed, and the vehicle left, headed away from their homes.

I looked around to see if anyone else was going. All I had at hand was Gramps's golf cart. It was raining and people scurried to their cars and trucks. No one seemed intent on going with La Donna and the chief.

Kevin put his hand on my shoulder, and I jumped. "Are you okay?"

"No. Do you have your pickup here?"

"Sure, but—"

"Let's go."

We climbed in his pickup and Gramps pushed me in the middle as he got in behind me. "Ronnie said they're on their way to the hospital."

Kevin turned the key, stepped on the gas, and we were gone.

"What happened?" Kevin kept his eyes on the road. "Did she have a nervous breakdown? Why did she start yelling about killing Joe?"

"I don't know. Maybe she was trying to take the burden away from Mad Dog." I didn't know what to say. "She wasn't herself this evening. Maybe she's ill."

It was the only conversation we had between Duck and Kill Devil Hills when we reached the hospital. We jumped out and ran inside, hoping there would be some word on her condition. We met Chief Michaels in the emergency room.

"I don't know anything yet." He took off his hat and smoothed his black hair back from his anxious face. "She kept repeating it all the way here. I don't know what she's talking about. I know she didn't kill Joe. We all know La Donna could never do such a thing."

We huddled together in the waiting room on the god-awful orange and green plastic chairs. The nurse told us there was coffee on the sideboard. No one had any idea how long it was going to take to figure out what was wrong with La Donna.

"She's been real depressed about this thing with Mad Dog." Chief Michaels held an untouched cup of coffee I'd made for him. "Sometimes she takes things to heart, you know? I'm always teasing her about being such a softy."

"I'm sure she couldn't take that disruption at the meeting." Gramps was sympathetic. "That woman won't wash a spider down her bathtub drain. You know she didn't kill Joe, or anyone else."

I went back to get Gramps a cup of coffee too. Kevin came up behind me and stood there, shielding us from the two of them.

"You know I like La Donna, right?" he whispered. "And you know I like and respect Ronnie. Dae, this is the perfect storm. We've already been asking questions about Ronnie's badge. You know La Donna was one of Joe's groupies. The only question I'd need to ask in this scenario—if she killed Joe—who buried him?"

"That's crazy." I made sure the chief couldn't hear the conversation. "They didn't double-team Lightning Joe. That didn't happen."

"You were okay accusing the chief of losing his badge at the crime scene. You said you thought a woman was involved and a deputy threatened Joe before he died. Do you see a pattern here or are you too close to admit it?"

"Not now." What he'd said made too much sense to me. I was heartsick with it. "We'll have to talk later."

# Chapter 24

The doctor came out a short time later and told us they were admitting La Donna. "She's severely dehydrated and exhausted. Do you know if she's been eating the last few days? She's going to need a complete workup to help determine the problem."

Chief Michaels tried to answer his questions as best he could. He seemed so distracted that it was hard for him to concentrate.

La Donna's husband, Chad, had died a few years back. They had no children and she lived alone. Gramps asked if Ronnie should call their mother and let her know. He wasn't keen on that idea, at least not until they knew something definite. "No point in kicking that hornet's nest."

As they talked about their family, I thought about Marjory, Chief Michaels's wife, and gave her a call to let her know what was going on. She thanked me and said she'd be at the hospital as quickly as possible.

The doctor told Chief Michaels he could wait upstairs in

La Donna's room while she was admitted. He told us to go home and come back tomorrow during visiting hours. They might know something more about her breakdown in the morning.

We decided to leave. Gramps and Kevin shook Chief Michaels's hand, and Gramps clapped him on the shoulder. It was weird, but I hugged Chief Michaels (and he let me) and told him to call the minute he knew anything else about La Donna.

I wanted to do something more. "Marjory is on her way. Do you need anything done at home? What about La Donna's cat?"

"Thanks for thinking of that, Dae," Chief Michaels said. "Marjory will take care of that."

"All right. Have Marjory call if you need me."

I hugged him again for good measure and hoped some of it would rub off on La Donna. I wished I'd had a chance to say something to her. What good were my abilities when I couldn't tell that a dear old friend was about to fall apart?

It was probably the dehydration and not eating that had made her think she'd killed Joe. It had to be a shock to her when we found her teen idol in the car. Even more of a shock when she heard that Mad Dog was responsible.

She'd be in good shape again in no time. We'd all look back on this as something strange that happened. She'd come home, and everything would be fine.

Gramps, Kevin and I went out to the pickup and left the hospital in silence. I was thinking over everything that had happened that night. I knew Gramps probably was too.

I was worried about what Kevin was thinking after his remark in the hospital. I hoped he wouldn't bring up his theory about La Donna again on the way home. I clenched my hands nervously in my raincoat pockets, hoping for once that I'd think hard enough about something to prevent it from happening. It had never happened before, but it was worth a try. It would be great if Kevin and I had a stronger psychic bond. He'd had that bond with Ann when they were engaged.

I didn't want to know what Gramps's response would be to Kevin practically accusing La Donna and Chief Michaels of killing Joe. I didn't allow for a lawman's train of thought.

"Well, isn't anyone else going to say it?" Gramps asked.

"Say what?" I darted a murderous glance at Kevin that I wasn't sure he could see inside the darkened pickup.

"La Donna has confessed to killing Lightning Joe. I talked to Ronnie today about losing his badge. He didn't know what happened to it and refused to talk about where he was the night after Mad Dog's wreck."

"I thought the same thing, Horace." Kevin's voice was pained.

I nudged them both in the sides with my elbows. "This is no time to think of that. Gramps, you were so sure Chief Michaels couldn't do anything like this. What happened?"

"I told you that people are capable of doing crazy things when the need arises," he replied.

Kevin nodded. "Exactly."

"Just listen to the two of you," I complained. "I can't believe you're saying this. La Donna is overwrought, not to mention all those other things the doctor said. It's a coincidence that we were looking into Chief Michaels's badge."

"I don't like coincidences," Kevin said. "They usually end up having some strings that were left untied."

"He's right." Gramps was as pragmatic as Kevin. "Dae, don't think I like this any more than you do. You're the one who's so sure that Mad Dog isn't guilty. *Someone* killed Joe. You said it was someone with a woman in their life that they were trying to protect. La Donna was crazy about Joe. If she killed him and called Ronnie, what do you think he'd do?"

This would be a good place to fade away and let Maggie

rattle on about anything in her head. One problem—I couldn't feel her inside of me at all. "I don't want to think about this. Let's at least not pronounce sentence on them until we find out all the facts."

Gramps and Kevin both shrugged. I wished this had come from Tuck Riley. At least I'd be able to understand how he could be so calm and objective about it. Gramps and Kevin were infuriating.

Kevin stopped to let Gramps out to retrieve the golf cart at the Duck Shoppes parking lot. I stayed in the pickup. Not that it mattered. I was already soaking wet.

"There can always be mitigating circumstances." Kevin followed Gramps to the house. "If you called me to come and bury a body, do you think I'd pick up the phone and call the police?"

"I don't know. I understand what you're saying. I'd feel the same way about you. I can't take it all in right now. I refuse to believe La Donna was that much different forty years ago because she adored a race car driver."

Kevin pulled the pickup into the driveway, stopping fast when Mad Dog's face was picked out by the headlights. He was standing there in the rain with his hand on his cane, insolently glaring at Kevin, as though daring the pickup to hit him.

Gramps had pulled to the side abruptly and left the golf cart where he stopped. "What the hell are you doing out here? You could've been killed. This is why God created telephones, you idiot. If you wanted to know what was going on, you could've called."

Mad Dog didn't look at all sorry for scaring us to death. "Is it true? Did La Donna kill Joe? Is it over?"

"I'm not standing out here talking to you in the rain." Gramps started toward the house. "Come inside like a civilized person or go home."

Kevin and I exchanged glances as we got out of the pickup. "I didn't know Horace could talk like that."

"Use your imagination." I walked toward the house at a fast clip. "He was the county sheriff for twenty years."

"I guess you're right."

Gramps disappeared to change his wet clothes. I put on some coffee then excused myself to change when he came into the kitchen.

"I might have something you can put on, Kevin." Gramps still sounded a little cranky. "Nothing for you to wear, Randal, but you're welcome to a hot cup of coffee."

Gramps got the clothes out of the dryer for Kevin while I found the muffins he'd brought home from the firehouse bake sale yesterday. I found a towel for Mad Dog. It was the least I could do.

He sat down with his cane in front of him, his bad leg out to one side. Just thinking about the accident that had done that damage made me wince.

"You haven't answered my question yet, Horace." Mad Dog pushed his luck. "Is it over? Did La Donna kill Joe?"

Before anyone could speak, there was a knock on the front door. I went to answer and found Sheriff Tuck Riley on the step.

"Hello, Dae. Heard you all had some fireworks out here tonight. Is that coffee I smell?"

"Sure. Come inside." He was already walking past me and into the kitchen. It appeared as though it was going to be a late night.

Everyone sat around the table with mugs of coffee as they talked about what had happened to La Donna.

I didn't want to listen, but I wanted to know what they were thinking. I could imagine that news was already traveling through Duck about La Donna's confession. By morning, as many people who were sure that Mad Dog had killed Joe would believe that La Donna had done it.

I couldn't help but wonder if those same people would also tie Chief Michaels to the murder. Everyone knew how close he and La Donna were. It seemed horribly possible.

"Quit teasing, Horace! Was there anything what Mrs. Nelson said at the meeting or not?" Tuck got down to the real question between bites of blueberry muffin.

"I don't know," Gramps said. "She wasn't herself. How can we count anything she said as gospel?"

Tuck looked at Kevin. "You got any ideas, Brickman?"

Kevin shrugged. "I don't know La Donna well enough to say."

Tuck sat back in his chair, obviously frustrated by their answers. He glanced uneasily at Mad Dog. "I don't know why you're even here, Mr. Wilson. This doesn't change a thing for you yet."

"Maybe it has." Mad Dog stared at him defiantly. "Maybe La Donna killed Joe. And I *do* know her that well. What's that everyone's been saying about me? Maybe she just *lost* it."

"Let's say she did." Tuck warmed up to his theory. "How'd she get the car in the ground with the body in it? You"—he pointed at Mad Dog—"I can see you using a backhoe to do the deed. I don't see a young girl knowing how, or carrying it out."

Gramps swallowed hard and looked at Kevin.

"What's up?" Tuck intercepted that look. "What are you all thinking? Do you think someone helped her?"

Tuck Riley's good-old-boy act was mostly a ruse. He wasn't slow-witted. It only took him a moment to put it together—even without knowing about the badge I'd found.

"Of course." He brought his hand down dramatically on the table. "Ronnie! He's her brother. Who else would she call?"

"Her parents were alive." I wanted to muddy the water. "What about a cousin or uncle? And she was probably already seeing Chad. Maybe he came when she called and buried the body for her. I'm sure there are other possibilities too."

"What's your point?" Tuck asked. "Are you saying that Ronnie *didn't* do it? Do you have some word from the beyond that confirms your conclusion?"

"I'm saying that all of you are assuming that La Donna killed Joe then called her brother to take care of the problem. You don't have any proof besides her crazy confession."

"They have less than that on me, but that hasn't stopped them," Mad Dog complained.

Gramps gave me his "you've said enough" look. "First of all, no one is accusing anyone of anything. This is only speculation."

Mad Dog puffed out his chest. "They not only *accused* me on less, Horace, they put me in jail."

"I'm talking about La Donna here, Randal," Gramps said. "Something snapped in her tonight. We have to wait until we find out what happened."

"I don't have to wait." Tuck not-so-subtly reminded them that he was the sheriff. "As soon as she wakes up, I'm going to question her."

"That gives Mr. Wilson's attorney grounds to ask for a dismissal." Kevin pointed out the legal ramifications. "Either he's your suspect or not."

"Whose side are you on anyway, Brickman?" Mad Dog demanded.

"No, he's right." Tuck played with his coffee cup. "Mrs. Nelson will have to answer some questions after dozens of people heard her confession."

The matter seemed to be settled, and the group began to break up. Kevin offered to drive Mad Dog home. Tuck said he'd keep in touch, and Gramps did his best to stand in front of the giant sticky notes we'd forgotten were on the wall.

When everyone was gone, we locked the door and turned off the light outside. Gramps leaned against the door. He looked tired and not as animated as usual.

"It's a bad business when friends are in trouble with the law. I'm glad I'm not sheriff right now. Tuck can have this whole mess."

"I know what you mean. I wouldn't want to have to decide if La Donna or Mad Dog killed Joe. I'm sorry I caused all of this by digging up the car. Sometimes I don't find exactly what I'm looking for, or what I want."

Gramps laughed and hugged me. "Isn't that the truth? You remember that time when you were about eight and you insisted on digging for something in the backyard. You were sure it was pirate treasure."

"I remember."

"There wasn't any treasure there—just some old fish heads I'd buried the day before. It was a while before you dug up anything else."

I smiled. "I wish this was as easy to fix. Good night, Gramps. I hope another alternative to Lightning Joe's death comes up."

"I hope so too, honey. Joe didn't get in that car and bury himself. Whoever is responsible—their lives will be ruined after all these years they'd thought they got away with it."

I understood what he was saying about someone having to pay for the crime. Maybe it was selfish of me, but I hoped it wasn't someone I knew.

The next morning, word was all over town that Mad Dog might be innocent of Joe's death. Even the media had picked up on it and were at the hospital, waiting to hear whether or not La Donna's outburst had been a true confession.

The phone rang as I was leaving to go to Missing Pieces. It was Pam Walsh wanting to know if she could meet with me again. I invited her to the shop for tea.

I was fairly sure she wanted to talk about the possible new developments after her outburst had triggered the chaos that had ended the town council meeting. I found out I was right after she got to the shop.

Pam was tearful and contrite. "I'm sorry. I was so angry that people weren't doing anything. Mad Dog came home and settled right back in like it was nothing. My brother will never come home again."

"I'm sorry that you've had to live with that all these years. But trashing our council meeting and accusing the wrong person of killing your brother isn't right either."

"I know. I didn't realize that other woman was responsible. I don't even remember her—she looks like all the rest of them. Otherwise—"

"Otherwise?"

"I—I did something. Maybe it was wrong as I look back at it, but at the time it seemed right."

I waited for her to tell me what she'd done. She obviously wanted to.

"I wanted to make sure he was going to be put away for good."

"Mad Dog?"

"Yes." She nervously sipped her tea. "I had Joe's car. I've had it all this time."

# Chapter 25

"What?"

"We found it." The words came flooding out of her. "Me, Mom and Dad. We found it on Highway Twelve, a few miles from home."

"When did you find it?" I was thinking about what Chief Peabody had said about giving Joe a ticket, in his car, a week after he was supposed to be dead.

"It was the next day after the race where Mad Dog was hurt. Joe didn't come home that night. He always came home. That was one of my mother's strictest rules. Even if he was late, he always came home."

Was she telling the truth? "So you went to look for him."

"Yes. We found his car. The keys were still in it. There was no sign of Joe, then or . . . until you found him. My father drove number twenty-three home and finally put it in the old shed out back. As long as my parents were alive, they made sure it was taken care of—in case Joe came back. I took care of it after they died."

"Can you prove when you found the car?"

"I don't know." She thought about it. "Maybe."

"So *you* put the car in Mad Dog's garage?"

She started crying again. "Yes. I thought it was the best thing to do. I thought if they found Joe's car there, they'd convict Mad Dog of killing Joe."

"Why are you telling me this? You have to know the police could arrest you for creating false evidence." I wasn't sure if that was really a charge, but I thought in this case it probably should be.

"You know everyone. I've seen you on TV. I was hoping you could tell the police. I know I may have to go to jail, but I don't want that evidence to help convict the wrong person."

*Now she thinks about that.* "I'll be glad to go with you to turn yourself in to the sheriff, but I can't take care of all of it for you. Sometimes you have to admit your own mistakes."

"You're right, of course. I want to do that. If you could come with me, that would be great."

We devised a plan that I would go with her to her house and she could show me where Joe's car had been before she'd moved it. I could also take her car back home for her, in case she was arrested. She was more worried about her car, it seemed, than about what was going to happen to her.

I closed Missing Pieces and let Gramps and Kevin know what was going on. Kevin agreed to come and get me when it was over, if I needed him to. I didn't want to drive Pam's car back to Duck.

Pam chattered all the way to Manteo. It was odd, but it was as though her life had ended at the same time Joe had disappeared. The event, and what had happened since then, was all she could talk about. Maybe it was the impression her parents had left with her. It sounded like their whole lives had been dedicated to finding Joe. Pam didn't seem to have a personal life or relationships with other people, even as an adult.

When I could get a word in, I asked, "Did you know your brother was married to Rosie Carpenter?"

She almost swerved her little car off the road. The expression she turned to me was one of horror and indignation. "*No!* He wouldn't have done such a thing. My mom completely disapproved of her."

I took the marriage license out of my pocketbook. "They got married right here at the courthouse two days before he died."

She had to pull over to control her breathing, snatching the paper from me to stare at it with anger.

"This is ridiculous. It was probably some kind of stunt. Joe wouldn't have—he *couldn't* have. He wouldn't have hurt me and my parents this way."

"I'm sorry. He obviously loved Rosie and wanted to spend the rest of his life with her."

Pam screamed as she ripped the marriage license to shreds. She had to get out of the car and walk around in the abandoned parking lot where she'd stopped.

I got out with her, worried what she might do. Obviously, she was having a hard time realizing that there was more to her brother's life than her and their parents.

"How could he? She pounded on the hood of the car. "I can't believe he was going to leave us for that tramp."

"I thought you said you couldn't tell them apart."

"Oh, *her*. That's different." Pam laughed a little hysterically then paced the parking lot where grass was growing through the old concrete. "I remember *her*. Everybody knew her. Of everyone who followed him around, she was the worst. This was exactly what Mom and Dad were afraid of. She got her hooks into him but good."

"It's been over for a long time." I glanced at my watch. "We need to get to the sheriff's office and sort through this thing about Joe's car. Are you ready?"

"Doesn't it seem a little ironic that I might go to jail for trying to make the police put my brother's killer in jail when all the time he meant to leave us?"

I didn't know what to say. It seemed Pam had crossed a line that had taken her to another place. I wasn't sure if she could come back.

I offered to drive. She didn't care. She directed me to her house, and we got out to look in the garage where Joe's car had been. She wanted to make sure the house was locked up when she left too.

The home was an older split-level that she'd inherited from her parents. It appeared as though time had stopped here forty years ago. Most of the furniture was covered with old sheets. Cobwebs hung between lights in the ceiling and against the wall. There were still yellowed newspaper clippings from before Joe's death on the refrigerator.

The only room that looked used at all was Pam's bedroom. Even there, everything was dated from her childhood up to Joe's disappearance. The walls were filled with pictures of Joe, their family and friends. Many of them had faded until they were barely visible.

I sat in a chair by the door, waiting, while Pam bustled around the room trying to find the key for the garage. I was beginning to think we should go to the police first and let them deal with it.

"I wonder how long I'll be in jail." She looked dazed and confused. "What do you think?"

I wasn't sure she could handle that type of stress. I realized that they might have to find a spot for her at the hospital. Finding out about Joe's marriage seemed to have devastated her. No wonder, since she had no life without her memories of him. I really wanted to get her someplace where professionals could evaluate her.

"I took all of these pictures with my little Kodak camera my parents gave me for my birthday." She forgot about the key and pointed proudly to the wall. "I loved my brother so much. I guess he didn't really love me."

I didn't correct her. I stood at the wall and exclaimed over her photos. Even though it had been many years, it was easy to spot La Donna—a young, shapely La Donna—who wore a lot of bathing suits and short sundresses. She'd aged very well and still wore her hair in the same basic style. It was hard to imagine that Rosie Carpenter was more attractive.

I asked Pam which of the hundreds of girls was Rosie. She didn't say anything, just pointed her out. Once I knew what she looked like, I realized how many of the photos she was in with Joe.

"I know I should take my own toothbrush with me." Pam wandered into the bathroom. "I'll be done after this and we can go."

I moved closer to a group of pictures that showed Rosie clowning around with Joe. Her signature short-shorts weren't so bad by today's standards. I thought La Donna's dresses were much more provocative.

One thing teased me about Rosie. She looked vaguely familiar. Maybe not familiar as in someone I passed every day, but someone I'd seen before. It made me wonder if maybe she'd taken over her father's car dealership and was doing commercials that played late at night when Gramps was watching *Gilligan's Island*.

She'd be older, of course, like La Donna. It might be that Rosie had aged as well as La Donna and that's why I'd recognized her.

"I've seen both of them," Maggie whispered as I searched the photos. "Here, let me—"

"Okay. I'm ready." Pam stood at the door holding her toothbrush. "I wish I would've done more with my life. I would've if I'd known I might spend the rest of it in prison. I guess it's too late now."

"I know exactly what you mean, lady," Maggie commiserated with her. "My life was over before it began."

Pam's reddened eyes narrowed as she stared at me. "Who is that in there with you?"

"No one." I pushed Maggie back. "Let's go and get this over with. I don't think you'll spend the rest of your life in prison. What you did was wrong, but I think the sheriff will take everything into account. You'll have time to do some things with your life. You have to get past Joe."

She agreed and we got in the car together. Was Pam psychic? She'd reacted differently than most of the people who'd heard Maggie speak through me. Could she see spirits?

In less than ten minutes, we were at the sheriff's office, waiting to see Tuck Riley. I thought there was no point in talking to a deputy. This way, Pam would know something about her fate in less time.

Tuck strode in a few minutes later with his customary grin, holding his tie against his chest as he went around his desk and sat down. "Mayor O'Donnell. Always good to see you. I don't believe I've met your friend."

He reached across the desk to shake Pam's hand. "Sheriff Tuck Riley, ma'am. And you are?"

Pam held her hands out. "Guilty."

He glanced at me. "Everyone is guilty of something, ma'am. Let's start with your name and address, if you don't mind."

He wrote down Pam's information. "That's right. You're Lightning Joe's sister. I know your name. Exactly what crime have you committed, Miss Walsh?"

Pam told him what she'd done in a surprisingly calm tone. "I wouldn't be sorry except that now it looks like one of Joe's old girlfriends may have killed him instead of Mad Dog. My mother told him those girls would be the death of him."

Tuck grinned and looked at the information he'd written. "This is a serious offense, ma'am. Tampering with evidence is a big deal. I understand your anger and frustration. We can't work around the law, can we? It's all that keeps us from running wild in the streets."

"Yes, sir. I know." Pam hung her head.

"I'm sure you're contrite about this lapse. I do suggest you retain an attorney in case something comes up about it during the trial—whoever the defendant is. In the meantime, we'll keep your brother's car in the impound lot. It will be released to you after the trial is over."

Pam lifted her head. "Is that it? You aren't going to arrest me?"

Tuck grinned. "No, ma'am. I feel sure this won't happen again. We needed that car anyway. No harm, no foul."

I don't think she could quite believe it. I was surprised too. I was glad he'd taken everything into consideration—Pam wasn't a criminal. I hoped she'd be all right though.

"Thank you very much, Sheriff Riley." She jumped up and shook his hand. "I appreciate you going easy on me—especially since I didn't vote for you in the last election. I will in the next one."

Pam turned to head out the door, and I started to go with her.

"Mayor," Tuck called me back. "If I could have a few

more minutes of your time. I'll make sure you get home, if you need a ride."

"Sure." I turned back and Pam was gone. "What can I do for you?"

"It's what I can do for you." He grinned. "Sit down a minute, will you?"

I took my chair again as he walked around the desk and closed the door to his office. Whatever it was, he seemed to be more serious about it than usual. Surely he wasn't upset because I'd brought Pam there.

"I heard a disturbing rumor about some federal agents operating in my county without telling me they were here." He sat back down and stared at me. "Do you know anything about that?"

I cleared my throat and hoped I didn't look guilty. "I don't think so. I'm not sure I'd know a federal agent if I saw one. Maybe they're friends of Kevin's."

"It's rude for federal agents to invade a county without briefing the local law enforcement. Whatever they're doing here, it may be below board. A person would be foolish to get involved in a clandestine operation of that sort. You aren't involved in that sort of operation, are you, Mayor?"

Obviously he knew something about Agents Moore and Jablonski. He also knew I couldn't say anything without getting into more trouble. What was he up to?

His phone rang before I could think of a polite answer to his question. He took the call after excusing himself and spoke in low tones for a moment before he hung up.

"I'm sorry, but we'll have to have this conversation at another time. You might as well know that Mrs. Nelson has come to her senses and made a compete confession to Joe Walsh's death."

# Chapter 26

The Dare County deputy sheriff who drove me back to Duck was not a talkative person. Traffic was heavy for that late in the year, creeping almost bumper-to-bumper between Manteo and Duck. I couldn't see anything that would cause the backup, but the deputy answered his radio a few times. He obviously didn't want to share any information he'd received.

My worst fears had been realized with La Donna's new confession. I cautioned my overactive imagination to wait for the facts. As we'd been discussing the last few days, anyone could make a mistake.

Did this involve Chief Michaels? Had La Donna told Sheriff Riley how Joe had ended up buried in the car? I didn't want any of it to be true.

I realized that I hadn't even had a chance to tell Tuck about the two different stories involving Joe's race car. I guess it wouldn't matter anyway, if La Donna was confessing. Forty years was a long time to remember if Chief Peabody had given Lightning Joe a ticket the night after he'd been killed or a week later.

The same thing could be true for when Pam recalled her parents finding the car. She was only a child. Her life was suddenly very stressful. Her memory might not be clear either.

Traffic was still heavy when we reached Duck. Not wanting to go through one more silent moment with the deputy, I asked him to let me off at the boardwalk. I thought Nancy might have more information on what was going on. She usually did. Being the town clerk, she heard everything. She didn't always want to share, fearful that people would call her a gossip. Unless she knew something for fact, she rarely indulged in idle speculation.

Though she could be *persuaded*.

"Dae." She smiled when she saw me. "I'm glad to see you. I suppose you've heard that the DA has dropped all charges against Councilman Wilson. It's crazy. Now La Donna is saying she killed Joe Walsh. I thought she'd flipped out at the meeting from the stress last night, you know? I can't believe she could kill anyone, can you?"

I sat down at her desk. The office was empty. Chris was probably out supervising something. He was very hands-on, which was what made him such a good town manager.

"I was with Sheriff Riley when he got the call about La Donna." I explained about Pam having her brother's car towed to Mad Dog's house. "Something is still wrong."

"What's wrong?" Mad Dog's booming voice interrupted our conversation from the doorway.

I'd had Chris put WD-40 on the office door last week because it was squeaking. My mistake.

"Go on, ladies." He sat down near us. "What doesn't

seem right? That La Donna Nelson killed Joe Walsh instead of me? Why? I've never hurt another human being in my life. I thought you were on my side, Dae."

"I'm not against you, Mr. Wilson." I tried to be polite about it. "I know you didn't kill Joe. I trust the things I see more than any police report. That doesn't mean I can imagine La Donna killing him either. Can you?"

He looked away, studying his walking cane for a moment. "I'm not saying she did it—she's saying it. Not that I'd think of her as being a killer, but it always seems as though it's easier to imagine a man committing violence."

Nancy's expression was carefully guarded. She didn't want to lose her job.

I had no such issues. "I'm sorry. It made sense, looking at the facts. I'm glad you've been exonerated. Please don't expect me to like the idea that La Donna could go to jail."

"Bah." He got up and waved his cane around. "You're sorry I still have some time to campaign. I could still win this election."

Nancy and I watched him walk out the door before saying anything else. Nancy even made sure the door was closed all the way.

"I guess that's who he is." She shrugged as she sat back down at her desk. "What are you gonna do?"

"Beat him in this election anyway. It's what I was going to do to begin with. At least now, people will feel like it's fair and that I didn't find the car with Joe in it to ruin Mad Dog's life."

"You go, girl." Nancy grinned. "Oh, I forgot. A woman stopped in here to talk to you. I sent her down to Missing Pieces. I guess you weren't there either."

"That's okay. I'm headed that way now. Thanks."

"You're welcome, sweetie."

I couldn't stand it. I had to know. "Have you heard anything about Chief Michaels being part of this thing with La Donna?"

She stared back at me with her pretty brown eyes. "No. So far, everyone is saying she did it. I'll keep my ears open."

I hugged her. I hoped not to hear that news.

I walked down to Missing Pieces and found my big buyer of the Lucian Smith estate waiting patiently on a boardwalk bench outside my door.

I panicked for an instant—I hoped she didn't want her money back. I'd already given a large portion of it to Dillon.

Then I looked more closely at her. The years had been kind. Rosie Carpenter was still youthful. After Pam pointing her out in the old photos, I realized that's why I'd recognized her. Her name wasn't Carpenter anymore. That had been a long time ago.

She stood when she saw me. "Hello, Dae. I wanted to come back and clear up a few things. I meant to do it when I was here before and I got sidetracked. Could we go inside and talk?"

I opened the door and hung up my coat. Rosie, now Barbara Rose Carpenter-Walsh-Reece, took off her jacket and made herself comfortable on the burgundy brocade sofa.

"I came down here to see what was going on." She fiddled around with the cuffs on her pretty green sweater. "I was as much in the dark as anyone else. Unlike Joe's sister, I thought he'd abandoned me. After all, we were both very young and I didn't expect it to last."

"So you never looked for him?" I put some water on for tea.

She smiled sadly. "I've looked for him every day that we've been apart. I went on with my life when I realized he probably wasn't coming back for me. Not a day has passed that I haven't wondered if he'd pull up in that old black car and take me away. I love my husband now, Dae. But not like I loved Joe."

I made two cups of tea and sat beside her. "So you came down here when you heard I'd found him. In some ways, that must've been a relief."

"In some ways. At least I knew it wasn't his choice to leave me. I knew I could stop looking for him too."

"Do you have any idea what happened that night after the accident at the track?"

"Not exactly. Joe and I left the track together. He took me to my dad's trailer after we had dinner. He said he was coming up to Portsmouth the next day. He was going to talk to my father about us. He never got there."

"His sister said she and her parents found Joe's car on the side of the highway the next day. They took it home with them. You never heard from him again?"

"That's right."

"Do you know of any sheriff's deputy here that Joe had trouble with—especially one that might have been interested in you romantically?"

"Oh, honey, every deputy had trouble with Joe." She laughed. "He was a very bad boy. That's why all the girls loved him. As far as a deputy being interested in me, you might not be able to tell it now, but they all had crushes on me. There was one who actually asked me out—Deputy Rogers. He seemed so old. He was probably thirty. At that time, he was ancient to me."

"Did Deputy Rogers ever threaten Joe over you, that you know of?"

"Not as far as I know. Joe probably wouldn't have told me if he had. He never threatened Joe in front of me. Why are you asking all these questions? I understood that they arrested Donnie for killing Joe now. I would've put money on Mad Dog myself. I can't imagine Donnie killing anyone. She worshipped Joe."

"Donnie? You mean La Donna?"

"Sure. She's the one who started calling me Rosie. I called her Donnie."

I thought about it for a minute. "You two were friends, even though you were both in love with Joe?"

"We were. He was our Archie. We were his Betty and Veronica. We would've done anything for him."

I started to ask her what changed, what had made Joe choose her over La Donna? Then the door opened, and a tall, thin man with black curly hair came to find his mother.

"I need to get back, Mom," he said.

He was an exact copy of his father, only older with a few gray strands tucked into the black curls.

Rosie smiled and introduced her son, Joseph.

It seemed I had my answer.

# Chapter 27

"She bore him a son." Maggie kept repeating the words as though it astounded her. "He was trying to do right by her then. Not up and leaving her. You have to find the rotten sot who killed that baby's father!"

"That's what I'm trying to do."

Rosie's words gave me a lot to think about as I received packages from Stan and sold a few trinkets to some teenagers whose parents were visiting Duck.

"I wish I'd had Thomas's son." Maggie forced me to slow down so she could look at herself in the mirror. She smoothed her hand across her flat stomach. "I would'a made a good mother. Thomas would'a made a handsome lad."

La Donna's lawyer was all over the TV, joined by photos of her and Joe from the past, and a recent photo of her that looked like the one from the Duck Web site. She was still in the hospital.

Chief Michaels refused to answer questions as he walked

out of the building with their mother. Luke seemed to be in his element, explaining how La Donna's confession had brought real justice to the case. He also noted how difficult it was to take on a case where the murder had happened so long ago.

There was no mention of how Joe had come to be buried in his car. Luke didn't give anything away as far as other suspects that might have helped her.

Kevin walked into the shop as the news turned to weather, and I switched off the small TV. "I thought you hated the news. Or is it that you only like Duck news?"

"I need to get into the hospital to see La Donna."

"I don't think that's possible. I'm sure she's well guarded."

"Anyone can walk into the hospital." The scheme was forming in my mind. "All I have to do is get in there and sneak into her room."

"What would this accomplish?"

"By holding her hands, I might find out for sure if she killed Joe. He was lost to her. It's possible."

Kevin sat down. "Let's think about this for a minute. La Donna has confessed to killing Joe. She must think she did it. I don't know what else you could hope to see. I know you really like her and she's your friend—"

"It's not just that. I don't particularly like Mad Dog, and I wouldn't really call him a friend, but I tried to help him because he needed me. I have to see if I can help La Donna."

"You know, I heard they're having a rally for you at Duck Park this afternoon. The election is tomorrow, Dae. I know you want to be mayor again. Maybe you should concentrate on that today."

"Thanks for reminding me about the rally. I forgot. Cailey will kill me if I don't show up."

"Good. Then that's settled."

"I have plenty of time to go to the hospital, see La Donna, and come back for the rally. Or I will have if you volunteer to drive me to Kill Devil Hills. If I have to waste time trying to find someone going that way, it might take too long."

He got to his feet. "All right. I don't want Cailey to kill you. I'm ready when you are. You're lucky I brought the pickup instead of the cart."

I laughed and started to close down the cash register. "No, you're lucky. It's a long ride from Duck to Kill Devil Hills in a golf cart. Believe me. I've done it too often."

I still had two more browsing customers who came in before I could change the sign from open to closed. Mrs. Fitzsimmons, who'd recently moved from Florida to Duck, also came in to pick up her UPS package. She complained, as she always did, that she had to come out to get her package instead of receiving it at her home.

I explained, as I always did, that she and her sister didn't live off of a real road, more a sand track, so Stan couldn't deliver to her house.

"Well, it wouldn't have been that way back home," she fussed. "I think Duck needs to catch up with the rest of the world. My sister and I will bring that up at the next town council meeting."

She walked out with her package, banging the shop door closed behind her.

"She didn't even say thank you," Kevin said. "Maybe I should ask the town council to pass an ordinance about that."

I finally turned the open sign and ushered him out the door so I could lock it. "Okay. Just do it when I'm not there."

"I've never seen you miss a meeting."

"That's right. Let's go."

When we were in the pickup headed toward the hospital, Kevin asked if I was trying to prove to myself that La Donna was really guilty.

"I guess so. Or maybe there might be something that I could pick up on in her memories of what happened. Memories aren't always exact. I'd like to see for myself that she really killed Joe. I think that's the only way I'll ever believe it."

"You know you're asking to be disappointed. Sometimes bad things happen. You called it right with Mad Dog. Most of the list of suspects are people you look up to and care about. All of them can't be innocent."

"I guess we'll see."

I knew he was right, but it made me angry. I stared out the window and thought about La Donna and all the times she'd been there for me. I hoped to see something else when I held her hands.

"Can you think of anyone La Donna could be trying to protect by confessing?" Kevin asked.

"I think we both know the answer to that."

"Are you going to feel any better about this if you hold her hands and see Chief Michaels either killing Joe or helping her get away with it?"

"Will you please stop being so logical?" I requested, only half joking. "I wish I had a better plan. This is all I've got."

"Sorry. Sometimes you have to let go."

"Not yet."

"What was that about the gambling casino at the meeting before the fight broke out? Where did that come from?"

"It's the first I've heard of it." I was glad he'd changed the subject. "The man presenting the project works with Dillon."

"That's interesting. How likely is it that the council would pass that kind of project?"

"Not likely at all. Duck was incorporated to fight off that kind of development."

"Has Guthrie contacted you about it? He might want your help trying to pass it."

I didn't want to get into a conversation with him about Dillon. There was too much about him that I didn't want Kevin to know.

"I'm only trying to do what the ATF wants me to."

Kevin pulled the pickup into the hospital parking lot. He shut off the engine and started to get out.

"You don't have to come in with me. I'll be fine. If you have something else to do, I could call you when I'm ready to go."

He opened the door. "The only thing I need to do here is make sure I don't have to bail you out of jail. I'm coming in too."

His phone rang, and I waited impatiently for him to answer. I could tell it wasn't good news. "I guess you get your wish. A pipe broke and water is flooding the first floor. I have to go back to Duck. Call me when you're ready anyway and I'll come and get you."

I kissed him quickly, knowing I wouldn't call. He'd barely be getting back to the Blue Whale before I'd need to leave. I'd find a ride back.

There were reporters in the hospital lobby, waiting for any developments in the case. I wondered what it was that made them so interested in this particular instance. We had things going on all the time in Duck. None of them caught the press's fancy like this one. Maybe it was the whole bizarre nature of it. I wished it could be better publicity, but as I'd found with Missing Pieces, even bad publicity was better than none.

Sheriff Riley got off the elevator, and the press moved in to question him. I noticed Chief Michaels coming from the stairway and considered that this might be the best way to get into La Donna's hospital room.

I grabbed his sleeve as he started to walk by me. His face was a mask of exhaustion and fear when he turned back.

"Mayor O'Donnell. What are you doing here? Is there something I can do for you?"

"I know you don't believe that the things I see are real, at least not all the time." I rushed into my speech before he could walk away. "I want to see La Donna. I want to hold her hands and see what she's talking about. I know you can't believe she killed Joe."

He rubbed his hand across his face. "No, I don't believe she killed anyone. The important thing is that she believes it. Even if you could look into her thoughts, I'm afraid that might be all you'd see."

I stared hard into his brown eyes. "You didn't kill him, did you? She isn't covering up for you."

I thought he might be offended. He barely seemed to notice the accusation.

"No. I didn't kill him—but if I'd known she was going to do this, I would've confessed to the whole thing. I'd do anything to keep her out of prison."

"Then let me see her, Chief. What can it hurt? If I see her killing Joe, we're no worse off than we are right now."

He put his hand on my shoulder, and I jumped.

"Okay. What do you need?"

I rode up the elevator with the chief and a group of deputy sheriffs. It almost seemed too easy. I thought convincing the chief would be much harder. I hoped he didn't have his expectations set too high.

The deputies looked at me like I didn't belong there

when we all got out on the same floor. It was like a prison environment already with at least five deputies standing outside La Donna's hospital room door. The chief explained to the captain that I was the mayor of Duck and had demanded to see my constituent.

I wasn't sure if Sheriff Riley would have gone along with it if he'd been there, but the captain agreed, and the chief and I went into the room.

They left us alone with La Donna. She was sitting up in bed beside a window. She was actually pretty in her green hospital gown. Her thick brown gray hair was pulled back from her face with a black headband. She looked sad and pale.

Chief Michaels took one of her hands as he approached the bed. She smiled at him and turned to me.

"I'm so glad to see you, Dae. It's lonely here—when people aren't asking me questions."

"Who was here asking you questions this time?" Chief Michaels was still trying to protect her, even though it was beyond him now.

"Don't worry. It's the same old questions from the DA. I guess you have to expect as much when you've confessed to a crime."

"There's no point in them badgering you about it," he growled.

"I'm fine." She touched his worried face. "Really."

I hated to be the one who needed to ask her more questions, but that's why I was there. "We were so worried about you after the meeting. Are you okay now? What happened?"

She closed her eyes for a moment. When she opened them, she was trembling. "It's been hard keeping this secret for so many years. I went on with my life, acting like everything was fine, when I knew it wasn't. When I heard Joe's sister accuse Mad Dog again, and they started arguing, I couldn't do it anymore. All the strain from telling myself it should be me in Mad Dog's place spilled out. What kind of person am I who could let him go to jail for my crime?"

Chief Michaels smoothed his hand down her hair. "You were scared, that's all. Anyone would be. I've seen grown men cry when they realized they were caught."

"I was terrified," she admitted. "I think I managed to convince myself that it never happened. Joe was gone. No one knew what had happened to him. Everybody guessed that he'd left town, since Mad Dog couldn't race anymore. I thought many times that it didn't really happen at all—until you found him, Dae."

That made me feel incredibly guilty. It seemed finding Joe had brought such heartache to so many people. It was wrong for him to be down there, under the sand, all those years with no one knowing what had happened to him. Still, I was sorry I'd been involved.

"I know everyone keeps asking, La Donna, but could I *see* what happened to Joe? He was lost to you. You know I find lost things. If you think of him that way, it might work."

"What good would that do? I know what I did. I didn't want to admit it, but I *know*."

"La Donna." I took her hands in mine. "How did Joe get in Mad Dog's car? How did you bury him?"

"Dae—" Chief Michaels started to warn me.

"It's not like she's the first person to ask, Ronnie. I've answered this question a dozen times already."

He nodded, grudgingly, his usually square shoulders drooping.

"I've thought a lot about it." Her eyes unfocused as she held my hands tight. "I think I blacked out. I found out that Joe had married Rosie and that they were going away together. I was so angry, so hurt. I wanted to hurt him the way he'd hurt me. After I did—after I hurt him—I guess I couldn't cope with it. I forgot the rest. The doctor I've talked to here at the hospital said it isn't unusual."

"I can't tell you how many people come to me thinking they know the whole story of how they lost something. When I look at it, there's more. I might be able to help you fill in the gaps that you can't remember."

She stared at me for a long moment. "All right. I've looked at the rest of this ugly time in my life. I suppose I might as well let you look too."

"Think back to what you lost that day. Think about Joe."

I closed my eyes. Sometimes it takes a few minutes to make a connection. This time was almost immediate. I had that strange feeling of slow motion and cold that shivered through me. La Donna's thoughts of when she lost the man she loved took us right to the spot.

*"I'm sorry, Donnie, really," Joe said. "It just wasn't meant to be, you know? I'm married to Rosie now. We're going to have a great life together. You have to move on. Find someone of your own. You're beautiful. It should be easy."*

*Joe Walsh's wildly handsome young face was earnest as he pleaded with her. La Donna was the gorgeous young woman she'd been in the photos on Pam's bedroom wall.*

*"You said you loved me," La Donna cried. "How could you marry her? How could you choose her over me? Don't you love me anymore?"*

*Joe flashed a wicked smile then turned back to look at Mad Dog's smashed car. It was up on a flatbed truck. "I'm sorry, Donnie. What can I say? I do love you, just not like I love Rosie. Can you believe what a wreck this is? I wish I was going to race again so I could see his face."*

*La Donna was standing behind him, sobbing so hard*

*she was having a hard time catching her breath. Her gaze fell on an old tire iron that was brown with rust. Her thoughts were random as she picked it up. She wanted to hurt him. There seemed to be no other way.*

*While Joe kept going on about the car and his opponent who'd been injured, La Donna swung the tire iron up toward him. It was almost too heavy for her. There was no real strength in the blow that brushed his shoulder.*

*"Hey! Are you crazy or what? Put that down, Donnie, before you get hurt."*

*"You deserve to be hurt." She tried again. The second blow was no better than the first. But it got his full attention.*

*Joe struggled with her, trying to take the tire iron away. He bent over as though he meant to pick her up or knock her off her feet. She lifted the tire iron again at the same time. It came down on the back of his head, and he dropped to his knees.*

*There was blood everywhere—on his hair, the ground, the tire iron in her hands. La Donna screamed and dropped her weapon. As she turned to run, the last image she saw of Joe was him crawling toward his black number twenty-three car.*

The connection between La Donna and me was severed as she screamed and put her hands against her chest. "He was still alive! Oh my God! I didn't kill him! Now I remember."

# Chapter 28

Two of the deputies ran into the room and looked around, their hands on their weapons. Chief Michaels explained that everything was okay. They cautiously left us alone again.

"I didn't kill him there, did I, Dae?" La Donna was excited. "You were there. You saw it. He was still moving."

"You're right. You hurt him but he was still alive. You ran away when you saw the blood."

Chief Michaels hugged his sister. I reminded myself that Kevin had been right. La Donna had been pushed to a place where she could hurt another person. Maybe not kill him, but at least injure him. People *were* capable of anything.

"I don't want to spoil the moment," Chief Michaels said. "This is all well and good, but I only deal in facts, and so do those deputies out there. It may make you feel better, honey, but we can't prove any of this. And now that you've confessed—"

La Donna wiped away her tears. "I remember now. I left Joe there and caught a ride home. I cried myself to sleep that night after I'd scrubbed the blood off my hands. Someone must have seen Joe after it happened. He might have gone to the hospital. If anyone knows, it would be Rosie. They were supposed to leave together. Joe was going to work for her father in Virginia. There has to be some way to prove it."

"Rosie doesn't know. She never saw Joe again."

"You know her, Dae?" La Donna asked in surprise.

I explained our meeting. "She came back to Duck today. She wanted to talk about Joe. There was a reason Joe chose her over you. She was pregnant with his son. His name is Joseph. He looks like an older version of his father."

La Donna started crying again. "Oh my God, I can't believe it. They had a son together. Joe never saw him."

"Which puts us right back where we were," Chief Michaels interrupted with his staid pragmatism. "Who else might have seen Joe after you assaulted him?"

"I'm not sure, Ronnie. You know there were a lot of people at the track all the time. Mad Dog's car was close by. Anyone could have seen him there."

"Who gave you a ride home?" I wondered.

"One of the deputies. I don't really remember which one. I was upset and desperate at the time. I don't know. He helped me get cleaned up and told me it would be all right."

"I'll check with the hospital to see if Joe came in and was treated for a head wound." Chief Michaels came up with a plan. "If Joe went to the hospital, it could've been overlooked with all the other ruckus. His injury must not have been too bad. The ME didn't report a fractured skull or any other serious head injury."

"At the time, I really thought I'd killed him," La Donna

said. "Now I know, looking back on it, head wounds always bleed a lot, even when they aren't serious. I've been such a fool all these years not telling anyone."

"Not that it would've meant anything until Dae found the body." Chief Michaels said the words with pride and in an unusually pleasant tone. "Thank you, Dae. I hope we can find justice for Joe's killer."

"You're welcome, I guess." I smiled a little self-consciously. "I kind of feel like I stirred the pot a little more, not really much help. I hope it can calm down now."

La Donna laughed. "You've saved me from a lifetime of guilt, my young friend. No matter what happens next, I'll always be grateful to you for that."

"And you're sure you can't remember who drove you home?"

"Dae has been exploring all the deputies who could have been there that night." Chief Michaels frowned. "Including me and her grandfather. She's very thorough. I can tell you she doesn't play favorites. When Horace told me she all but accused him of killing Joe, I almost busted out of my britches laughing."

"I found a badge," I told La Donna. "It was at the crime scene. There were ten possibilities for the person who wore it. Now you're saying a deputy gave you a ride home that day. It seems to fit."

She searched her memory again. "I'm sorry. It's not there. Maybe it will come to me later."

"You should probably rest now." Chief Michaels kissed her forehead. "Let me see what else I can find out. I'll keep you posted."

"All right. I'm glad you could be here. It's nice to have a know-it-all for a brother once in a while."

Marjory came into the room as we were going out. She

grabbed my arm. "Be sure you're at Duck Park for the rally later. It will look bad not to have our candidate there."

"Don't worry. I'll be there."

Chief Michaels headed toward the hospital records room. He asked me if I needed a ride home. I didn't want to bother him, so I told him I could find my own. Someone that I knew was bound to be around. Last resort, I could call Kevin to come and get me.

I was in the lobby, waiting to see if there was anyone I knew, thinking about what had happened to Joe.

It seemed to me that it would be easy for a person who loved La Donna to see that she was in trouble after her attack on Joe. That person might even have seen that Joe was injured and taken advantage of the situation after he'd dropped La Donna at her home.

Seeing the number twelve car on the flatbed made even more sense—that's why Joe wasn't buried in his own car. It had nothing to do with whose car it was—it was a matter of expediency.

Whoever buried him wasn't worried about him being found either. That's why Joe's car was left out by the road. People could look all they wanted to and never find him— at least not for forty years.

I looked at the short version of the list of possible lost badge holders. I crossed off Gramps and Chief Michaels. Wally Newcastle probably had an alibi. Blackie Rogers and Marvin Taylor were dead, although I couldn't quite cross them off altogether.

That left four badge holders either unaccounted for, or unquestioned. And, of course, Chief Peabody, who'd said he'd given Joe a speeding ticket a week after everyone else had theorized that Joe was dead.

I looked across the crowded room and saw Chief Peabody

talking and laughing with some sheriff's deputies. I wondered if he might be headed home. He could drop me off on his way, and I could question him a little more about that speeding ticket.

"Don't go!" Maggie started talking.

I turned to face a large plastic plant that hadn't been dusted recently. "I need a ride home."

"I know, Dae. I'm begging you not to go with *him*."

I tried to see Chief Peabody again without looking like I was trying to see him. "Why?"

"I believe he killed the lad's father. Think on it."

"I have. You know I've thought of almost nothing else for days."

"Which is why I'm still trapped here instead of in the gentle earth with my Thomas."

"I'm doing the best I can." I considered her request. "Why do you think Peabody did it?"

"I seen it in his eyes when you talked to him the last time. He is the one who done it!"

"Why didn't you say so then?"

"I tried. You told me to hush!"

"Just a minute." I dialed Chief Michaels's cell phone. When he answered, I asked him if he'd heard from Chief Peabody about the night he claimed to have ticketed Lightning Joe.

"I haven't heard anything like that, Dae. Are you sure? It wouldn't be like him not to tell me something that important to a case."

I mumbled something about misunderstanding and hung up. "Great."

"You'll find another way home? Please do." Maggie quietly urged me to change course.

"That's not what we do when something like this happens," I explained.

"What do we do then?"

"We find a way to prove it."

"Oh no!"


"Chief Peabody." I approached him with a smile. "I was wondering if you might drop me off in Duck, if you're headed that way."

He didn't look very pleased with the idea. "I have to make a few stops. It might be better if you find someone else. I don't want you to be late for something on my account."

I put on my big mayor's smile and reminded myself that he could be the killer. This could be the big break I'd been looking for. "Please, Chief. I have an election rally and I don't see anyone else I know. I don't mind waiting for you to run your errands."

The other deputies were badgering him about taking me. He finally had to give in or look bad. He decided he could stand being with me more than losing face with his law enforcement buddies.

"Okay. I'm ready to go now. I hope you are too." He turned and walked outside.

I followed quickly and got in the squad car right away before he had a chance to change his mind. "Thanks so much."

What was I going to say to him? How could I get him to confess?

He responded by making a grunting sound and starting the car. I wondered what kind of errands he had to run. I could still end up missing the rally if he took too long. Of course the same thing could've happened if I'd waited at the hospital too long.

I tried to engage him in conversation. His replies weren't

helpful. He kept his eyes on the road and never even sneered at me.

Of course I had other ideas. "You know, I was talking to La Donna Nelson. I think she may finally remember the night Joe Walsh was killed."

We stopped at a red light. "What do you mean? I thought she'd confessed to killing him? How can she not remember?"

I knew I had him hooked. There's nothing lawmen liked to talk about more than a good murder case. "It seems she remembered attacking Joe with a tire iron. She thought she'd killed him because she couldn't remember what happened after that."

"That's probably because she didn't want to think about it."

"You're probably right." I was on a roll. "But someone had to drive the rollback with Mad Dog's car on it to Duck then bury the car so it wouldn't be found. I can't imagine La Donna knowing how to do that, can you?"

"I don't know. Women do crazy things."

"She was only a kid." I smiled at him. "I have another theory."

"I'm a captive audience."

"I think I found that old badge I showed you because one of the ten deputies around at that time knew La Donna had hurt Joe. He picked her up, took her home, then went back and killed Joe. He didn't know he'd lost his badge. Not that it mattered because all of you on the list had put in for new badges. There are two things that really stand out for me."

"And what are those, Sherlock?"

"The first one is that everyone knew Blackie Rogers was interested in Rosie Carpenter. He even asked her out."

"Blackie was interested in anything that wore skirts. What else?"

"You said you gave Joe a speeding ticket after he disappeared. Almost everyone thought he died that night after

Mad Dog's wreck. Your speeding ticket, a week later, changes the timeline."

"Not really." He was starting to turn into a narrow drive that probably led to a house farther back beyond the thick bushes at the road. "There's no way the ME can call time of death with any real accuracy from bones after forty years. A few days wouldn't make much difference."

"I suppose that's true. Where are we going?"

"I told you I had a few errands to run. One of my officers lives up here. He's been out sick. I thought it might be good to pay him a visit and see how he's doing."

I was surprised. I never guessed that Chief Peabody would be sympathetic to something like that.

"Leave him alone," Maggie murmured.

"What did you say?" he asked.

"Nothing. Just muttering about finding Joe's killer."

"I don't know why Ronnie puts up with you getting into his cases. I wouldn't."

We'd reached the house, which was in bad condition. It didn't even look like anyone had ever lived there. There was no car in the drive, and the whole place was overgrown with vines and grass.

"I think you and me need to have a little talk, Dae." He got out of the car and came around to my side.

"It's okay, Chief Peabody. It was probably an accident. You didn't mean to kill Lightning Joe, did you?"

He frowned and shook his head. "All these years, I thought I was safe. Why'd you have to find that, of all things? Why couldn't you mind your own business for once?"

"I'm sorry. I didn't go out looking for this. The whole thing was a mistake. I was looking for something else."

He stared vacantly off into the distance. "You know, I loved La Donna. I wanted her to marry me. She only had eyes for Lightning Joe, just like all the other girls."

"You dropped her off and went back for him."

"I sure did." He wiped his hand across his mouth. "He was a brash, skirt-chasing— You know the type. He would've never made her happy. I finished the job she started. I realized that she finally saw him for who he was. I thought maybe, when he was gone, she'd turn to me, like she did that night. But no, she met Chad. That was it."

I still hadn't gotten out of the car. I hadn't even unfastened my seat belt. It would have to be harder for him to get me out of it and drag me into the house and shoot me, right? I was pretty sure that was on the agenda.

"So you loved her, but you let her suffer all these years, believing that she had killed Joe." Gramps had told me long ago that the best thing to do in this type of circumstance was to keep your captor talking and look for an opening to escape.

"How was I supposed to know she thought she'd killed the boy wonder? He was clearly still alive when I got back. He was a little woozy though. It was easy to put him in Mad Dog's car and drive the rollback to Duck. They were doing work on the beach where the park went in later. As soon as I saw the backhoe, I knew what I needed to do."

"I'm sorry, Chief."

He drew a deep, ragged breath and looked at me. "I've known you all your life, Dae. I have great respect for Horace."

*I knew where that was leading.* "Don't go out this way."

"I can't take the blame for this. What would my wife say? People would hate me, like they did Mad Dog."

*Stay calm. Take deep breaths.* My heart was still pounding.

"I don't want to hurt you. I wish it could have been someone else that found out."

# Chapter 29

I knew I couldn't fight off Chief Peabody. I didn't have a weapon. He was much stronger than me. For all the talk of holding a key between your fingers and going for the eyes, I didn't have a key, or even a can of hairspray that I could set on fire with my Zippo. All of these were ideas from a self-defense course I once took.

I wasn't even wearing heels that I could use against him.

I imagined my headstone would say something like, *Here Lies Dae O'Donnell. She asked too many questions and one of the answers killed her.*

I thought about Maggie. She was screaming inside of me. We both knew if I died, she'd die along with me. Her bones would never get their proper burial. And all of my treasures at Missing Pieces would be auctioned off. Gramps would take care of Treasure, but I wouldn't be there. And Kevin . . .

All of these things went through my head as I looked at

him. I saw his hand on the gun that he carried. I knew he was thinking the same thing.

Yet, deep inside, I believed Walt Peabody was a decent man, despite having once killed Lightning Joe. That was in a fit of jealous rage. For forty years, he'd upheld the law. He didn't want to kill me.

"We should go. Gramps will be expecting me." It was mundane, but it was all I could think of.

"I know." He shook his head, his eyes tearing. "I know I've been harsh with you, Dae. It's been for your own good. I know you've done fine things for Duck."

This was getting closer to a farewell speech. I didn't want to know how it ended.

"Please let me go. You're a good man. Do the right thing."

"I can't." He sniffled and drew his gun. "I just can't."

I could feel something welling up within me. I didn't know what it was. It felt like a storm, strong and powerful. It swelled and burst with a ferocity I didn't know could come from a person.

It didn't come from a living person, I realized. Maggie wasn't willing to see what came of this moment either.

"I've had enough!" Maggie burst forward like a beacon of light on a cloudy day. "You shall not take this woman's life! Look at me, human man. Face me, if you can!"

Her spirit grew, larger than me, swirling and growing dark like a thundercloud. There were jagged edges and bursts of lightning. Her face was terrible, transformed from the face I saw in the mirror to something from a horror movie. She reached out for Chief Peabody with clawlike hands.

Chief Peabody screamed and threw down his gun. "No! Stop! Get away from me!"

"Think you can save yourself?" Maggie growled. "There is no escape from my wrath!"

The strange voice was convincing. It sounded like it came from a deep empty space, echoing across the yard.

"No!" He ran to the abandoned house and locked the door. He yelled for me to stay away from him.

Maggie changed back to her normal self and dusted her hands. "That should take care of him. He didn't scare me."

I shivered as I picked up my cell phone. "Maybe not, but you scared me! Let's not do that again."

Later Chief Peabody said that it was like a cursed spirit had risen from the grave, a hideous sight that he thought I'd conjured up from my gift. It was the truth. I'll never forget it.

I called Chief Michaels, who was there with Sheriff Riley in record time. I told him what I knew, what Chief Peabody had confessed to.

"We already figured that much," Tuck Riley drawled.

"I checked into what you said about Walt giving Joe a ticket a week later," Chief Michaels told me. "When I spoke with Ms. Walsh, she had the tow truck receipt to prove when her parents found Joe's car. When I called Walt's home, I found out he'd already confessed once—to his wife, Patsy. It didn't take much to hear it all from her."

I glanced at my watch. My hands were still shaking. "I have to go to Duck Park for the rally. I'll never hear the end of it from Marjory and Cailey if I don't show up."

"I'll have Tim take you." Chief Michaels signaled to the car behind his. "You okay?"

"I will be. Thanks, Chief."

He started to say something then shrugged. "No point in me telling you not to let this happen again. It's like shouting into the storm."

"I can say it." Tuck hitched up his pants. "Quit meddling! You're gonna get yourself killed!"

Tim talked about Trudy and their marriage plans the rest of the way back to Duck. I didn't say much, just trying to take the whole thing in. People changed with time, I realized, thinking about what I'd seen La Donna do and what Chief Peabody had done. I wondered how I would change in the next forty years.

I didn't have to worry about no one showing up for the rally. There were at least a hundred people with signs and banners at the park. Most of them had my name on them—a few said vote for Wilson. When they saw me, almost everyone started cheering and applauding. It looked like not all of Duck hated me for finding Mad Dog's car after all.

I said a few words, which were greeted by more applause. Marjory, Cailey, Mrs. Euly Stanley and Shayla stood around me like guardian angels, beaming on my presence.

I saw Kevin in the crowd and smiled at him. I could tell by the look on his face that he knew something about what had happened and had plenty of questions. Gramps pulled up in his golf cart a few minutes later while members of the Duck High School band serenaded us.

I really felt that it might be possible to win the election after all. It was a warm feeling in my chest that made me proud to have been the mayor of Duck for the last two years.

The band got quiet, and the applause died down. Marjory introduced me again to speak. But before I could say a word, Mad Dog had pushed himself between me and the makeshift podium.

"I'd like to take a minute to say thank you to Mayor O'Donnell for her hard work in keeping Duck growing and thriving. But there's always room for progress. I hope you'll vote for me tomorrow when you head to the polls. I'll make you proud as your mayor, and together, we'll sail into the next century."

I was up early the next morning, wrapped in a shawl and looking out from the widow's walk on top of my house. It was early—the polls weren't open yet. The sky looked clear and blue even though the temperature was cold.

I'd know by that night if I was elected as the new mayor. The crowd yesterday seemed to think I should be. They booed Mad Dog away from the microphone, and a large group of us went to the Blue Whale for dinner afterward.

It was so quiet on the roof. A few cold seagulls dipped through the sky around me. If they had known what a storm was coming later that day, they would have raced away.

After I went to the polls, I was supposed to go to Chief Michaels's office right away to give my statement about Chief Peabody. Then there would be a dozen small parties, which was traditional. Some of them Mad Dog and I would attend together. For most of them, we'd be apart.

Treasure meowed and looked out of the shawl where he'd been hiding from the cold. It was going to be a crazy day but also a good one.

La Donna had called to say that she was coming home. She wasn't sure yet if Luke Helms was going to press charges against her for that long-ago fight with her boy friend. Even if he did, she'd get through it. She was that kind of woman.

Maybe best of all, the Duck Historical Society had come through for me. Barney had called to let me know that they'd found the grave of Thomas Graham. The tiny cemetery was located behind James Millford's old shed where three generations of his family had made illegal moonshine.

"Dae?" Gramps called from inside the house. "Get down here. You have to vote. This isn't the time to be standing up on the roof, daydreaming. Pancakes are almost ready. Get dressed."


Hours later, I was finally finished with the polls and my statement to the police. I tried not to wonder how many of the people at Duck Elementary School were voting for me.

We'd found the tiny cemetery. Most of the headstones were falling apart, but enough information could be seen to declare it a historical site.

I'd buried almost all of Maggie Madison's earthly possessions along with her bones in an earthen wine jug that Kevin had found for me. I kept some of them that weren't personal. A few I planned to sell. The rest I donated to the museum.

Barney and Mrs. Euly Stanley had walked with me and Kevin to the old cemetery. Mr. Millford wasn't interested. He waved us on from the kitchen window when he saw us on his property.

"There was a little chapel out here, according to records we found from the 1700s," Barney said. "Several members of the Madison family were buried here. But so was your sea captain."

"I have my doubts that Thomas Graham wasn't just another scallywag pirate." Mrs. Euly Stanley took pictures with her new camera. "Nice trees, anyway. What is that you're burying, Dae? I think we should include it in our cemetery log."

Maggie, who was reluctant to go now that we were here, came to the front. "It is but a little-known woman who loved well and died unfortunately. I have enjoyed being here. I never thought to feel the kiss of the sun again or a man's arms about me. Farewell to you all."

I shuddered as she left me. I'd hoped to see some misty-colored light as she went to be at peace with her lover. There was nothing.

Nothing except the stunned faces of my companions.

"My, you are going to be excellent in that play." Mrs. Euly Stanley patted me on the back.

"Thanks." I started filling in the hole where the clay urn would rest, hopefully for another four hundred years at least. Barney helped me too.

I felt a little empty when Maggie was gone. It had certainly been an experience having her inside me.

I said good-bye to Mrs. Euly Stanley and Barney at the road, and we went separate ways. Kevin had to go back to the Blue Whale to get ready for the party later. He dropped me off at Missing Pieces, more to calm down than anything else. I planned to have a quiet, solo cup of tea before the next election party. I knew it was unlikely there would be any customers that day. That was okay.

The Currituck Sound was a smooth, glossy surface leading to the horizon as I walked down the boardwalk. All the shops were closed. There was one woman standing at the railing in front of Missing Pieces. She was looking out over the water, as I had been. She wore a dark purple suit with an amazing hat that matched it.

She turned to me as I came closer. "Hello. I've been waiting for you."

I thought she was wearing a marmalade-colored scarf around her neck, but it moved. A large cat looked at me with lazy green eyes.

"Do I know you?" I thought she looked vaguely familiar. Maybe a former customer.

"Yes. We met a few years back. I see my shop still bears

my name." She glanced at Shayla's shop—Mrs. Roberts, Spiritual Reader.

"I remember you. You opened the shop and then moved to Wilmington. Have you moved back to Duck?"

"Not exactly. Baylor and I will be here for a while. Something quite large and possibly dangerous is about to happen here. Maybe you've heard something about it from the horses. Goodness knows, news travels fast."

At that moment, a large fish jumped out of the sound and seemed to fly through the air toward her until it finally dove back into the water, inches from the boardwalk.

She laughed. "You see? Everyone knows. I'll wager your little Treasure has been talking about it too. Don't worry. We'll handle it. I think you have some prehistoric horse figures we need to examine. I hope you have some tea."

FROM
# ELLERY ADAMS

## BOOKS BY THE BAY MYSTERIES

### A Killer Plot
### A Deadly Cliché
### The Last Word
### Written in Stone
### Poisoned Prose

elleryadamsmysteries.com
facebook.com/TheCrimeSceneBooks
penguin.com

M1322AS0513